The
Silence
of the
Loons

The
Silence
of the
Loons

NODIN PRESS

ISBN 10: 1-932472-36-3
ISBN 13: 978-1-932472-36-3

Cover photograph © Craig Blacklock
Loon image © John Ford
Book design: John Toren

Sixth Printing, 2019

Nodin Press, LLC
5114 Cedar Lake Road,
Minneapolis, MN 55416

www.nodinpress.com

Printed in USA

The Minnesota Crime Wave dedicates this anthology to the following:
First and foremost to readers, readers of all sorts of literature, but most especially, of mystery fiction. Without readers, we don't have much reason to hang around. We also dedicate this anthology to publishers, printers, distributors, bookstore owners and workers, to reviewers, book artists, and editors and clerks and to all the authors whose work is represented in this modest volume. And even to non-Minnesotans.

Editors' Note

We are Ellen Hart, Deborah Woodworth, Carl Brookins and William Kent Krueger. More notoriously, we are the Minnesota Crime Wave.

How did the Crime Wave come to be? The story we tell is that we met in the Hennepin County drunk tank. It's a good story, but it's not true. As a part of the Twin Cities mystery writing community, we've known one another a long time. Four years ago it occurred to us that the lonely, expensive and time-consuming business of book promotion might better be done in consortium.

One night, with the help of some bottles of wine, we birthed the Minnesota Crime Wave. From the beginning it has been a fine experience, one that we intend to continue until our creative ideas die—or we do.

Why this anthology?

It began with a discussion as we speed across the flat farmland of the Midwest in Carl's Crimemobile while on one of our signing tours. We wanted to bring the Minnesota Mystery community together in order to showcase the talent of these wonderful writers and friends. A short story anthology seemed the perfect way.

But that, in itself, was too easy. These are writers used to dealing with locked rooms and battling serial killers. We realized we needed to give them an additional challenge, something that would, in its way, unify the collection.

This was the challenge. We created a set of eight clues or elements, a pool which each author had to dip into in order to construct their stories. We asked each author to include at least four of the clues in the story. We knew it would be exciting to discover how creative minds used the same elements to construct vastly different tales.

We're not going to tell you what the clues are (though the insatiably curious might want to inspect the last few pages of the book). In the end, in one story or another, all the clues were used. As you read the stories, you'll pick up on a few of them, at least, and you'll be amazed at how ingeniously they have been incorporated into these engaging tales.

This is an all-Minnesota project—editors, authors and publisher. Reading the stories, we think you'll find there's more to Minnesota than green pines and blue water. There's plenty to be afraid of here. We offer occurrences more haunting than the cry of a loon and crimes more lethal than a lump of lutefisk.

TABLE OF CONTENTS

Introduction

R.D. Zimmerman
AKA Robert Alexander

I've often heard it said that there are only two types of books, those of character and those of plot. In my mind, however, there are actually two more—those written by friends and those set in Minnesota. Throw in a little crime and you have the perfect story to while away a quiet afternoon at the lake or pass a cold winter's night.

What all mystery writers strive to do, of course, is not write one type of story exclusive of the other. If a novel is all character development and introspection with no discernible plot, there's nothing to pull the reader along. Or if the book has so much action yet is devoid of people to care about, it turns into nothing but a cheap ride. Wonderful crime fiction, as you're about to find in the following pages, pulls from both camps. The mysteries in which we care about the characters not by what they blah-blah-blah about, but by what they do, are the stories that we stay up reading until the last page and are the ones that stick in our mind.

I don't know why our state has so many crime writers. Is it the emphasis and appreciation of the arts? The great pleasure so many find in reading? No one seems to be able to put their finger on it, but I find Minnesota the perfect place to work because the creative environment is stimulating without being distracting. And here I might add that one of the greatest unspoken benefits of being a mystery writer in this northern place is that you get to meet lots of other mystery writers because there are indeed a lot of us and we (really, truly) are a friendly bunch. And while there's nothing more I love doing than sitting around with a bunch of authors yakking about book biz, I also love picking up a friend's mystery or thriller. Not only does it feel as if the story were written just for me, it's also as if that writer were sitting right by my side reading aloud to me and me alone. Like magic, each line comes to life in an entirely special way, resonating with that friend's voice, passion, and compassion. For this reason I encourage all of you to get to know your favorite mystery writer, not just in the following pages, but at your local bookstore, library, or book club. Trust me, there's nothing more that nine out of ten crime writers love than coming out of quarantine and talking about their work.

Hand in glove with reading stories written by authors you've met is reading a mystery set in a place you know. Again, another dimension of the reading experience opens up, making the images richer and more real as you follow characters through familiar landscapes. (But God help the author who gets it wrong, who does something unforgivable like having a victim mugged at Dayton's in 2005!)

So turn the page and sink into this wonderful collection of fine writers who use Minnesota to bind mystery and mayhem, crime and chaos, characterization and humanity, pace and plot, all into a delectably rich stew of entertainment.

The
Silence
of the
Loons

M. D. Lake

M. D. Lake is the pen name of Allen Simpson, who taught Scandinavian languages and literature at the University of Minnesota for twenty-seven years. When a Physical Education professor got a grant to write a book on "The Kantian Imperative and the Hegelian sittlichkeit as the foundation of morality in sport," Simpson felt it was time to explore other career options, settling finally on writing mysteries. He has written ten of them, all set on a fictitious Midwestern university campus with a large river running through it, that feature a red-headed campus cop named Peggy O'Neill, and a number of short stories. Two of his stories have won Agatha awards, one of his novels was given the American Mystery Award for best paperback original, and some of his work has been translated into French, Russian and apparently (he has no proof, just a little royalty check) Bulgarian.

The story in this anthology features two characters, Mrs. Newman and her grandson Zeke, who appeared in Lake's first published fiction, "Special Effects," published in Alfred Hitchcock's Mystery Magazine in 1988 and anthologized several times since.

Lake has two children and four grandchildren and lives in Minneapolis.

Holiday Murder at
Harmony Place

M. D. Lake

Most of the regulars were already in the lounge when Mrs. Newman came down from her apartment after dinner. They were talking about the Talented Youth Symphony Orchestra's annual holiday concert that some of them were going to attend the next morning. They attended it every year, of course, weather permitting, but this year was special: Fiona McClure's granddaughter Kathleen was going to play her first clarinet solo.

"I'm so proud of her!" Fiona said, waving to Mrs. Newman. Fiona, a short, robust Irishwoman with a tipped-up nose, green eyes and an untidy mop of reddish-gray hair, was one of Mrs. Newman's best friends at Harmony Place, the senior citizens' high-rise on the edge of downtown Minneapolis.

"I'll bet she inherited her musical talent from you, Fiona," Hulda Jonsson said. "Didn't you say once that you played the recorder in college?"

Fiona laughed. "Every college girl played the recorder back then! It was just a short-lived hobby."

"I've never really cared for the clarinet," Agnes Bixler said from an easy chair a little apart from the others, where she was working a crossword puzzle. "It has a tendency to squeak, especially in the hands of children." She accompanied her words with a gentle, almost remorseful smile, as if to show that, while it was important to tell the truth, she was aware that it could sometimes hurt. She was a petite woman in her late sixties, with expensively colored and coiffed hair, and always dressed to the nines.

Fiona's eyes flashed. "I've never heard Kathleen's clarinet squeak!"

"But there's always a first time, isn't there? That's what makes listening to clarinets so nerve-wracking. You never know when they're going to squeak. Besides, the clarinet's not an appropriate instrument for a girl. The piano, now, is so much more appropriate, don't you think? It encourages good posture, for one thing. You simply cannot slump and play Mozart."

"And for another thing?" demanded Clarence Dalquist, the retired judge.

"What?"

"You said, 'For one thing.' Is there another?" Clarence had the craggy face of a man accustomed to meting out long sentences to convicted felons.

"Oh." Agnes collected her thoughts. "Well, for another, you have to keep your legs modestly together when you play the piano."

Anna Larson looked up from her crocheting and said, quietly, "It's too bad you never learned to play the piano, Agnes."

Agnes flushed and Doris Wilkinson, a bird-like woman in her seventies with sequined glasses that made her gray eyes seem enormous, had to cover her mouth to keep from giggling. The newspaper Anna's husband Einar was holding up in front of his face rustled slightly.

The biggest scandal to rock Harmony Place in months had taken place in October, when Agnes began flirting with Einar, a retired pastor who was still quite an attractive man for his age, if a bit too innocent for his own good. Before anything serious could happen, as far as anybody knew, someone (Doris was suspected) had whispered a few words into Anna's ear. Anna had nipped it in the bud and told Agnes off in no uncertain terms. Those who happened to overhear it were amazed that a pastor's wife could have such a colorful vocabulary.

Mrs. Newman, who tried her best, within reason, to spread sweetness and light, asked Agnes if Ernest, her son, played an instrument.

"Ern played the trombone in the school band and was quite good," Agnes replied. "But he had more important things to do with his life. There's no money in music."

"What does he do?" Doris asked, gazing up at Agnes from her book.

"Works at a job that keeps him half a world away from his mother," Fiona muttered, not quite under her breath.

Before Agnes could respond to that, Mrs. Newman asked, "Is it next Friday he's coming home, Agnes?"

Agnes's face softened. "Yes—I'm counting the days!"

"I'm looking forward to meeting him," Mrs. Newman said.

Several of the others nodded. Fiona grunted.

Agnes and Fiona, almost from the moment Fiona had moved into Harmony Place, had disliked one another. Why? Who knew? Perhaps because Fiona was so outgoing and made friends so easily, a skill Agnes had no talent for at all. Or maybe it was because Fiona talked so much about her grandchildren. The others had no problem with that—Fiona, after all, had so many more than they did, it was natural she'd need more time. They just waited eagerly for their turns.

Not only did Agnes have no grandchildren, but she rarely saw Ernest, her only child. He was a bachelor who did something in international business and lived all over the world. The others felt sorry for Agnes, but she exasperated them too, for she did so little to make her life enjoyable—unless finding fault with just about everything at Harmony Place was her idea of fun, which it might well have been.

Instead of grandkids, Agnes had dolls. Dolls of all kinds and from all over the world.

"They're from Ern," she told them. "He gives me a new doll on my birthday and for Christmas, and at other times as well—just to let me know he's thinking about me. He's such a thoughtful boy."

Her apartment was full of them, still in their boxes, unopened, untouched.

"They freaked me out," Mrs. Newman's grandson, Zeke, told her one evening. "They made me think of Snow White in her little crystal coffin, except you know that Prince Charming isn't ever going to show up to kiss 'em back to life."

Zeke was a house painter by trade, but currently "into" (as he put it) feng shui. A few months earlier, on one of his visits, and newly armed with his feng shui lore, he pronounced Harmony Place a hotbed of bad chi. Mrs. Newman wasn't quite sure what chi was—something to do with the life force, she thought—but it seemed that, under certain circumstances, it could turn on you and,

M. D. Lake

like cucumbers and cabbage, cause unpleasantness. To offset this, Zeke offered to redo Mrs. Newman's apartment to improve what he called "the harmonic energy flow."

Well, she'd been thinking of repainting her place anyway, so she hired him to do it, but she had to keep a close watch on him to make sure he didn't do more than she wanted, such as install a fish tank in her living room that he said would attract good chi. Mrs. Newman had no intention of spending her so-called "golden years" taking care of fish, so they settled on a fern that Zeke said would have the same positive effect, chi-wise, but wouldn't require much in the way of care. He did such a good job painting her apartment that some of the other residents overcame their prejudice against a young man with facial jewelry and spiked hair the color of a rainbow and hired him to paint theirs too.

Mrs. Newman's friend Fiona, for example, hired him to redo her kitchen. She told Mrs. Newman afterwards that he'd wanted to paint the drawers a red that he claimed would stimulate her mentally, but she told him mental stimulation was the last thing she wanted in the morning before she'd had her coffee, so they compromised on orange, a symbol of sociability, which suited Fiona to a T, for she was a very sociable woman.

When Agnes heard that her son was coming on vacation and planned to stay with her, she decided to surprise him by turning her late husband's bedroom into a room that looked the way Ernest's room had looked when he was a child, so she hired Zeke to paint it, but unfortunately it didn't work out. Zeke took one look around her place and warned Agnes that it was a feng shui disaster waiting to happen, and he urged her to allow him to set off some firecrackers to drive out the evil spirits. Agnes declined, somewhat frostily, and much to Zeke's dismay said she'd find someone else to paint the room. He hadn't meant to hurt her feelings.

He told his grandmother afterwards that Agnes's apartment collected evil spirits the way alley cats collect fleas. "She's saved a lot of her son's stuff from when he was a child," he said. "Model airplanes, rock star posters, comic books, and tried to arrange it the way he'd had it arranged thirty years ago. I'd like to see that kid's face when he walks into that room!" Zeke shuddered at the thought.

6

Mrs. Newman (mercifully, she thought afterwards) couldn't attend the Talented Youth's holiday concert the next morning because she had her Stock Market for Seniors class during that time and it was the last class of the session, but she was in the lounge when those who did attend returned. She was drinking coffee and watching Larry, the custodian, trim the Christmas tree, supervised by Mr. Foy, Harmony Place's manager. Larry was tall, thin and dour—it was hard to get a word out of him—whereas Mr. Foy was short, round and jolly, and liked to visit with the tenants whenever he had the time. Larry had just got the lights arranged to Mr. Foy's satisfaction when Fiona came stomping into the lounge, red-faced from more than just the cold. "I'll kill her! I'll make her wish she'd never been born!" she hollered.

Clarence followed on her heels, propelled along by his cane. "Let's have no talk of violence, Fiona!" he said, as if demanding order in the court. "Not even in jest!"

"Who's jesting?" Fiona called back over her shoulder and then, ignoring Mrs. Newman's invitation to come and sit down and tell her all about it, stalked out of the room. As she passed him, Mr. Foy started to intercept her, but thought better of it and began hanging ornaments on the tree.

A moment or two later, Opal Furlong came in, her soft mink hat snow-powdered on her brassy orange hair, followed by some of the others who'd gone to the concert that morning. They all looked subdued.

Mrs. Newman asked what had happened and Opal bellowed, "Agnes!" Opal had lived a checkered life, and always talked as though trying to make herself heard in a noisy bar.

"What's she done now?"

"Coughed."

"What?"

When they'd taken off their coats and hats and got coffee to warm up with, they took turns telling Mrs. Newman what had happened.

Orchestra Hall was well within walking distance of Harmony Place, so they'd walked and all the way there, Fiona had chattered on about how nervous she was on little Kathleen's behalf, and how proud she was too. "You know how she does," Hulda told Mrs. Newman.

"She made us all nervous," said Doris, who was a naturally nervous person herself.

They were surprised when Agnes joined them, considering how she felt about grandkids and what she'd said the night before about girls who play the clarinet, but no one suspected her motives.

"Orchestra Hall was very well decorated," Clarence pronounced judiciously. "A winter motif, with snow and pine boughs scattered around the stage."

"Then the curtain went up and there all the children were," Anna said. "The boys in white shirts, dark pants and bow ties, the girls lovely in their long gowns and black, patent-leather shoes." She smiled at the memory. "Fiona pointed out little Kathleen over in the woodwinds section—a pale, freckled child with curly red hair parted in the middle and held at the temples with barrettes, one a treble, the other a bass clef. She looked just the way Fiona must have looked at that age. Some of us waved, but she was too busy with her reed to notice."

The orchestra played a number of holiday songs from various cultures and traditions, and the chorus sang, and finally it was little Kathleen's turn to play her solo.

"I could never play in front of people when I was Kathleen's age," Doris said, adding that she'd played the flute. "But she didn't seem frightened at all."

The orchestra leader set up Kathleen's music stand for her and then the orchestra began to play. Kathleen stood there, concentrating for all she was worth, then put her clarinet to her lips as the orchestra quieted down. She watched for the conductor's signal, took a deep breath, her cheeks filled with air and, just as she sounded the first note—

"Agnes coughed," said Opal.

"Of course," Clarence reminded them, "somebody always coughs during crucial moments at concerts in Minnesota, and not just in the winter, either. A lot of people seem to regard Orchestra Hall as a kind of respiratory vomitory. But this wasn't an ordinary cough. This cough was remarkable even by Minnesota concert standards." He glared around the group, daring anyone to challenge his words.

No one did. "And it was perfectly timed," Hulda Jonsson said grimly.

"The squeal from the poor child's instrument was one of the loudest sounds I've ever heard from that instrument," Clarence went on, "a testament to her lung power and the hall's quite remarkable acoustics."

"What made it worse," Hulda said, "was that the hall was packed with children on the last day of school before the Christmas break."

"And you know how cruel children can be!" Doris managed to say through pursed lips. "They broke into laughter and it was a while before their teachers could restore order."

The conductor whispered some encouraging words to Kathleen, raised his baton again and began the piece over. It went all right after that, but it was clear that Kathleen's confidence had been shaken, and there were some unfortunate squeaks, just as Agnes had predicted.

"Who could blame Kathleen?" Doris asked. "I saw tears in her eyes when she took her bow. Who knows what effect it will have on her future musical career?"

While getting their coats afterwards, Agnes apologized to Fiona. She claimed that it was saliva that had gone down the wrong throat and that it could have happened to anybody. No one believed her, of course. Fiona glared at her and said, 'You did it deliberately."

"I most certainly did not!" Agnes replied. "My cough had nothing to do with the girl's squeaks. She just needs more experience playing in front of audiences, where things like coughs can happen. But I can see that you don't believe me—none of you does. Well, I'm sorry, but that's just too bad!" And with that, she turned and walked the other way, saying she had to do some last minute shopping downtown in preparation for her son's visit.

Hulda, whose two grandchildren were grown but still lived close enough so that they could visit regularly, said she understood Fiona's anger. "If Kathleen was my granddaughter, I'd murder Agnes!" Hulda was an Icelander and Icelanders are said to be quite fierce, descended as they are from the Vikings, who rarely took prisoners.

"We don't talk like that at Harmony Place!" thundered Clarence, pounding his cane like a gavel.

Harmony Place stayed calm until Monday, and then, as some of them were having their mid-afternoon coffee in the lounge, holiday music playing softly in the background, Agnes appeared in the doorway, scanned the room with a frosty eye, and demanded, "Who is responsible for this?" She held up a crumpled piece of paper and, like a magician, pulled something small, pink and silky out of it.

"What is it?" someone asked.

"A ballet slipper—from a doll!" Agnes stared at Fiona in a meaningful way as she spoke. "I found it as I was leaving my apartment a few minutes ago, half stuck under my door. Assuming it was just trash that Larry, with his usual incompetence, had overlooked when he vacuumed the hall, I was about to kick it away, but something made me hesitate. I opened it and found the slipper. You don't happen to know anything about this, Fiona, do you?"

"No," Fiona replied contemptuously.

Mrs. Newman asked Agnes if it was from one of her dolls.

"Mercifully not! But until I checked my ballerinas, my heart was pounding! Anyway, this one is much the worse for wear, probably played with by a thoughtless child with grubby little fingers. My dolls are all NRFB."

"They're what?" Anna asked.

"Never Removed From Box. They're worth at least twenty percent more in NRFB condition."

"Well," Opal said, "maybe somebody found the slipper and thought it belonged to you and slipped it under your door."

Hulda was examining the paper the slipper had been wrapped in. "It's a page torn from a dictionary," she said. "One of the words has been underlined in red."

"What does it say?" demanded Agnes.

Hulda hesitated a moment, then read: "'Jezebel. From the Bible. 1. The wicked woman who married Ahab, king of Israel. 2. Any woman regarded as shameless and wicked.'"

Anna laughed. "Well, Agnes, whoever delivered that to your door got the address right!"

Her cheeks suddenly bright red, Agnes retorted, "And who would think of calling me a Jezebel but a pastor's wife!"

"I'm a *retired* pastor's wife," Anna replied with a smile, "and I know a shorter word for what you are than Jezebel. You know that!"

Her husband groaned.

Mrs. Newman happened to glance over at Doris, a novel by George Eliot lying open on her lap, and saw a little smile on her face. Doris, she knew, disliked Agnes because Agnes had once made a slurring comment about Precious Moments figurines, which Doris collected assiduously.

Still steaming, Agnes marched to the coffee urn and tried to pour herself a cup of coffee, but the urn was empty. Muttering under her breath, she hollered to Larry, waxing the floor down at the other end of the room, to make a new pot, then went over to her corner of the lounge with her cross-word puzzle book, rustling it noisily to let the world know she was not happy.

That was Monday.

The next afternoon, they were in the lounge as usual and Hulda had just remarked to her friend Doris that if she ever heard Bing Crosby croon "White Christmas" again—it was playing softly in the background—she'd take an axe to the loudspeakers, when Agnes came charging out of the elevator as if blown there by a high wind, her eyes blazing, her face contorted in rage. She was trailed by Mr. Foy, the manager, almost running to keep up on his short legs.

"What now?" Opal wondered aloud.

"Look!" Agnes hollered. 'Look at this!'

She brandished a doll. It was dressed in a gauzy material of pink and green stripes, and the legs were bent into a ballerina's position, a pink toe slipper on one foot, the other foot bare. It looked as though it were poised to leap out of Agnes's hand except for one thing: its head was missing.

Mrs. Newman, sitting next to Doris, heard Doris's sharp intake of breath and gave her a curious glance. "The poor thing!" Doris said quickly, her eyes skittering away from Mrs. Newman's.

"This is terrible," Mr. Foy said, wringing his hands, something Mrs. Newman had never seen before, only read about in books.

"Terrible! Isn't there enough violence in the world? Does it have to invade this peaceful retreat?"

Agnes was having trouble breathing. "I came out of my apartment this morning, suspecting nothing," she finally gasped, "and found this affixed to my door with tape!"

She let her eyes sweep slowly over all of them. "One of you doesn't, perhaps, have a grandchild who is missing a Peppermint Candy Cane Barbie, by any chance?"

"My grandchildren have never played with Barbies," Fiona said.

"I've never heard of such a doll," Hulda said.

"Of course you haven't," Agnes snapped, "since it comes from *The Nutcracker,* a famous ballet. What would you know about—?" She broke off and turned to Doris. "Didn't I see one of your grandkids playing with a Peppermint Candy Cane Barbie last summer with her sticky little hands?"

Doris stuck up her chin and, her lips trembling, said "I have no idea what kind of Barbies my granddaughters have."

"Ladies! Please!" Mr. Foy pleaded. "This must stop!" He gave his standard speech, whenever dissension broke out, on the need for all of them, friends and neighbors, the citizens of Harmony Place, to live up to the ideals embodied in the very name of their residence.

"I'm very much afraid that someone among us is not being a very good citizen and I call upon her—" he let his little round eyes behind the rimless bifocals roam from one face to the other, pausing just a moment longer than necessary, some of them thought, on Fiona— "or him, to put the good of the entire community above her, or his, real or imagined grievances—especially at this time of the year, the season of peace on earth and good will to men."

"Hear! Hear!" cried Judge Clarence, as Mr. Foy disappeared back into the elevator, shepherding Agnes before him. As the elevator doors were closing, Agnes shouted back, "If you think you can drive me out of Harmony Place with childish pranks like this, you're very much mistaken!"

That evening, Zeke took his grandmother to dinner at a nice Mexican restaurant in downtown Minneapolis, for Mrs. Newman loved Mexican food and it goes without saying that it never appeared on the menu in the dining room at Harmony Place, for most of whose residents "fine dining" brought up memories of lutefisk suppers in the church basement.

After dinner, they went to a movie at a nearby theatre and then strolled arm in arm back to Harmony Place along the brightly decorated Nicollet Mall. It was starting to snow, but there was no wind and the temperature, hovering close to thirty, was almost balmy. It was a lovely walk, reminding Mrs. Newman of winter strolls long ago with Zeke's grandfather, down this same street, when they were young.

Zeke (whose real name was Bernard) had devoted his life to finding himself, first as an artist, then as a film maker and photographer, and now, of course, as a feng shui house painter. Although some people couldn't get beyond his outrageous exterior, he was, at heart, a very nice boy and his grandmother was proud of him for doing his own thing, or whatever the current term was for going your own way.

When they reached Harmony Place, Mrs. Newman invited him up to her apartment for a cup of hot cocoa and he agreed, largely, she suspected, because he had nothing to go back to his place for, since Nadia, his girlfriend, was in India at something called an ashram, doing whatever it is they do in places like that.

It was late, almost eleven o'clock, and nobody was about. "Spooky!" Zeke said in a hoarse whisper. "Very spooky! Why don't they build these big apartment houses with halls that curve? Good chi loves curves."

"Good chi in *China* loves curves," Mrs. Newman retorted, "but maybe it's assimilated here, as immigrants usually do, and has learned to love straight lines and right angles."

"Efficiency experts who design buildings like this love straight lines and right angles. Chi doesn't."

Mrs. Newman just laughed and gave his arm a squeeze and said, "I think my chi must be very good." The elevator doors opened softly and they headed down the carpeted hall towards her apartment.

They had just passed Agnes's apartment when Zeke slowed and looked back. "Her door's not shut all the way."

The door was open a crack, the room beyond it dark. Mrs. Newman went back and knocked softly and, when there was no response, pushed the door open a little, just enough to stick her head in, and called out softly, "Agnes."

"She's down the hall, visiting somebody," Zeke said, trying to pull his grandmother away.

"She wouldn't leave her door open."

"She probably didn't realize she did."

"I think I'll just check to be sure," she said, and stepped into the room.

"Agnes won't be happy, finding you prowling around in there," Zeke called after her. "I'll whistle if I hear her coming."

Gray light filtered into the apartment through the falling snow outside the living room windows. "Agnes?" she called and, when there was no answer, repeated it more loudly. Glittering dolls' eyes seemed to be watching her from boxes on every flat surface in the living room, giving her goose-pimples.

The kitchen was on the left, around the corner from the entryway. She glanced in.

"Zeke!"

"What?" He came up behind her, peered over her shoulder. In the otherwise tidy kitchen a drawer was lying upside down on the floor, knives and other kitchen utensils scattered around it.

Mrs. Newman turned and rushed down the hall.

"Wait!" Zeke hollered. "I'll go first!" She ignored him, glanced into the spare bedroom as she passed, saw it was empty and continued to Agnes's bedroom.

"Oh, dear God!"

Agnes was lying on the floor at the foot of her bed, on her back, and something black was sticking from her chest, the handle of a knife.

Zeke called 911 on his cell phone and then, after looking in the closet and under the bed, said, "Let's get out of this room, Grandma," but she shook her head and stayed with Agnes, she couldn't say why. Zeke left her there and went back down the hall to look around. The police, when they arrived, regarded him with suspicion and might have arrested him just on general principles, had Mrs. Newman not been able to vouch for him.

The residents of Harmony Place, brought closer together by the tragedy, did their best to keep open minds all the next morning, but that became harder to do later in the day, when the afternoon news programs announced that the police had found Fiona McClure's fingerprints on the knife drawer on the murdered woman's kitchen floor, and Fiona had been brought in for questioning.

"Neither of them came down for dinner last night," Clarence observed darkly.

"Fiona often doesn't," Anna reminded them. "She doesn't like the food and she's a good cook."

"Agnes didn't come down for coffee yesterday afternoon, either," Anna said. "Poor woman, probably lying there in her own blood all that time! I didn't like her, of course, but she didn't deserve to die like that."

"We should all keep our minds open," Opal said. "It doesn't have to have been Fiona, you know."

"How do you explain the fingerprints?" demanded Clarence, whose greatest sorrow was that he'd been a hanging judge in a state without the death penalty.

Opal thought a moment. "Maybe she cooked for Agnes once when Agnes was sick."

"Tell that to the judge!" Clarence said.

"I hope she can explain it," Hulda said. "I'd miss her if she had to go to prison. She's got a temper, no question about that, but I can't believe she'd commit murder—not in cold blood, anyway."

"If she didn't kill Agnes, who did?" the judge asked. "You don't seriously think it could have been one of us?"

"No!" Doris said, suddenly sitting up straight and looking around fiercely. "Some of us are always letting strangers into the building, even though we're told not to. We're just too polite or too cowardly to tell them we can't let them in when they're standing there claiming they've come to see one of us. Remember last February, when Hulda came upon that thief wandering around on the second floor, checking doors to see if any were unlocked? Helen Lindbloom later admitted that she was the one who'd let him into the building because she'd always liked men with ponytails and besides, he wore a tattoo that said 'Mom,' so how could he be evil? Turned out the hair was a wig and the tattoo was fake!"

"You may be right, of course, Doris," Anna said. "It's possible that somebody who knew Agnes got in that way and killed her—maybe for the dolls. I wonder if the police are checking to see if any were stolen. Agnes said some of them are valuable."

"But Agnes also insisted she would never open her door to anybody she didn't know," Opal reminded them.

Anna looked at Mrs. Newman, who'd been sitting there without joining the conversation, lost in her own dark thoughts. "Did you happen to notice if any of her dolls were missing, Florence?"

Mrs. Newman shook her head and then said, "Fiona didn't do it."

They all turned and looked at her questioningly.

"How do you know that?"

"I know Fiona. We all do. We all know she didn't do it."

"But the fingerprints . . ." Anna said, her eyes big.

"They can be explained."

"How?"

"I don't know. Yet."

Fiona posted bail, according to the late local news, but she didn't return to Harmony Place. The next morning Mrs. Newman asked Mr. Foy if he knew where she was, and he said he'd been informed that she was staying with one of her daughters.

"Frankly, I think it was a wise decision on her part," he added. "While I'm sure that all the good people of Harmony Place are more than willing to grant her the benefit of the doubt, there is, nevertheless, a miasma of suspicion hanging over her head. How could there not be? It would be most unpleasant for her—for all of us—if she were to return here before this—this possible misunderstanding is cleared up."

He wiped his jowls, which had a tendency to perspire under stress, with a handkerchief, then gave Mrs. Newman Fiona's daughter's telephone number.

"I'm fine! How do you think I am?" Fiona roared when she came to the phone. "Has Clarence set the execution date yet?"

Mrs. Newman ignored that. "Fiona," she said quietly, "did you kill Agnes?"

"Of course not! Maybe I wanted to kill her for a couple of hours—hell, for a couple of days--but I didn't have any plans to do it. Would you kill anybody for something so trivial? Kathleen got over it—she's looking forward to playing another solo next week at church—so why wouldn't I?"

"What about your fingerprints being on—"

"Those aren't my fingerprints! It's got to be a mistake, damn it! I was never in that woman's apartment in my life!"

Mrs. Newman couldn't think of anything to say to that, because it seemed unlikely to her that there could be a mistake about something so basic as fingerprints.

Subdued, Fiona said, "I know what you're thinking. It's hard to believe, isn't it, that I didn't do it."

"Not nearly as hard as believing you did do it. I'm going to talk to my grandson about it. Zeke got me out of a similar predicament last year. Maybe he can come up with something."

"Thanks, Florence," Fiona said. "In the meantime, I'm getting the best lawyer my kids can afford." She tried to laugh, but it didn't fool Mrs. Newman.

Mrs. Newman and Zeke met at Zeke's favorite eatery, the Languid Sprout, for lunch. "This case," he said, "presents some features which make it absolutely original in the history of crime."

Mrs. Newman, looking up from a salad that claimed (somewhat redundantly, she thought) to be organic, gave him a puzzled look. "It does?"

He shrugged. "Probably not. That's just something Sherlock Holmes was known to say." He shoved something called a tofu-veggie wrap with tahini sauce into his mouth, bit off a piece, and chewed it with every appearance of finding it good. "If Fiona McClure didn't murder Agnes Bixler, who did? Ernest, her son? Was Agnes loaded and threatening to disinherit him for neglecting her all these years? He's supposedly on his way to visit her, right? But did he perhaps arrive in town early, pay a nocturnal visit to his mom?"

"I'd like to think so," Mrs. Newman replied. "As far as Agnes was concerned, he could do no wrong, but it wasn't hard to figure out that he kept as much distance between himself and her as he could. But I don't think she had enough money to kill for, even if Ernest needed money."

"I've made it a life-long practice," Zeke said, "never to trust men named Ernest Bixler. Do you know if Agnes had friends outside Harmony Place?"

"I never saw her with any. She played Bingo a couple of nights a week at a church down the street, but she never talked about any of the people she met there. She made friends quickly, but lost them even faster." Speaking these words, Mrs. Newman realized, for the first time, what a lonely and unhappy woman Agnes must have been.

"What about in the building?"

She told him about the scandal that had rocked Harmony Place in October that involved Einar, Anna's husband, and Agnes.

Zeke said that might be a promising lead. "At least," he added, "it might explain the Obsession."

"What obsession? Whose?"

"Agnes's. The perfume. No doubt she wore it to make herself irresistible to retired pastors named Einar."

"What're you going on about, Zeke? Agnes didn't wear perfume! She was allergic to them."

The remains of Zeke's wrap froze halfway to his mouth and his eyes got a faraway look in them. "You're sure? How do you know?"

"Because she told us. She demanded that all scented perfumes, deodorants and aftershave lotions be banned in the building. It annoyed a lot of people, of course, but I sympathized with her because I'm allergic to cats and I know how hard it is to get people who aren't to believe it. Why'd you think she used Obsession?"

"Because I smelled it in her apartment when we were in there. In the kitchen."

"Oh." Mrs. Newman thought about that a moment. And then she said it again, "Oh."

"You didn't kill her, dear Grandma, did you?"

"No."

Zeke leaned forward across the table, looked into his grand-mother's eyes. "No? Just 'No.' What's wrong?"

"Nothing."

"Not nothing, Grandma. If it wasn't Agnes' Obsession, and it wasn't yours, whose was it?"

She flared. "How should I know?"

He watched her a moment, unblinking, but she refused to meet his eyes. Finally, she said, "I gave my Obsession to Fiona."

"You gave Fiona the perfume I gave you for Christmas last year?" Zeke cried. "How could you?"

"I'm sorry. I've never much cared for perfume or cologne, but I didn't have the heart to tell you. Zeke, you must be mistaken! Fiona didn't kill Agnes. Besides, why would she put on Obsession to go down and kill her? They say Agnes was killed sometime during the day."

They sat in silence for a minute and then Mrs. Newman, uncomfortable, started to say something, but Zeke held up a hand to stop her. He closed his eyes and seemed to be concentrating on something. She watched him nervously, picked at her salad.

"There was a small pile of comic books on the table in that bedroom she was fixing up for her son," he said, slowly, as in a trance. "I asked her about them and she said they'd been his." Absently, he bit off a piece of his wrap, chewed it, his eyes still closed. "I'm visualizing that room when I explored the apartment after we found her body." His eyes flew open. "I don't think the comic books were there!"

"She could have put them somewhere else."

He shook his head. "She told me she'd put them there because that's exactly where Ernest—Ern, she called him—kept them on the table in his room when he was a kid."

They sat there in silence a few minutes longer, and then Mrs. Newman said, "Well, maybe you're right, Zeke, but we still haven't figured out the answer to the most important question, how Fiona's fingerprints got all over Agnes's knife drawer. Fiona wasn't interested in comic books and she didn't need money badly enough to kill for it."

"Oh, that," Zeke said airily. "That's easy."

"What's easy?"

"The fingerprints on the knife drawer. Haven't you figured that out yet?"

"You know I haven't, Zeke!" Mrs. Newman said angrily. "Stop playing games! This is serious."

Zeke leaned across the table and said, quietly, "If it's true—as you insist it is, and I always believe everything you tell me, Grandma—that Fiona didn't kill Agnes and never touched Agnes's knife drawer, then it has to follow that the drawer with the fingerprints on it isn't Agnes's—it's Fiona's. The killer switched them."

"Switched—?" And then the realization hit her, her face lit up and she cried, "Oh, Zeke, you're a genius!" She reached over and picked a piece of mung bean from the corner of his mouth.

Then her face clouded over. "Oh, but you painted Fiona's kitchen drawers, remember? If Agnes's were painted at all, it probably wasn't with the same paint as Fiona's. The drawers wouldn't match."

He rolled his eyes with comic exasperation. "The Obsession, remember, Grandma? The killer didn't have to use one of Fiona's *kitchen* drawers, he could've used one of her *bathroom* drawers, where she must have kept her perfume. When I was painting your apartment, I noticed that the bathroom and kitchen drawers were interchangeable—just what you'd expect in a building designed by bean counters. Furthermore, every apartment's cabinetry in this place is the same wood and the same stain, unless the tenant has it painted, as you did."

Mrs. Newman laughed. "The killer took Fiona's bathroom drawer up to Agnes's kitchen and put Agnes's knives in it without noticing, or thinking anybody else would notice, the smell of perfume. Then he replaced Fiona's drawer with Agnes's kitchen drawer!"

Zeke swallowed the last bite of his veggie wrap. "There's really only one person who had the means to do all that with the least chance of discovery, you know."

Mrs. Newman thought about it a moment. "Larry?"

"Exactly. The custodian."

"I suppose so. He's always around, replacing a burned-out light bulb here, vacuuming a floor there. He's almost invisible—and he has keys to all the apartments."

"He helped Agnes bring up her son's stuff from her storage locker in the basement, she told me. He might have spotted something valuable—the comic books, probably."

They got up and bussed their dishes and put on their coats. "But before we go to the cops," Zeke said, "we ought to make sure we're right about the drawers matching—just in case—and see if the comic books are still there. We'll ask the manager, what's-his-name, to let us into Agnes's apartment."

"Mr. Foy?" Mrs. Newman was doubtful. "Maybe it was him who killed Agnes."

"Possible, of course. I'll keep an eye on him. But he's the least likely suspect, and they only do it in books."

Mr. Foy was in his office, watering the large pot of bright red poinsettias on his desk, when Mrs. Newman and Zeke knocked on his door. He gave them a welcoming smile and asked them to come in. Mrs. Newman explained what they wanted, and why. As she spoke, the expression on his face became increasingly concerned.

"If we're right," she finished, "the smell of Obsession will still be there too. And who knows, maybe the killer was so confident that his plan would work that he didn't bother to wipe Agnes's fingerprints off the drawer that's now in Fiona's bathroom."

"But even if he did," Zeke added, "there's bound to be evidence that the drawer in the bathroom was once in a kitchen—maybe bread crumbs in the cracks, or something. These days, you shed a nose hair at a crime scene, the cops'll find it."

Mr. Foy leaned his chin on his clasped hands and pursed his lips. "Your theory seems far-fetched to me," he said. "Larry's been here longer than I have and I sincerely doubt that he's capable of murder. He's one of the sweetest men I know! And murder for what? Comic books, you say?" He shook his head. "Surely not."

"I think the old ones can be worth a lot of money," Zeke said.

"Anyway, it couldn't hurt, could it, Mr. Foy, to let us into those apartments—just for a few minutes?" Mrs. Newman pleaded.

Mr. Foy gave her a pitying look. "Fiona McClure's a close friend of yours, Florence, I know. And I can understand your loyalty to her.

But sometimes, something happens and people snap. Maybe what happened at the concert was the last straw—"

Zeke interrupted him impatiently and turned to his grandmother. "Let's call the police and tell them what we think might've happened and ask them to check it out. We'll use your phone, okay, Mr. Foy?"

Mr. Foy heaved a long sigh, then got up slowly. "All right," he said, his voice filled with infinite resignation. "We'll take a look. I'll get my keys."

He rummaged in a closet behind him and when he turned back to them, he was holding a shiny little pistol that he pointed at Mrs. Newman.

"Close the door quickly or I shoot your grandmother," he said to Zeke. "I have nothing to lose."

"Is that real?" Zeke asked, his eyes wide.

"I'll count to three. One . . ."

Zeke closed the door.

Mr. Foy no longer looked like the friendly rotund manager Mrs. Newman had known for years, eager to please, the man who played Santa Claus on Christmas Eve for those residents who didn't have families to spend it with. Now his chubby face was pasty and glistening with sweat, his button eyes narrowed and frightened, and the pistol trembled dangerously in his hand. "Get over there!" he ordered, pointing across the room, and, as they moved away from the door he backed in front of it, to keep them at a distance.

Zeke said, "You'll never get away with this."

Mr. Foy licked his lips. "Please be quiet," he said. "I must think this through."

"Tell us why you did it," Mrs. Newman said, trying a ploy that characters in books often used in this situation, to stall for time until rescue arrived.

"Why should I?" Mr. Foy asked. "You're just trying to stall for time until somebody—"

There was a sharp rap on the door behind him and somebody pushed it open, almost knocking him over.

"Mr. Foy—." It was Hulda Jonsson and, trying to peer around her, her friend Doris. "Doris has something she wants—*Mr. Foy!*"

He looked back and, as he did, Zeke grabbed the pot of poinsettias off the desk and broke it over his head, and he went down in a heap.

As Zeke had guessed, Mr. Foy killed Agnes for the comic books. Early the week before, Agnes had asked him to come to her apartment to discuss the possibility of getting her late husband's bedroom painted to match the color of her son's room when he was a child. He saw the comic books on the table and asked her about them and she'd told him they'd belonged to her son. She'd found them in her storage locker in the basement of Harmony Place when she was going through a box of things from her old house. She assumed Ernest had forgotten all about them.

Mr. Foy made the mistake of telling her he'd collected comic books as a child too, and asked to look at them. He didn't recognize the first few, he said, but then he came across one that shocked him: The first issue of "Vipers of Vengeance," a series featuring a seemingly ordinary suburban family—mother, father, sister and brother—that could assume the guise of a nest of poisonous snakes in their crusade against evil. He'd recently read an article in a magazine on the Viper series, which was soon to be made into a motion picture featuring some of Hollywood's biggest stars. It claimed that the first issue was now worth over fifty thousand dollars to collectors, with several of the following issues, which he also found, worth nearly as much.

"And who knows how much some of the other comics in the stack might be worth?" he told the police, hoping for some understanding, if not complete sympathy.

Ernest had been very fond of the Viper comics, Agnes told him. He'd be surprised and thrilled to see them again, just as he'd left them, in a room that looked just the way his did when he was a child. She took the comics gently out of Mr. Foy's hands and replaced them lovingly on the top of the stack.

That was what doomed her, for Mr. Foy was sure she'd know it if the comics were missing, and know who'd stolen them.

The thought of those comic books haunted him. He'd owned them himself as a child—bought them for twelve cents apiece— twelve cents! he repeated, shaking his head in amazement—and read them and lost them, the way most kids do. He imagined that, if somehow he got hold of them, he might not even sell them now, just keep them and, maybe, sell them someday when he got old and needed the money so, he said, he wouldn't have to spend his old age in a dump like Harmony Place.

"I would *not* have killed her," he assured the police, trying to salvage a vestige of his honor, "had I been able to come up with a less drastic alternative." But he didn't have the time, for Agnes's son's arrival was imminent.

That was what was on his mind when Fiona came storming back from the concert last Friday, raging at Agnes and threatening to kill her. He decided he might get away with murder if he could blame it on Fiona. It was important for him to keep the police from looking for the killer elsewhere in the building, for Mr. Foy had a record: He'd spent six months in the workhouse in another state for embezzlement and had only escaped a prison term because, on the advice of his attorney, he'd let Christ into his life.

He decided to torment Agnes with the Barbie doll, hoping the police would conclude that Fiona was behind it, working herself up gradually to a homicidal frenzy.

Then, on Tuesday, after the scene with the headless Barbie doll in the lounge, he'd accompanied Agnes back to her apartment, taken a knife from her knife drawer (he'd asked her if he could get a glass of water), gone down to her bedroom where she was getting ready to lie down and rest, and killed her, using gloves, of course, so he wouldn't leave his fingerprints on the knife. Then, checking to make sure Fiona was still down in the lounge, he'd switched the drawers.

And that was that. It was risky, yes, but he'd taken risks before with the law and, except for that one short stretch in the workhouse, gotten away with it. Great rewards, he'd read somewhere, usually involved great risks.

Zeke, who told his grandmother all this over the combination plate special—two tacos and an enchilada, black beans and rice—at her favorite Mexican restaurant, added, "Poor Agnes! She should have let me set off some firecrackers."

Mrs. Newman shook her head sadly. "He gave such a moving speech in the lounge Tuesday afternoon—about the need for us to live in harmony together, especially at this season of the year. And yet, the entire time he had murder on his mind!"

"He should have gone into politics," Zeke said. "Who knows how far he could've risen?"

After Mrs. Newman paid the bill and they were outside on the street, he added, "The only thing Mr. Foy insists he didn't do was put that little ballet slipper under Agnes's door, wrapped in the 'Jezebel' paper. He claims he found the doll in a pile of leaves last fall—he thought maybe a dog had been at it—and the slipper was missing. He'd meant to throw it away, but forgot about it until somebody put the slipper under Agnes's door. But if it wasn't Mr. Foy who did it, who could it have been?"

"Doris," Mrs. Newman said.

"Doris? That little woman who came in and distracted him?"

She laughed. "She came in to confess to Mr. Foy that she was the one who'd done it. She thought what Agnes did to Fiona's grand-daughter at the concert was terrible—not to speak of the scandal involving Einar. Plus she was still simmering at Agnes for having made slurring comments about "Precious Moments" figurines. So she sent the page from the dictionary to her with "Jezebel" circled and threw in the ballet slipper for good measure, knowing how much Agnes loved dolls. She'd found the ballet slipper under her couch, where one of her grandkids must have lost it. She had no idea what had happened to the doll until Agnes came charging in with it, accusing us all of trying to drive her away."

"Doris saved our bacon," Zeke said somberly. "I almost got us killed, thinking the killer was the custodian."

Mrs. Newman smiled and hooked her arm through his. "Nobody's perfect, dear."

Zeke was startled to hear that. "How can you say that about your only grandson?"

"It'll be our little secret," she said, as they made their way through gently falling snow back to Harmony Place.

Mary Logue

Award-winning poet and mystery writer Mary Logue was born and raised in Minnesota. She has since lived in New York City, France, Belgium, and Tucson, Arizona, but has always come back home to roost. She has written seven mysteries—Red Lake of the Heart, Still Explosion, *and five in the Claire Watkins series:* Blood Country, Dark Coulee, Glare Ice, Bone Harvest, *and* Poison Heart.

Dark Coulee *won the Minnesota Book Award for popular fiction in 2000. She has also published three books of poetry,* Discriminating Evidence, Settling, *and* Meticulous Attachment; *a book on her grandmother,* Halfway Home, *and many children's books.*

She has taught writing at the Loft and Hamline University for many years. She lives with the writer Pete Hautman and their toy poodles Rene and Jacques in Minnesota and Wisconsin.

Loon Lodge

Mary Logue

The first thing Claire saw as they pulled up to Loon Lodge was a headless Barbie doll swimming through four inches of snow that had sifted down the previous night, the only snow that had fallen all February.

Claire wondered how her fourteen-year-old daughter Meg would view the grand old lodge. She could not help but see it through her own fond eyes: the large log structure nestled under long-needled white pines on the edge of Winnebagoshishama Lake.

Claire had started coming to Loon Lodge when she was five and then had continued almost every year of her childhood. But those family vacation had been during the heat of mid-summer many, many years ago. She noticed the lodge had not fared well in the meantime.

As they got out of the car, Meg picked up the maimed Barbie doll and stuffed it in her pocket. She didn't say anything as they walked into the lodge.

Standing in the lobby, Claire looked up the old moose head over the fireplace. A veritable moth wonderland, it looked hopeless and forlorn.

Meg followed her mother's eyes and said, "Eyew, that moose reminds me of you trying on your mother's old fur coat."

A few months ago, Claire had modeled her mother's old mink stole for her daughter. They had laughed together over how outdated it looked, but the painful question remained—what do you do with your mother's old, well-loved, but beyond fuddy-duddy, mink? She couldn't bear to throw it away, and so it hung at the back of the coat closet like an animal carcass aging.

Her darling daughter Meg had entered her teen years with a thump. Her sense of humor was sharp and pointed and often aimed at her mother. Claire had decided that they needed an outing together over President's Day. What better trip than back to her old lodge?

Now, staring up at the moth-eaten moose, she couldn't believe she had done this: dragged her teenaged daughter away from her friends for a weekend to sit in front of a drafty fireplace at this old resort. They had brought their skis in hopes of getting out to cross country, but with this little snow, she didn't think it would happen. It was going to be a long, long weekend.

"Let's check in," she suggested.

Meg rolled her eyes. Claire could hardly say anything without Meg lifting her eyes to the heavens and then letting them drop dramatically to the floor.

"I'm hungry," Meg whined.

"We'll eat as soon as we're settled."

A woman who introduced herself as Mrs. Lundquist was waiting for them at the desk, blond hair pulled back in a neat ponytail, royal blue sweater highlighting the blue of her eyes. Claire guessed the woman was her age. Mrs. Lundquist looked tired under her efficient smile, but Claire thought she recognized her.

"Aren't you Bonnie Sandier?" Claire asked.

The woman looked up at her. "Was once. Do I know you?"

"Oh, you probably wouldn't remember me. We used to come here when I was a kid. Claire Watkins. Your folks were running the place then."

"Yes, my husband and I took it over about fifteen years ago when dad died. Nice to have you back with us."

"Do you still live in the lodge?"

"On the other side of the lobby from you. If you need anything, we're always available."

When they got to their room—two twin beds dressed in black and red gingham spreads—Meg flopped down and closed her eyes.

"Tired?" Claire asked.

"Bored."

Claire decided it was time for one of those small talks that she gave to her daughter fairly infrequently, trying to remind her that mothers had feelings too. She knew the talks were dumb and accomplished nothing, but she couldn't stop herself.

"I brought you up here because I wanted you to see a place that was important to me when I was your age. I thought we might have a chance to hang out together and talk."

Meg sat up and glared. She held out her hand with three fingers pointing up. "First, that was too many years ago to think about. Second, we communicate plenty well at home. Third, I had important things to do this weekend."

Claire could see this was hopeless. She had failed as a mother. They might as well go to dinner. She was hungry too.

"Let's go eat."

They trooped out of their room and ran into a girl about Meg's age with long blond hair and very short bangs. Her odd haircut gave her an astonished look.

"Hi," the girl said as they walked down the hall. "I'm Brigitta Lundquist."

Meg mumbled something about "Princess Kay of the Milky Way" under her breath.

The blond-haired girl stopped and said, "No, just a runner-up." Then she ran down the hall in front of them, her hair flowing like a flame.

"Meggy," Claire admonished.

"What a priss."

"You don't even know her."

"You can just tell."

Claire stopped and grabbed Meg's shoulder, causing her to spin and face her in the dark hallway. "Your attitude stinks, Missy."

"Missy Pissy to you."

Claire couldn't help herself. She started laughing. Meg could always do that to her—surprise her and remind her that her daughter was her own person. "Well, cool it."

"I'll try. But I'm getting my period."

"Listen, you don't want to go there. You don't know from period until you're not getting them anymore."

"Truce."

They slapped hands and walked down the hallway.

"Walleye," Claire said.

"What?"

"I want walleye. It's so good here."

As they walked through the lobby, the main door gusted open and two men came in. On second glance, Claire could see that it was an older man, about her age, later forties, and a teen-aged boy, a little older than Meg. But tall and skinny. With dyed black hair and a earring in his nose and through his eyebrow and, she suspected, in his tongue. They both had suitcases and went to the desk to check in. Meg gave the boy the once over as they passed in the lobby.

The restaurant had changed little since Claire had last been there: big heavy oak log tables with equally large chairs that were almost impossible to move, a roaring fire in the stone fireplace, and a marvelous view of the lake. Too bad there weren't more people to enjoy it.

As soon as they sat down a waitress scuttled up to them with two menus. Her name tag read "Karen." She was a thin wisp of a woman with short dark hair. She took their drink order: a ginger ale and a beer.

Without even looking at the menu, Claire said, "And I'd like the walleye."

"Oh," the waitress's hand went to her mouth. "I'm afraid we're out of the walleye." Claire looked around the room. The only other people were a couple sitting close to the window. "Out of the walleye?" she repeated. "Will you have it tomorrow night?" "I hope so." Claire opened the menu with resignation. This was going to be a very long weekend.

Meg had talked to the dark-haired boy in the front of the fireplace for an hour or so before bed. His name was Ned, and his favorite ice cream was plain chocolate. Figured, anything dark he'd like. He wrote poetry and wanted to go to India before he went to college. He was a junior and two years older than she was. She suspected she might be a little in love, but she didn't want to get her hopes up. She had hardly ever fallen in love in her life.

She had even come to have fond feelings for the moose. They

had named it Hank the Hardly-haired moose. When she walked down the hallway to her room, she was humming a little tune she had made up.

Her mom was sitting up in bed reading.

"Hey."

Her mom turned her head and smiled. Meg couldn't get used to the fact that her mom now wore glasses when she read. It made her look like a librarian or school teacher, not a cop.

She had told Ned that her mom was a cop, or rather a deputy sheriff. He was suitably impressed. He had said that it made him feel safer to know there was a cop in the lodge.

When Meg had asked him if there was any reason not to feel safe, he said, cryptically, that there were stories, and then went on to explain.

As Meg pulled on her pajamas she asked her mom, "Did you know that a woman was killed here?"

The book lowered and the glasses came off. "No, when?"

"I guess about five years ago. Might even have been in this very room."

"Who told you that?"

"Ned. The waitress told him. His father is maybe writing an article on this place—if he can find a story. So Karen, the waitress, told him about the murder. But he said it might be too far in the past."

"Did they solve the crime?"

"I don't know. Maybe you should look into it tomorrow. Give you something to do."

At three o'clock in the morning, a shriek rent the night, a woman's scream, which sounded like it was right in their room. Claire sat up in bed with her heart at full gallop. She could see Meg was up too.

Then silence.

Meg whispered, "What was that?"

"Sounded like a scream."

"Duh."

"What'd you want at this time of night? CSI?"

Claire forced herself out of bed and went to the door.

"What if she's out there?" Meg squeaked.

"We'll invite her in," Claire said and opened the door. The hall was empty.

Claire shut the door.

Meg was staring at her. "Did you see anything?"

"Nope."

"Aren't you going to investigate?"

Claire looked down at her snowflake pajamas and her bare feet. "I don't think so."

"Mom, you're the law."

"I'm on vacation. At the moment, I'm only a tired, cold, nearly naked woman who wants to crawl back in bed."

"Then I'm going to look."

Claire climbed into bed and pulled up the covers. "Fine." Her daughter left the room.

Meg couldn't believe her mom. Where was her sense of duty? Where was her sense of adventure? Where was her sense of motherhood? She had let Meg come out on her own to look for what might be a deadly killer. Or worse yet, a horrible ghost.

Meg walked down to the end of the poorly lit hallway and as she turned the corner, she ran into someone.

As they bounced off of each other she saw that it was Ned. His dark hair, instead of being slicked back, was tousled. He had removed the ring from his eyebrow and his nose. And he was wearing candy-cane pajamas. He looked younger and quite sweet. She liked him even more.

"Did you scream?" he asked.

"No, are you kidding? I just got up to see who did."

"No one down this way," he told her. "But it sounded like it was right outside our room."

"I think she was running as she was screaming, because it sounded right outside our room, too."

"What's your mom doing?"

"She went back to sleep. Some cop."

"My dad was out of the room when it happened, getting ice. But he heard it, too."

Ned looked down at her pajamas. There were small black poodles with big purses on a pink background and the word "Shopping" on it. "Cute," he said.

She nodded at his pjs and didn't feel like she even had to say anything.

He stepped back. "So, see you in the morning."

"Yeah, good night."

As she watched him lope down the hallway, her heart lifted in her chest. Yes, love was like all she had read about. Even though it was deep winter outside, in her heart it felt like spring.

The next morning broke brighter and crisper than Claire could have hoped. The breakfast at Loon Lodge was as good as she remembered: blueberry pancakes with real maple syrup, American fries, and piping hot, if not very strong, coffee.

Meg was nearly sunny, chatting away about everything, sharing the paper with her mom, even took the possibility of a walk later in the day under advisement.

Ned showed up at their table as they were finishing breakfast. He too had brightened up, not resembling the sulky, sinister creature that had strolled through the door last night. His hair was freshly washed, his eyes bright, no scowl on his face, and many of the facial adornments were gone. Claire had the good sense to leave the two of them to drink more coffee and fight over the paper.

She headed for the desk and found Bonnie bent over some bills. Bonnie did not look like she had had a good night.

"We heard a scream last night," Claire told her.

Bonnie looked up and nodded her head in weariness. "The writer told me about that."

"What's going on?"

"I don't know."

"Has this happened before?"

"No. Nothing quite like this. But strange things have happened."

"Like what?"

"Strange sounds, things missing."

Claire couldn't help the laugh that slipped out. "A poltergeist, a ghost?"

Bonnie shrugged. "Or someone trying to ruin us."

Claire decided she should tell Bonnie what she did for a living. "I haven't mentioned this, but I'm a deputy sheriff in Wisconsin. So I could help you out here if you have any suspicions about what's going on."

Bonnie seemed to shut down with this new information.

"My daughter told me that someone was killed here about five years ago."

"Yes, it was awful. A waitress, a friend of Karen's, was murdered by her ex-husband right after she got off work. Her throat slit. Then he blasted his head off with a shotgun down by the lake. People stopped coming here. It hasn't been the same since."

Right after breakfast, Meg saw Brigitta standing in the lobby, looking out at the snow. She decided to do some sleuthing.

"Did you hear the scream last night?" she asked.

"No," Brigitta said. "But I heard about it. Ever since Barbie was killed, weird things have been happening here."

"Did you know her well?"

"Not really. She didn't live here. She just came in to work. But she did babysit me a couple times. That was great. She would bring some of her Barbie dolls for me to play with. I loved those dolls."

"I never played with Barbies. I played with horses."

Brigitta was still looking out the window when Meg walked away.

After a good day spent reading, hiking the lightly snow-covered ski trails, a meal of hamburger and fries, and a rousing game of Scrabble with Ned and her mom, Meg didn't want to go to bed. But her mom dragged her off around midnight.

Now the two of them were deep under the covers in their matching twin beds. Claire was reading some mystery novel and Meg was thinking about Ned. He was nearly perfect.

Except he lived in Alexandria, Minnesota, which was about five hours away from Fort St. Antoine, her hometown in Wisconsin. One more day and then they might never see each other again. Thank god for the Internet.

"What're we going to do if we hear the screams tonight?" Meg asked her mom.

"The door is locked."

"We need a plan, Mom."

"Okay. You run to the left and I'll run to the right. Maybe we'll catch the person."

"What if it's a ghost?"

"Well, then you have nothing to worry about. I've never heard of a ghost hurting anyone."

The scream pulled Claire out of a very deep sleep. It felt like she was coming up through layers and layers of snow, as if she'd been buried under an avalanche.

She woke up gasping. Looking over, she saw that Meg was still asleep.

The scream didn't come again, and Claire almost fell back to sleep, but her curiosity got the best of her. She stepped into her slippers, pulled on her bathrobe and went down the hall. Walking into the lobby, she saw no one, heard nothing.

When she looked outside, she noticed it was snowing. She walked to the lobby door and saw footprints, fresh and deep in the newly fallen snow. She wasn't going to follow them, but they reassured her. She tried the door and found it locked.

There was no ghost, but whoever the screamer was, they either had a key to the lodge or were staying there.

When Claire got back to her room, she noticed something on the floor right next to the door. She bent down to pick it up and saw that it was a doll's head, a Barbie doll's head. The neck was red and sticky. Claire lifted it to her nose and sniffed. Just as she suspected, ketchup.

Meg couldn't believe she had slept through the scream, but her mom told her about her discoveries: the footprints, the doll's head. Her mom had cleaned off Barbie's head and now the body was sitting propped up on their dresser, holding its own head like a modern Ichabod Crane.

"Mom, you washed off the evidence."

"Sweetie, I don't like the screaming, but I don't think it's a crime to scream in the night."

"I'd call it disturbing the peace, at least."

Meg was so excited to see the snow. About eight inches had fallen overnight—enough snow for good skiing, but not enough to worry about being stuck at the lodge.

Her mom was great about letting her go skiing with Ned. She actually got the impression her mom was relieved to have a little time to herself.

That night Ned and his father, Art, joined them for dinner. Art was happily married and her mom was happily living with Rich, but the two of them seemed to enjoy each other's company. Art talked about a novel he was working on, and then talked about his article for *Minnesota Living*.

Karen waited on them as usual.

Art asked her, "So do you think there is a ghost?"

"Like I told you the first night, ever since that woman died here, things have been a little strange. The screams in the night are the latest thing. Are you going to put that in your article?"

Art nodded and said, "Exactly the kind of thing I was looking for. Something out of the ordinary. It makes for good atmosphere."

"Oh, that's what folks will get here—really good atmosphere."

Meg couldn't believe how much Karen was talking. She had never said more than two words to them.

"We got a special delivery of walleye. Nothing too good for the writer," Karen announced. Her mother clapped her hands and then they all four ordered walleye.

After dinner, they decided to play Pictionary. In a corner of the lobby, Meg found a dictionary lying open to the Bs. Meg was surprised to see the page torn in half. She showed her mom.

"Some kids, more surprising it's even still here."

Meg was pleased to see how quickly Ned picked up the game. He won with thirty points, her mom came in second with twenty-seven points, Meg was third with twenty-five points, and

Art trailed with twenty-four. "Embarrassing for a writer," he said.

Then it was time for bed and Meg didn't want to go. She had to think of a reason to stay up with Ned for a few minutes longer. It was their last night together.

She couldn't believe it when her mom said, "Hey, Meg, why don't you keep Ned company for a little while. I'm going to take a bath. Don't be too long, though."

Art waved good-night, too.

Meg sat on the couch in front of the slowly fading fire and felt Ned walk his hand down her shoulders.

"We're leaving bright and early tomorrow," he said.

"We are too."

"This has been great."

"Yeah, great."

"Let's try to catch the screamer tonight," he suggested.

"Okay."

Then he kissed her. It wasn't a wet kiss, it wasn't a pressure kiss, and it wasn't a groping kiss. It was a perfect kiss: slow, thoughtful with a little nibble. It left her breathless and wanting more. She had been kissed before but never by someone she liked so much and never so well. When the fire died, they stood up and held hands and he walked her to her room.

He leaned down for one final kiss and someone screamed.

Meg jumped. Ned ran toward the sound and she ran after him. It had come from the other hallway. They went around the corner in time to see a flowing mane of blond hair disappear in the dark. They ran after it, but by the time they got back to the lobby, she was gone. Meg saw that a long blond hair was on the corner of a log where the screamer had run too close to it. She grabbed it and wound it around her fingers. A clue.

When Meg walked back to her room, she found her mom in the hallway, holding a note in her hand. On it were written the words, "The cry of the banshee."

Ned said goodnight and they went into their room. Meg told her mom about seeing the blond hair on the screamer running down the hall.

"So it must be Brigitta," her mom said.

"I thought so too, but now I'm not so sure," Meg sat on the edge of her bed, holding a long blond hair. "Do you have a match?"

The next morning they all gathered for their last breakfast. Karen waited on them and looked as tired as they all did.

"Hey, Karen, we heard the screams again last night," Meg said.

Karen ran a hand through her short, dark hair. "The woman must be in torment. Not sure what draws her here."

"Do you think she's a banshee?"

Without a blink, Karen said, "Could be. Banshees wail a warning when someone's about to die."

"It would make a good story, don't you think? Might bring up more people to stay at the Loon Lodge. I think Art is going to write about the banshee in his article."

"That's great. We need more people to come and stay. We've been hurting badly. Maybe Bonnie will change the name of the place to Ghost Lodge."

Meg reached into her pocket and pulled out the deconstructed Barbie doll. "I thought you might want this doll back. I'd recommend you try to keep walleye on your menu. Might be a better way to pull people in than screaming in the night."

Claire watched her daughter say good-bye to Ned, but tried not to let her know she was watching. She sat in the car with the motor running and looked forward to getting home.

When Meg piled into the car and they were on their way, Claire said, "You're not thinking of going into law enforcement, are you?"

"No way. I learned that trick in Home Economics, how to check to see if a piece of fabric is a hundred percent wool or if it has some synthetic material in it. Wool or hair has a distinctive odor when it burns. That piece of hair felt odd to me—too elastic.

"Once I knew the screamer was wearing a wig, it all fell into place. The ketchup on the doll's neck. Karen had easy access. The footprints in the snow you saw—everyone else except Karen was staying at the lodge. The page torn from the dictionary—I figured she might not know how to spell 'banshee.'"

"So I guess it was as simple as she saw any opportunity to give a writer what he wanted—a good story. The Loon Lodge could use more business, Karen would make more money." Meg added, "And her friend wouldn't be forgotten." She snuggled into her coat and fell asleep.

As Claire drove out of the north woods, she glanced at the sweet face of her sleepy daughter. Finally a little quiet time with Meg.

William Kent Krueger

Raised in the Cascade Mountains of Oregon, William Kent Krueger briefly attended Stanford University—before being kicked out for radical activities. After that, he logged timber, worked construction, tried his hand at free-lance journalism, and eventually ended up researching child development at the University of Minnesota. He currently makes his living as a full-time author. He's been married for more than thirty years to a marvelous woman who is an attorney. With his wife and two children, he makes his home in St. Paul, a city he dearly loves.

Krueger writes a mystery series set in the north woods of Minnesota, hard up against the Iron Range. His protagonist is Cork O'Connor, the former sheriff of Tamarack County and a man of mixed heritage—part Irish and part Ojibwe. His work has earned him two Minnesota Book Awards, the Loft-McKnight Fiction Award, the Barry Award and Anthony Award for Best First Novel, and the Friends of American Writers Prize.

Before Swine

William Kent Krueger

When Sheriff Amundsen telephoned that morning just as I was pouring coffee and said to me, "Bad news, Earl. Adolph Burmeister's been ate by his hogs. Better get your ass over here," I knew it was going to be one strange day.

I was still a bachelor back then, so had no wife to apologize to for leaving abruptly. I strapped on my gun belt, put on my leather jacket with the Holmes County Sheriff's Department patch on the right shoulder, donned my flat-brimmed uniform hat, and headed out the door just as the sun was coming up.

Burmeister's farm was six miles outside of Plainview. It was a spare-looking place, especially at the end of winter. Most of the snow had melted, leaving the land looking hard and bare. As I drove up, all I saw were flat empty fields, dull fence lines, and Burmeister's drab farm buildings, long in need of fresh paint.

Sheriff Amundsen's Buick was parked in the yard between the house and barn. I didn't see him anywhere. I figured maybe he was inside talking with Burmeister's wife, Marta. There was a gray feather of smoke sticking up from the stove pipe, and I smelled sausage cooking.

"Out here, Earl." The sheriff's voice came from the other side of the barn.

I found him in Wellingtons, calf deep in the muck of the hog pen. He had himself a pitchfork and was going over the pen carefully, sinking the tines into the mire, drawing the big fork back. Out and back, out and back, in the way of a man patiently casting for trout.

This was nineteen and twenty-five. I'd lost both my parents to the influenza epidemic several years before while I was in college. After that I went to Europe and spent a year trading shots with Germans across farm fields so devastated by war I couldn't imagine anything ever growing there again. I planned on law school when I returned, which was my father's deepest wish for me. Instead, I came home to Plainview, Minnesota, and took the first job offered to me: deputy to Rolph Amundsen. He'd been sheriff nearly twenty years. He was so well thought of he usually ran unopposed. He'd also been my father's best friend.

I leaned over the top fence rail. "What are you doing?"

"Looking for Adolph," he replied.

The hogs had been moved to the next pen, but they were all lined up with their snouts between the rails, staring at the sheriff and grunting in a resentful way.

"He's in there?" I asked.

"What's left of him."

"How do you know?"

"Because of that." He pointed toward a boot sitting on the corner fence post.

I went over and took a look at the boot, which wasn't exactly empty. It was full of blood and mud, and Adolph's foot was still inside. Other men might have been startled, but it was nothing compared to the things I'd seen in the war.

"How'd you find him?" I asked.

"Bill Knieff called me," he said, still casting the pitchfork. "He brought a load of corn seed over just before daybreak. Roused the missus who says Adolph's out feeding the animals. Bill goes to the pens, sees the hogs here going crazy, spots Adolph's jacket. He wades in, shoos the animals away, finds what's left of Adolph, which isn't much, gives me a call. By the time he gets back out here, the hogs have pretty much finished Adolph. Except for that boot. I'm just checking to see if they overlooked anything else." He finally stood up straight and shook his head. "Looks like they made a pretty good meal of the man."

"Ironic when you think about it," I said.

The sheriff smiled, a little grimly. "That it is. Adolph was awful fond of a good pork loin."

He waded toward me through the muck, a sucking sound at each step. I unlatched the gate and let him out.

"Where's Knieff?" I asked.

"Sent him home. He was pretty shook up. Sorry to tap you for this," he said. "I know you just finished your shift."

Being the only bachelor in the department, from the very beginning I drew the graveyard shift so that the married men could be home nights. I didn't mind. After the war, I often had trouble sleeping anyway.

"Truth is you got more brains than anybody in the department. Say, what time do you have?" he asked.

"I don't know. I misplaced my watch."

"Your father's watch?"

He said it with a note of disapproval. It was a fine gold timepiece. My father had given it to me before I headed off to college. Even in the trenches in France, I'd managed to keep it safe through a lot of fierce fighting. Then I'd lost it thoughtlessly in quiet Plainview.

"How'd you know when your shift was done?" he asked, slipping off the Wellingtons and putting on his own boots, which he'd placed beside the gate.

"I heard the whistle of the five-fifteen going through town."

"Ah," he said with a nod, and bent to tie his boots.

"So what do you think about Adolph?" I asked. "Heart attack?"

"Gonna be impossible to tell without a body."

"What now?"

He straightened up and looked toward the house. "I think we should talk with the widow."

We crossed the yard. It had snowed lightly overnight, a dusting fine as flour that covered the mud of early April, except along the path to the barn which was a mess of muddy tracks. We walked to the farmhouse door. The sheriff knocked. A moment later, Marta appeared.

"Gut morning." She had a fine, soft voice that carried strong echoes of her German homeland. Her brown hair was braided and coiled on her head. Whenever she let it down, it reached to her waist. She had on a plain, gray shift. Sundays when she accompanied her husband to Good Hope Lutheran Church in Plainview she wore a long almond-colored dress with yellow flowers embroidered on the collar. It was the dress she'd been married in, the only nice dress she had. Adolph said one good dress was plenty for any woman.

Around Plainview, everyone knew about Adolph Burmeister. That's why he had to go buy himself a bride from the old country. He was older by twenty years, and his wife was his wife because after the war Germany was in bad shape and people were desperate. Burmeister's distant cousins had sent their daughter to him in exchange for much needed money. I'm sure they were hoping for a better life for their daughter in America. If she'd ended up anywhere but on Adolph's farm she might have had it.

"May we come in?" the sheriff asked.

"Yah," she said, and stepped aside.

Before he married, Adolph had kept house like a bachelor. No—worse. I'd never had occasion to visit myself, but other bachelor farmers who did joked about how awful the place was. Marta had changed that. Though it was not a well-appointed house—Adolph bought only what he believed was absolutely necessary and never spent extravagantly on anything—it was clean and neat.

"Coffee?" Marta asked.

"Obliged," the sheriff said.

She smiled at me weakly, this new widow. "And you?"

"I could stand a cup, thanks."

The sheriff and I sat down. Marta brought us coffee and stepped back, like a servant.

"Would you sit with us?" the sheriff asked.

She did, folding her small rough hands in her lap and looking down at them.

"So," the sheriff began, "you told me earlier that Adolph went out to feed the livestock. What time was that?"

"I don't know," she answered softly. "After de rooster crowed. Before de sun vas up."

"You were awake?"

"Adolph, he did not like for me to be in bed after him. He feeds de animals. I make de breakfast."

"What kind of a sleeper was he?"

"I do not understand."

"A sound sleeper?"

Her delicate brows furrowed in confusion. "Does he sleep good?" I said.

The sheriff shot me a stern look. This was his interrogation.

"Ah," she said, brightening. "Yah. He drinks his viskey, goes to bed, sleeps like a big rock until de rooster crows. Every night."

The sheriff pulled at his big walrus moustache. "Some men his age, they get up in the night to take care of business. How about Adolph?"

"Business?"

"The chamber pot," I said.

"Oh." She shook her head. "Like a rock until de rooster crows."

"How about you? How do you sleep?"

"Not so good as Adolph."

"When your husband didn't come back from feeding the stock, what did you do?"

"I vait. Adolph, if I come looking, is angry."

"Why would he be angry?"

"Adolph is a man I do not understand. So much anger. De eggs are too hard. De coffee is too bitter. I try, but I cannot please him."

It was well known in Plainview that Adolph Burmeister was prone to strike his wife. We'd all seen the bruises on her pretty face when she came to church. I thought about what her life was like isolated there with Burmeister. A prison sentence couldn't have been any worse.

"So," the sheriff went on, "you didn't know anything was wrong until Bill Knieff came banging at your door?"

"I did not know."

He stood up without having taken more than a couple of sips from his cup. "Thank you for the coffee. We still need to look around a bit more, do you mind?"

"No." She looked up from her hands and said, "I cooked breakfast. For Adolph, but..." She stopped and dropped her eyes again. "I have food if you are hungry. I have kept it varm."

"That's a mighty nice offer, Mrs. Burmeister," the sheriff replied, "but we still have work to do. By the way, is that Adolph's shotgun there by the door?"

"Yah."

He picked it up from where it leaned against the wall, cracked it open, and found two unfired shells.

"For intruders?" he asked.

"He vas always vorried someone vould steal his animals."

"Ah." He nodded as if he understood about Burmeister.

"Are you all right?" I asked Marta.

She gave me a small smile. "I am fine. Thank you."

Outside we put our hats back on. The sheriff looked around the bleak yard, finally settling his gaze on the barn. "Let's have a look in there."

The sun had risen fully and threw a bright rectangle of orange light through the big door, illuminating the barn, the stalls inside, the hay loft, and the hay mound. The sheriff walked around a bit, scratching his unshaved jaw. He'd probably come straight from home. He was a widower, had lost his wife in the same flu epidemic that claimed my folks. He hadn't remarried, but not because he didn't have the opportunity. A man like Rolph Amundsen was a catch. I think he was devoted to his wife, a romantic man. He still kept her photograph on his desk at the office. He was always after me to court some young woman. "A man ought not to waste his youth, Earl," he'd say, offering me the same advice I'm sure he believed my father would have. "Life's like a shooting star. Seems like only a moment after you take notice, it's gone."

He scrutinized a pile of hay in one of the stalls, lifted a blanket folded over the low dividing wall, then noticed something hanging on a nail in one of the support posts.

"Take a look at this, Earl." He lifted a pair of soiled pink ballet slippers. "I'll be."

"Marta's?" I guessed.

"I'd be mighty surprised if Adolph wore them."

He hung the slippers back on the nail, walked to the big empty area in the middle of the barn, and carefully studied the ground. "Look here." He pointed to a configuration of curving lines, circles, and small shallow depressions in the dirt. "What do you think?"

"Looks like somebody's been drawing."

He glanced back toward the slippers. "With her toes," he said.

It took me a moment, then I understood. "She dances here?"

"I imagine a man like Adolph would consider ballet a waste of her time. She said she had trouble sleeping at night. What do you bet she sneaked out here to dance while Adolph snored away." He shook his head. "That poor woman."

I could hear the hogs outside grunting and snorting restlessly. The sheriff crossed to a side door that opened toward the pens and swung it wide. He stepped out and I followed.

"Careful," he said and nodded toward a single line of tracks in the snow that led from the barn to the hog pens. "I imagine he came along here."

He studied the tracks all the way to fence and stood for a while gazing at the empty pen where Adolph had literally given himself over to the feeding of his hogs.

"A heart attack? Maybe a stroke?" I speculated out loud. "He goes down among his hogs, who are looking to him for food, and feed them he does."

"Sounds reasonable," the sheriff said. "Only…"

"Only what?"

"Those Wellingtons I put on to wade in the muck of that pen, they're not mine. I found them in the barn. I'm guessing they belonged to Adolph."

"So?"

"So if he was coming out here to feed his hogs, why didn't he put them on?"

"Never struck me as a particularly careful man," I said.

"Go get me that boot of his."

I went to the fence post, lifted what was left of Adolph Burmeister, and brought it to the sheriff. He knelt and set the boot into one of the tracks coming from the door of the barn.

"Boot's smaller than the track. What do you make of that?" He looked up at me.

"It happens sometimes when snow melts. Prints get bigger."

He nodded and stood up, leaving the boot on the ground. "Maybe."

I followed him back to the barn. Inside he returned to the stall where he'd found the mounding of hay and the folded blanket. He lifted the blanket and held it out to me.

"Take a whiff, Earl," he said.

The blanket smelled not of the barn but of some delicate floral scent. I looked at him with surprise. "Perfume?"

"That's what I'd say. And like the slippers, I'm guessing it wasn't Adolph's."

"She put on perfume to dance?"

"To dance?" He looked as if he were going to laugh. "Earl, you got a lot to learn about life. That's not just the smell of perfume. That there's the smell of Obsession."

"I don't understand," I said.

"That pile of hay, what do you think it's for? You see any animal in this barn?"

"What are you saying?"

"I'm saying that a woman in love—in love with a man who's not her husband—and obsessed with being with him, would find a way. Even if it meant a pile of hay in a cold barn in the middle of the night."

"You're saying she was with someone here?"

"For a college man, you catch on mighty slow."

He put the blanket where he'd found it, stepped to the middle of the barn again, and motioned me over. He bent, ran his fingers through the dirt, and came up with dark clods.

"I noticed this earlier. What do you make of it?"

I shrugged. "Mud."

He shook his head. "Mud is dirt and water. If this is water mixed in here, then I'm Mae West. It's blood, Earl."

"Could be from one of the livestock."

He looked at me like I was dumber than Adolph's pigs. "Come on." He moved to the barn wall opposite the stall and stood a couple of feet to the right of the door that opened toward the pens. "These holes, I spotted 'em when we headed out."

There were two of them, small with splintering at the edges.

"Bullet holes, wouldn't you say?" He waited for me to say.

What I said was, "They could be from anything."

"Really? Sure look like bullet holes to me. See, this is what I figure." He turned and looked back at the whole of the barn, as if watching it all play out in front of him. "Mrs. Burmiester said that Adolph was a sound sleeper. I believe she sneaked out here in the night to be with someone, a man. While they were…involved… Adolph came out and caught 'em. Maybe he suspected and was waiting for his chance. I don't know. But being the kind of man Adolph was, if he did, in fact, suspect his wife, then I'm guessing he brought something along to take care of things. Probably that shotgun of his we saw inside the house. Now, this lover, I'm figuring fate was on his side, because he had a gun, too, and before Adolph could discharge his shotgun, the lover let fly a few rounds of his own. A couple went wild and hit that far wall, but at least one got Adolph and got him good.

"The lovers, they're pretty scared, I imagine. How do you explain Adolph? Well, a smart person might realize that if you don't have a body, you don't have to explain much. So the lover, he carts Adolph down to the hog pen and gives those critters an early meal."

I stared at him, aware my eyes were huge as a couple of fried eggs.

"I know," he said, waving it off. "Sounds pretty far-fetched. Chalk it up, if you want, to a sheriff who's never dealt with anything much worse than drunk farmhands."

He stood with me a moment in the barn, the sound of Adolph Burmeister's greedy hogs coming from outside. Inside there was only the soft breathing of him and of me.

He spoke quietly, almost affectionately. "This is what I'm going to say officially. Adolph Burmeister had a heart attack while feeding his hogs and became a victim of the animals' hunger. End of story."

He took a deep breath and put his hand on my shoulder. "Why don't you go tell Mrs. Burmeister the news. And, Earl, I wouldn't be judging time by the five-fifteen through town for a while. I got a call from Burlington Northern a couple days ago. The five-fifteen's been rerouted for a month while they work on the trestle in Ansonville. Here, this is a much better way of tracking time."

He reached into his coat pocket and drew out a gold watch covered with muck from the hog pen. He dropped it into my palm.

"You know what your father might have said. He'd say there's little chance anybody can be happy in this life, but if the opportunity ever comes your way, the worst crime of all is to let it pass you by."

He walked away into the morning sunlight that streamed through the barn door like a river of gold.

Judith Guest

Judith Guest was born in Detroit, Michigan and graduated from the University of Michigan with a BA in Education. She has taught school in Royal Oak and Birmingham, Michigan.

Her first novel, Ordinary People, *published by Viking Press, won the Janet Heidinger Kafka Prize for best first novel in 1976. It was made into a movie that won six Academy Awards, including best picture and best director. Her novel* Second Heaven *was selected as one of* School Library Journal's *Best Books for Young Adults.* Killing Time in St. Cloud, *written with novelist Rebecca Hill, was published in 1988.* Errands, *her fourth novel, was published by Ballantine in 1997.* The Tarnished Eye, *a novel of suspense, was published by Scribner in June of 2004.*

She has written several screenplays, one of which was based on a trio of short stories by Carol Bly and made into a movie called Rachel River. *She and Rebecca Hill teach seminars on novel writing. She divides her time more or less equally between Minnesota and Michigan.*

The Gates

Judith Guest

The day the city of Edina became a gated community was a red-letter day for Archie Trebold. He had grown up in this elegant and urbane borough; his parents and both sets of grandparents had been born here; he was what was called a 'native'. For years he and others like him had petitioned the city to do a traffic study of its shady, curving avenues in order to determine how many transients were using the thoroughfare system for their own purposes. Of course it had turned out there were many, passing through in their Hondas and Toyotas, having no intention of settling down, but merely wearing out the roads and adding to the general disorder and confusion.

Archie's letters to the editor of the *Edina Sun* on the behalf of the long-time residents, along with his pervasive presence at the city council meetings had finally made an impression. He was not at all insulted by certain council members referring to him as the personification of the Chinese water torture. *Whatever it took.* He felt a certain pride in this outcome; he had asserted himself, as every good citizen should.

Of course there were some who had protested the gating, even going so far as to sport bumper stickers reading *Don't Fence Me In!* or *What next—an effing moat?* They said they preferred to broaden their children's experience of the world rather than narrow it, but Archie didn't believe it for a second; these were the very same people complaining about the presence of RVs on the city streets or unbagged leaves clogging the curbs. *There goes the neighborhood*, they'd say. And they'd be right. After all, the Gates Project was placed on the city ballot and duly voted for, and those who didn't approve should simply pack up and move back to where they came from.

It was a brisk morning in November and Archie was walking to his office, which was situated at the corner of Halifax and Fiftieth, catty-corner from D'Amico's Italian Restaurant and just inside the eastern gate. It was the last of the four to be completed, owing to the protests of a number of businesses in the 50th and France area who refused annexation and invoked the Business Opportunities Law, which declared that any industry or trade that deemed itself harmed by enclosure could petition to remain outside the confines of Edina proper. The West Gate, at Brookside and 44th, was installed on February tenth of this year; the North Gate, at Browndale and Excelsior, a few weeks later; the Southview Lane Gate on July fourth. *Independence Day.* Archie appreciated the poetry of this. And of the attractively decorated tollbooths erected at each of the gate sites and staffed by native sons and daughters, or *Gatesters,* as they were called. It was a cushy job and they had many applicants for it. Archie was proud of his unique addition to the system: an electronic windshield sticker that enabled the residents to pass through unimpeded. No need to stop and be identified or to fumble in one's wallet for the toll.

He turned up the driveway that led to the bank and the Post Office, admiring the row of arborvitae planted along the western berm, shielding the houses on fiftieth from the view of Minneapolis. As he walked along the curving asphalt, he noted the footprints in the snow—large and clumsy-looking. It had snowed last night and the temporary tattoo in the pristine whiteness wound around the circle of blue mailboxes. He recognized the boot prints of his old enemy, Dank Wagner.

What was he doing around here? He thought he'd seen the last of Dank when his letter was published last year in the *Sun* excoriating the 'artificial aristocrats of a certain suburb who were determined not to mingle with Minneapolis' mediocre minions.' What a colossal misstep that had been for Dank! For weeks people had marched up and down in front of his house waving their green and white beanies in the air and demanding that he apologize and resign his position on the Edina Standards Board. The last Archie had seen of him was his little green Volkswagen high-tailing it out of Hennepin County in high dudgeon. Good riddance to bad rubbish. Dank didn't belong here anymore, that was plain. If he wanted to be an *Everyman*, he should go do it in St. Louis Park or Fridley. Or Bemidji for that matter.

Archie hurried toward the Post Office, skirting the vehicles parked by the drive-up bank. He usually waved to the tellers working behind the plate glass, but this morning the windowpanes were dark.

Odd since it was nearly ten o'clock. Was it a bank holiday? Surely he would have known that. Did they close for Veteran's Day? Of course the closings didn't affect him since he did all of his banking by telephone anyway, and had done so for years. So easy, and so much less personal. Some days he simply didn't feel like talking to anyone, and the soothing voice of the pseudo-teller on the telephone suited him to a T.

The lobby of the Post Office was deserted, but the new automated machines stood at attention, waiting for him. He rested his burden on the weigh scale and inserted his credit card. The machine asked if it was a letter or a package, and he pressed his finger to the glass over the word 'package' and heard the reassuring *ping* as it registered the information. He typed in the zip code and instantly his postage was printed. He affixed the label to his parcel and slid it through the gaping maw of the machine. *Mission accomplished*. All in a matter of seconds. Amazing how efficient this was, compared with the time formerly wasted waiting in line in the Post Office. And there was no need to speak to anyone! No small talk, no inane asking of how people were or what kind of day they were having. What freedom!

He exited the building and thought for a moment that he saw a car glide around the corner and head for France Avenue. The exact same thing had happened last week at just about the same time. Who would be circling the border of the city at this hour of the day? And why? It was something to ponder. And ponder he would as soon as he got back to his office. *The price of freedom is eternal vigilance.* He remembered this from a course in Political Science he took in college. It formed the heart of his belief system—a motto to live by.

The sound of a train whistle echoed in the stillness, eerie and elusive. Hard to tell if it came from the crossing at Brookside or further up the line, in St. Louis Park. He'd been working on a petition for rerouting the daily locomotive with its tanker cars carrying who-knew-what through the confines of the city, and making the B & O divert through Chanhassen. The tracks were ancient and in need of repair; the cars shipped nothing that was even remotely useful to the city, so what was the point? Let some other town handle the noise and the nuisance.

He bent to the pavement to retrieve a piece of paper that had been crumpled up and tossed into the street. Picking it up, he stared intently at it. A page torn from a dictionary. Not a regular dictionary, either, but a dictionary of familiar quotations. He scanned it as he quickly walked toward his office. The word that jumped out at him was *Obsession.* Circled in red pen, along with its accompanying excerpt: *That fellow seems to me to possess but one idea, and that is a wrong one.* –Samuel Johnson, from *Boswell's Life of Johnson.* What did it mean?

Archie had lived on this great round ball just long enough to realize that everything was connected; that there were no accidents, no coincidences; that all events contained meaning, hidden or no. The soiled ballet slipper he had discovered in the library last week had not been put there by chance. He had gone to check out a book that he had ordered online; when he received the email informing him his book was in, he went to retrieve it from the reserve shelf. Running it through the automatic checkout, he had glanced past the red electric eye and seen the slipper lying on the floor against the table leg. He had picked it up in order to return it to its owner, but looking around, saw that there were no other patrons in the library and no service people either. It had dawned on him that he hadn't seen a live human being inside the library for months, although he'd been coming here on a regular basis. The slipper wasn't here last month when he had come in to pick up his copy *of A World Without Conflict* by A. Lacka Peeps. Then how did it get here? And why did it appear on the day that he, Archie Trebold, had come to pick up his book?

Likewise the headless Barbie doll left lying on his front porch yesterday; that had been a communication of some kind, and it wasn't to send the message that all was well. Archie had an impulse to stamp his foot like Rumpelstiltskin. He had spent a lot of time and effort smoothing out his life, sanding and planing it down to a simple, rational set of rules and regulations. He suddenly felt as if someone was moving his arms and legs for him, maneuvering his very brain to veer off in a direction that he never would have chosen. *Damn that Dank Wagner! It had to be all his doing!*

He stepped inside the building and started up the steps that led to his office on the second floor. The scent of Obsession was in his nostrils, and he remembered now that Dank was the only man he knew who wore that femmy yet brawny-smelling perfume. All right, then he was ready for battle; if what Dank Wagner wanted was a showdown then he, Archie Trebold, would not disappoint. The city of Edina could only afford one King. And Archie intended to be it.

He approached the opaque glass wall of his office, behind which he could see a thin shadow of a man, hair standing on end. But that must be a wig! Dank Wagner's head, he knew, was bald as a billiard ball! What was he trying to prove? He wrenched open the door, let it bang against the outer wall as he thrust himself inside, dukes up, ready for the fight of his life.

The room was empty. Where was Madge? His secretary was always here, waiting for him in the mornings when he arrived. She had to have been the one who let the gatecrasher in—but no, he had fired her—when was it? Last month? Longer ago than that. It was after his last run-in with Dank. When he had accused her of siding with the enemy. And what had she said to him? Something about living in a world of his own. Well, of course he did! Who wouldn't, if given the opportunity, choose to? Absurd woman! It was her own fault she got fired. No doubt she had gone straight to Dank! He remembered her last words to him: *Dank Wagner is a figment of your imagination!* Figment shmigment. Right there was the proof of Madge's two-facedness and skullduggery.

He sat down at his desk and looked out of the window onto 50th street below him. Quiet, peaceful, uncomplicated. Not a car in sight. The clock on the wall ticked on with a tranquil rhythm that he found soothing. Even the traffic light obliged him as he watched it, changing from green to yellow to red. He could hear the distinct *glumpf* as the mechanism shifted. It had taken him half a lifetime to achieve this serenity and self-possession. The one imperfection, the fly in the ointment, was Dank Wagner. But he would find a solution to that particular problem soon. He wasn't worried about it. After all, he was the inventor of the Gated Toll Community within the confines of a city. There was no one more adept, more creative, more *ingenious* at Environmental Control than he, Archie Trebold, was. He was the absolute master of it.

Monica Ferris

Monica Ferris, an Illinois native, sold her first short story, "Pass the Word," to Alfred Hitchcock's Mystery Magazine, *in 1983, and has since sold more than two dozen short stories to anthologies and magazines.*

Her first mystery novel, Murder at the War, *appeared from St. Martin's Press in 1987 and was nominated for an Anthony as Best First Novel. Other novels followed, including* The Unforgiving Minutes, Ashes to Ashes, Original Sin, *and* Shoe Stopper.

More recently Ferris has collaborated with Gail Frazer on a series of medieval mysteries published under the pseudonym Margaret Frazer, among them The Servant's Tale *(nominated for an Edgar as Best Original Paperback of 1993). In 1998 Ferris began a new series for Berkley set in Excelsior, Minnesota, and featuring amateur needleworking sleuth Betsy Devonshire. The most recent,* Embroidered Truths, *appeared in June of 2005.*

Monica teaches widely in the metro area, does lectures and signings, and has appeared on many panels at mystery and science fiction conventions. She collects and is often seen wearing exuberant hats.

The Root of
the Matter

Monica Ferris

Has it stopped snowing yet?" asked Sigurd. Jill looked out the window.

"Yes. Want toast with your eggs?"

"All right." He came to the table with a slow, halting gait she had never seen on him before. He looked old, and tired. Perhaps he was ill.

Jill suspected her father had taken his wife's death last year hard; goodness knows Jill still mourned the loss, and she had been out on her own since she was eighteen. When Mama had gotten sick, most of the burden had fallen on Dad, who took early retirement from the police department to care for her. When she died, Dad, a typical Norwegian, had refrained from weeping where anyone could see or hear him. Then he had surprised Jill by selling his house, moving into his parents' old place in Hedeby, three hours from Excelsior.

He'd always been independent as a hog on ice, so she hadn't said a word—not that she would have anyway, being a good Norwegian herself. But then came the phone call from her brother, Eddie, saying Jill should go visit Dad.

She arrived later last night, after Dad was in bed. This morning, standing beside the old bottle-gas cookstove, she asked, "Dad, are you feeling all right?"

"You bet," he said, with a trace of his familiar smile. He sat down with an almost inaudible sigh, clutching his robe closed up around his neck, and suddenly she realized that he was acting just like she remembered Grandfather after Gammelor—Grandmother—died. Three months later Gammelfar followed her.

"Dad?"

"Yes?" he said, looking over at her, the smile peeping out again.

"How do you want your eggs?"

"Scrambled." He fell into a blank silence, from which he awoke with an effort. "What are your plans for today?"

She cracked two eggs into a bowl. "Well, I thought I'd do some grocery shopping for us and then maybe stop by a couple of places to see if anyone I know is around." Jill had spent many happy summers in her grandparents' house in Hedeby, and still exchanged Christmas cards and letters with friends she had made.

He nodded and then, again after a visible effort, said, "Maggie Riggsbruk is in Fargo."

"Yes, I know. They made her City Editor on the *Forum*." She and Maggie had been great friends.

"That's nice," he said blankly.

She asked, "How's her dad?"

He smiled. "Old Fred's crabby as ever, and twice as miserly." He fell silent for a few moments, then said, "Remember Wally Lundini, the dentist? He's still around."

"Good, I'll stop by and say hello."

★ ★ ★ ★

Fred Riggsbruk had toughed it out for four days, taking Bayer and Aleve and Excedrin Extra-Strength. Toothaches sometimes went away if you gave them time, but not this one. Daylight found him on the old sofa in the living room, sucking on cracked ice to cool his hot tooth and watching the Sunrise Farm Report.

Not that it mattered anymore; he was too old and useless to farm. He'd turned the land over to his son nearly ten years ago, and helped out with the harvest a few years after that, but now he mostly just sat around in this little cottage his great-grandfather had built. Where did the years go?

His stomach growled. He couldn't eat anything that needed chewing, so he went into the kitchen and heated up a can of tomato soup and drank it. When nine o'clock rolled around he called Hedeby's only dentist and described his symptoms.

The receptionist put him on hold and played classical music at him for a couple of minutes. She came back to say, "Can you come in at eleven? Dr. Lundini says it sounds like you may need a root canal. He'll see you on his lunch break."

"Is one a them expensive?" Fred asked cautiously.

"That depends on what you mean by expensive."

More than fifty dollars, you cow, he thought, but persisted, "How much?"

"Around fifteen hundred."

"*What*? Shit, that's anyone's idea of expensive, excuse my French! Maybe he could just pull it. Lemme talk to him."

"He's with a patient. Anyway, he couldn't tell you over the phone what treatment he'll use. You'll have to come in and let him take a look."

"All right, I'll see you around eleven," he grumbled, and hung up.

Then he remembered today was Wednesday. Bowling day. Lunch-in-Town Day. With Jackson.

Jackson French was a neighbor, also retired from farming. They had known each other, man and boy, for more than seventy years. But not steady, it was one of those off-on friendships. Once, they hadn't spoken for nearly three years. Currently, they were on, if not very warmly, and had a weekly engagement to drive to town for lunch at Marian's Café and then bowl a coupla lines while sharing a pitcher of beer. They took turns driving—today was Jackson's turn.

Maybe Fred could ask Jackson to come over early—no, the old fart wouldn't appreciate doing him a favor, not if there wasn't anything good coming out of it for him. Because Fred was pretty sure all he'd want after the dentist was a ride home.

Annoyed, Fred washed the pan, spoon and mug, occasionally picking up the old plastic glass with a ballet slipper painted on the side—leftover from when his granddaughter wanted to be the Sugar Plum Fairy—to tongue another piece of ice into his mouth. He remembered hearing a story about his grandfather using a hammer and chisel to knock out a sore tooth and wished he had the nerve to try that himself.

But he didn't. Turning into a wuss, he told himself. Using glasses with ballet shoes on them, sleeping in pajamas, going to the dentist.

He watched an old *I Love Lucy* rerun until it was time to leave.

Then he thought about Jackson again. The man would pull into the driveway at eleven and Fred wouldn't be here, and he'd be mad. No time to call—Jackson never spent less than twenty minutes on the phone, the old motor mouth.

Fred decided to leave a note. He found a pencil and cast around for something to write on and couldn't find anything. He picked up the dictionary that graced a corner of the kitchen and ripped a big corner off a blank page in the front.

Jackson, he wrote, have to see dentist. Can't make lunch today. He signed it, Fred. He would have explained that it was an emergency, but he wasn't sure how to spell it. Besides, Jackson would know it was an emergency or he wouldn't have left the note, right?

He stuck the note to his front door with an old thumbtack, went back inside for his glass of broken ice, went out to his old Ford, and started for town.

It had snowed yesterday evening, but the plow had been through and the road was okay.

He was about a mile down the road when he saw Jackson's car pulled over to the side, close to the tall rank of snow that lined the road. He nearly drove on by, but realized Jackson would see and recognize the car and have one more reason to be mad at him. So he slowed and pulled over down the road a piece and walked back. He brought the glass of ice with him to underline his dental emergency.

Jackson, a scrawny little guy, was wearing good pants, Sorel boots, and nice tan coat with a fake sheepskin lining. He was hatless and scowling. "What are you doing here?" he demanded as Fred approached.

"Got a toothache," said Fred, indicating his swollen jar with the glass. "Have to see the dentist right away. Left you a note at the house."

"You idiot, why didn't you phone?" Jackson shouted. "Look what happened when I started for your place, got a goddamn flat, it's given me snow up my back and down my boots."

"Look, I'm sorry—," started Fred.

"Sorry don't peel the parsnips, Fred!"

"Now, hold on a minute, I said I'm sorry, what the hell else do you want?"

"Why don't you give me a hand, huh? Why don't you get the spare out of the trunk? Why don't you let me sit in your nice, warm car while you handle this little problem all by yourself?" Jackson had been moving slowly towards Fred during this diatribe. "You and your damned toothache—." He suddenly reached out and smacked Fred right on his sore jaw.

White-hot pain splattered across Fred's face, blinding him with rage. He struck back impulsively, knocking Jackson off his feet with his fist. The man went down, rolling over once, but was back on his feet with surprising nimbleness. "You bastard!" he roared, and looked around for a weapon. The only thing near at hand was the flat tire. With anger-fueled strength, he picked it up and came swinging it at Fred.

Fred dodged backwards and fell. He scrambled sideways as Jackson approached, prepared to swing again. Fred's gloved hand felt something and grasped it—the tire wrench. He got up in stages, ducking another swing of the tire, and lashed upward with the wrench. Jackson, pulled by the weight of his tire, leaned into the blow, which caught him hard on the temple. He went down in a boneless way.

Fred straightened, gasping, his whole face ablaze with pain, then went to bend over the man.

"Jackson?" he asked, prodding with the wrench. But Jackson wasn't moving, not even to breathe.

"Ohhhhhh, shit," moaned Fred. "Oh, hell; oh, damn! Oh, Christ!" He knelt beside his erstwhile friend, shook him roughly by the shoulders. "Here, here, Jackson, come on, wake up! Don't do this to me!"

But Jackson was beyond hearing Fred's plea, and Fred, halfway to weeping, staggered back to his feet. He stood there a minute, trying to think. Suddenly the appointment with his dentist seemed more urgent than ever, maybe because he didn't want to stay here with Jackson. Pretty soon someone would come along and see this. He glanced up and down the empty road, then over at Jackson's car, looking for an idea.

The car was hitched up awkwardly on its back end—it was the left rear that had the flat. The trunk was open, the spare visible inside it.

It was then it came to him, a terrible idea, but no time to think of something else.

Grunting with the effort, he dragged Jackson's body the short distance to his car and jacked the car up some more. He arranged the body so its chest was directly under the brake drum. Then, squinting and turning his head away, he kicked the jack, hard. It moved, but didn't fall, he had to kick it again. He didn't look at the result, but hustled back up the road to his own car. He climbed in. It took him two tries to start his car, and he pulled back onto the road without looking around.

★ ★ ★ ★

Jill, done buying groceries, was enjoying her walk in the bitter cold down Hedeby's one commercial street. There wasn't much traffic, it being a weekday. She had coffee at Marion's Café, where she caught up on most of the news of Hedeby—there was a diner back in Excelsior that served much the same purpose, she noted with a faint smile—then went on to the Ben Franklin, to talk to an old high school chum.

Dr. Lundini's office was two blocks off Main, in a converted house. He had fixed a broken tooth for her the summer she turned eleven, after a fall from her bicycle. She had never forgotten his praise for her courage.

Now she went up on the porch with a smile of anticipation, and was reaching for the door knob when it opened and a medium-size old man in loose-fitting farmer's overalls under a heavy denim jacket stood in the doorway. His eyes were red-rimmed and his left jaw swollen, his expression that of having just suffered a dreadful ordeal.

"Why, Fred Riggsbruk!" she exclaimed. "How good to see you! Remember me? I'm Jill Cross, Per and Ingrid Cross's granddaughter!"

He glanced up at her from under shaggy brows. "Huh," he grunted, perhaps in recognition. "Yuh," he added, and brushed by her, stumping along the boards of the porch and down the steps. There he paused as if uncertain where he'd left his car. Then the wind touched his face and he winced and held a hand up to his jaw, turned and slogged off.

"Poor fellow," she murmured and went in.

★ ★ ★ ★

Fred was about a mile from home when he saw the cars. One belonged to the sheriff's department, one was a highway patrol car, the third a severely plain black hearse. And the fourth was Jackson's car, with people gathered around it, shoulders hunched.

He pulled over, got out, and walked up to the men around the car. "What's going on?" he asked.

The deputy, a very big man, turned with that slow and weighty authority they put on when ordinary folks poke their noses in, then his face changed. "Hello, Mr. Riggsbruk," he said. "Hey, what happened to your face?"

Fred couldn't think who he was, how he came to know Fred on sight. "Dentist pulled a tooth. We got an accident here?"

"I've got some bad news." He put a mittened hand on Fred's shoulder and turned him away from seeing Jackson's car. "You know Mr. French?"

"Course I know him, that's his car right there. Has something happened to him?"

"That's the sad thing, Mr. Riggsbruk, he had a flat tire or something, and he pulled over right there, and he was fixing it, and it fell on him."

Fred didn't have to put on a frown of dismay, he felt his whole face clench up all by itself. "Is he hurt bad?"

"I'm afraid he's dead."

Fred stared blankly at him, trying to think what to say. The wind stung his eyes, making them tear as he struggled to say something about how awful this was and how sad he was about it. And to not show how frightened and guilty he was. "No," he finally managed, in a whisper.

"It's true, Mr. Riggsbruk. I'm sorry to have to tell you that. You two were friends for a long time, weren't you?"

Fred nodded, blinking. "Near to seventy years," he said.

"Wow," said the deputy, gently touching him on the shoulder, "that's longer than most marriages."

Fred nodded, then realized the deputy wasn't just touching, he was guiding. Fred allowed himself to be taken back to his car. "What's going to happen next?" he asked, opening his door and then turning to stand behind it, hands resting on the top. The guiding hand fell away, but even so, the deputy, tall and broad, seemed to be pressing in on him, cold blue eyes boring into his brain, making it hard to think.

"We'll need to notify his family," the deputy said. He glanced over his shoulder and Fred, his scared fascination with the deputy's eyes broken, saw the name tag. "Cross," it read, a familiar name, he knew a Sigurd Cross with a daughter named Jill, though he still couldn't place this man, whose face came back to ask, "Do you know who to contact?"

"What? Oh, his son Andy—he farms his place," Fred said, trying to get his mind in gear.

"I know Andy, but who else?"

"Well, there's a daughter, Sue, and another son named Mark, but they don't even live in Minnesota. There's grandkids—Andy will know." Feeling suddenly overwhelmed by all these lives touched by Jackson's death, Fred sat down in his car. "So awful," he said, shaking his head. The work of a one furious minute, sickening. His jaw throbbed. He touched the place, and was surprised at the feel of a harsh fabric glove. He pulled it away and wriggled the fingers inside it to make sure they were his own. Then he realized how strange that was, to be thinking that way. Probably the pain pill he took in the dentist's office, messing up his thinking. He had to get away before he said something stupid.

"I want to go home," he announced, and turned the right way around, settling behind the wheel.

"Good idea, you go ahead," said the deputy, stepping back. "Take care of yourself, okay? Maybe call someone to come and be with you."

"Yes, yes, I'll do that," lied Fred, and he drove home, careful to stay under the speed limit.

★ ★ ★ ★

Wallace Lundini still had that off-set sense of humor Jill remembered from her youth. "Hard to believe Mr. Riggsbruk needed a root canal," he said with a twinkle, "since he came in without a cup of ice." He explained, "The pain and heat of the infection inside a tooth generally has a patient sucking on ice to cool and soothe it. It's practically diagnostic." He grinned and continued, "I almost sent him home again, but Aki, here, insisted we take an X-ray, and sure enough, there was a big ol' abscess going on." Aki, Dr. Lundini's Persian hygienist, smiled at him, her magnificent dark eyes amused.

Fred couldn't afford a root canal, Dr. Lundini said, and insisted the tooth be pulled. Dr. Lundini complied—one way or another, the infection had to be gotten at and cleaned out—and he had given Fred three strong pain pills and a prescription for amoxycillin, an antibiotic. Fred had taken one of the pain killers and stuffed the others in a pocket, but had managed to leave the prescription behind.

Jill said, "Tell you what, I'll pick it up for him and take it out there. I'm not surprised he forgot, he looked dazed when he came out your door a couple of minutes ago."

"Not much worse than when he came in," said Dr. Lundini. "And thank you for offering, he really needs the antibiotics. You're sure you don't mind?"

"No, not at all. I've known him for years; his daughter Maggie and I are childhood chums."

Jill was not far from the Riggbruk place when she saw the vehicles pulled off the road.

Naturally, she pulled off onto the opposite shoulder and strolled across to see what was up. "Hey, Thor!" she called, recognizing one of the men.

The tallest lawman, the deputy, turned and, after a start of recognition, gestured at her to come closer. "Well, if it isn't Officer

Jill!" he said with a grin. "How's it goin'? What brings you to town?"

"Visiting dad." Jill came forward, holding out a gloved hand for a brief shake. "What's going on here, cuz?"

"Dunno yet," he replied. "Probably some sort of accident. Evidence so far: flat tire, pulls off the road, jacks it up, takes off the tire, crawls under the car, jack slides out, car falls, man dies of crushed thorax."

Jill, taking this in with a series of nods, frowned. "Whoa, whoa, hold on," she said. "'Crawled under the car'?"

"Yeah, that's the hinky part," said Cousin Thor. "No need to crawl under a car to change a tire."

"So maybe there was some other problem?"

"Maybe. We haven't got that far yet."

"Who's the deceased?"

"Name's Jackson French— "

"No!"

"What, you know him?"

"I used to, back when I was a kid."

"What can you tell me about him?"

"Well, remember, I haven't seen him in years."

"Okay. But shoot." He nodded encouragement.

Jill paused to gather her thoughts. She spoke slowly, both to be sure she didn't misspeak, and because she rarely spoke at length. "He was one of those little guys with a big mouth, who never walked when he could trot. He was a hard worker, and he told funny stories, not all of them—nice." She arched a pale eyebrow at her cousin, who nodded comprehension. "His place is next door to Fred Riggsbruk's. Fred's daughter Maggie and I became friends back when I spent summers here with my grandparents, that's how I came to know Fred. We'd cross onto Mr. French's land sometimes, that's how I met him and Mrs. French, who'd invite us in for cookies and milk. I can't remember who told me what, but I came to understand that Mr. Riggsbruk and Mr. French were old friends who'd hunt together and borrow farm equipment from each other and have quarrels and not speak and make up again. They'd go to church together—when their wives could make them. Their wives were—are, for all I know

—great friends. I liked Mr. Riggsbruk better than Mr. French, and Mrs. French better than either of them. She used to let me help her in the garden and with the chickens."

"I'm afraid she died about six years ago."

"Aww." There was some feeling in that brief comment, and the two fell silent for a bit.

Then Jill shrugged almost invisibly and looked around her cousin's broad torso at the scene. "Anything to point at a suspect yet?"

"We're still collecting evidence. There's all kinds of footprints, but the people who stopped and found him did some trampling around of their own, and may have moved some things befoe they saw it was too late. It was a man and his wife and two teenage kids."

Jill nodded and looked around. They were sliding French's body into a bright blue body bag, crossing his arms on his crushed chest. She looked away, across the road to the ruins of a cornfield, where the wind was twisting translucent plumes of snow, like little ghosts, from the tops of low drifts.

★ ★ ★ ★

Fred's whole face hurt. He took a second pain pill and in about fifteen minutes the pain started to fade, leaving him tired and fuddled. He hadn't slept well in two nights. He went to lie down on his bed on top of the faded crazy quilt his grandmother had made from Granddad's old work shirts and overalls. There was even a steel buckle off a shoulder strap ornamenting the center—meant, if he recalled correctly, to prevent people sleeping on top of the quilt instead of under it. Smirking with satisfaction at disobeying his grandmother, even at this remove of years, he fell asleep on its surface.

He was dreaming of changing a tractor tire when the banging woke him, and it took him nearly a minute to come awake enough to realize someone was at the door.

He rolled over and nearly fell off the bed—he'd been sleeping way to one side. He sat on the edge for a few seconds, scratching his head and trying to understand why he couldn't wake up. Then his moving fingers slid down from his hair to the side of his face.

"Ow, ow, dammit!" he exclaimed. The movement of his jaw hurt some more. And he remembered.

Meanwhile the banging went on.

"All right, all right!" he yelled as loud as he could without opening his mouth very wide, and struggled to his feet.

The cottage was all on one level, which was good—he was so tangle-footed he would have fallen down any stairs. He got to the front door and wrenched it open.

He stood staring at the trio looking back at him. A woman, tall and blond, with light blue eyes—he had a feeling he should know her—and two men, both in uniform. But not identical uniforms, one was gray and the other brown.

"What's the matter?" he barked.

"May we come in, Mr. Riggsbruk?" asked the taller of the two men, the one in brown. He took off his hat, revealing very light red hair, cropped short.

"We'd like to ask you some questions, sir," said the other one, taking his hat off, too. The woman wasn't wearing a hat, and the wind was ruffling light strands of her straight hair around her ears.

"Yah, yah, come in, come in," he said, stepping back, sweeping them across the threshold with a straight-arm gesture.

The trio stood in the tiny parlor, which was already crowded with ancient maroon-plush furniture and dark oak tables covered with framed photographs.

Fred stood in the middle of the room, waiting for someone to say something.

"How's your jaw, Mr. Riggsbruk?" asked the female.

"Sore. Damn sore," he replied, squinting at her. "Don't I know you?" he asked.

"Yessir, I'm Jill Cross, I used to come ride your horses with Maggie."

He felt a sense of relief so bright he actually smiled just a little. "Why sure, I thought I knew you! You went off to college and then . . ." He looked from one of the two men to the other. "I heard you became a policeman—police woman in Minneapolis."

"Actually, I joined the Excelsior Police Department, west of Minneapolis," said Jill. "I'm here visiting my dad, who moved into Grandma and Grandpa Cross's old place."

"So why are you riding with these two?"

"I saw them out where Mr. French died and pulled over. This fellow here's my cousin Thor. I told him I knew the deceased—and I saw you in town, so he asked me if I'd like to come along to talk to you."

Fred pulled his eyebrows together in a deep frown. "I don't understand. What does your seeing me in town have to do with anything?"

"We're wondering if you saw Mr. French pulled over working on his flat tire on your way in," said the trooper.

"No," said Fred. "If I'd a seen him, I would've stopped."

"That's what I thought," said Jill. "But you can help us set the time of the, er, event. What time did you leave your house to go to town?"

He needed a moment to calculate, and reached to stroke his jaw, a thinking gesture, but yanked his hand away. "Let me see, the doc said to be in his office at eleven, and it's about fifteen minutes to town, so I left here about twenty till, to give myself a, a margin, ya know?"

"And you didn't see Mr. French or his car on your way in?"

"No." He couldn't believe they weren't here to arrest him. That they didn't even know it was a murder. Wonder and relief swept through him. He did touch his face, then, because he knew his expression might give him away. "Ow, ow, ow!" he muttered, and, crouching and wincing, turned away.

"Do you know of anyone who had a quarrel with Mr. French lately?" asked the trooper, who had stripes on his sleeve.

A cold fist took hold of his heart. He turned back around. "What?"

"Did he say anything to you about a fight or a quarrel he had with someone?"

Fred couldn't endure the look in his eyes and turned his gaze away. "No, I don't recall anything like that. Why?"

"When did you see him last?" asked Thor.

"Last week. We go into town on Wednesdays for lunch and to bowl a couple a lines, or take in a movie."

"But you didn't see him today?"

"No, he was supposed to pick me up, but I had this tooth." Memory struck. "I left him a note, on the front door." He brushed by them and opened the door. To his surprise, the note was gone. "Well, I'll be doggoned. I stuck it up with a tack." He touched the tiny round hole with a forefinger.

"You're sure you left a note?" asked Swanson.

"Well, a course I'm sure!" He couldn't think why it wasn't there.

"Maybe he came by and took it," suggested Jill.

"Yeah!" He jumped on that—too eagerly? He moderated his tone. "Well sure, that must've been what happened." Shaking his head at himself, he stepped back in and shut the door.

"What time was he supposed to pick you up?"

"Around eleven-uh-thirty," said Fred. "His place is only a couple miles up the road, he probably hadn't left yet when I went by." He touched his jaw again, more gingerly, just enough to produce a wince. "Anything else you want to know?"

"No, sir, we're just covering all the bases, that's all," said the Dan. "We'll be on our way, then. Thank you, sir." He closed a notebook Fred hadn't noticed before and the three of them filed out of the house.

He went into the bathroom and washed his eyes and forehead with cold water, then stared at himself in the mirror. He looked like a mug shot of a drunk and disorderly. Had they noticed how he stumbled over the time Jackson was supposed to pick him up? Cops could be stupid—and, they could be sharp. No telling with these guys. That question about a quarrel—they knew something was wrong. Maybe they did suspect him. Funny thing about that note. Where the hell had it gone?

★ ★ ★ ★

Jill went into the tall, narrow old house and found her father watching a soap opera. Or perhaps he was only watching the television make meaningless noises and colored shadows. Certainly his expression gave no indication he was watching with anything approaching interest.

"Can I talk to you, Dad?" she said.

He gave a little start; he hadn't heard her come in. "Why, sure," he said, and clicked the remote to shut off the set. "What's up?"

She unbuttoned her coat, stuffing her mittens into a pocket with her other hand. She felt something in the bottom and pulled them out again. With them came an orange-brown plastic bottle with a white cap. "Oh, gosh, I forgot to give this to Mr. Riggsbruk!" she said.

He said, surprised, "Since when did you become a Walgreen's delivery boy?"

"That's part of what I want to talk to you about. I ran into Mr. Riggsbruk as he was coming out of Dr. Lundini's office. Come on into the kitchen. I haven't had lunch." She continued with the story while she made a fat sandwich to share with him—he hadn't eaten, either. She didn't consider herself much of a raconteur, and so was pleased at his intent listening posture.

When she finished, he said in his old voice, the one she remembered from back when he was a detective sergeant, "So, you like Fred for this?"

"Well, he was awfully hinky coming out of the dentist's office, and later, at home. I almost think he was surprised we weren't there to arrest him."

"But do you have anything concrete to show me?"

"No." Jill said it simply, and stopped there, having also said it all.

"So what's next?"

She shrugged. "Nothing. This is out of my jurisdiction." She went to wash the plates, then said, "I'd better take those pills out there, he's supposed to be taking them to cure an infection in his jaw."

"I'll come along, if you don't mind."

Jill turned away to hide her smile of pleasure. "Fine. I'll get our coats."

Less than twenty minutes later they were out on the road, almost to Mr. Riggsbruk's place when Jill's father said, "Stop here."

Jill, noticing they were about to pass the place where Jackson French's body had been found, obediently slowed and pulled onto the shoulder.

The sun, well south, was starting down the sky, and they cast long blue shadows on the pinking snow as they walked across the road. Jill was content to follow in silence as her father slowly walked the scene, the snow groaning and crunching under their feet. Here were the marks of Mr. French's tires, here feet had skidded, here a tire had lain, here were footprints crisp and clear near the tire tracks, and here was the outline of a man's body. Not much blood on what would have been the shoulders, but some.

Jill's father stood a long time looking down at that sad outline. Then he turned and went still again while his eyes moved slowly around. He stiffened as they focused on something a little distant. He walked to it. Jill, maintaining silence, followed.

He stooped and gestured at something half-buried under wind-swept snow. "See that?" he asked.

Jill came to look over his shoulder at an old plastic glass. It was clear with what looked like a well-used ballet slipper printed on it, the ribbons rising and making a circle up near the rim. There was something gray-white and lumpish inside, a frozen liquid.

"I think Dr. Lundini was right," he said. "Go find me a long stick or something to mark the place."

Jill looked around. Down in the ditch beside a culvert was a big cluster of cattails. She started down, setting her heels deep in the snow to form a kind of staircase, but near the bottom the snow broke loose, and she fell. She wasn't hurt, but she looked up angrily at her father. He was grinning. She snorted, then grinned back, and broke off a couple of cattails, their brown tops half open and spilling their light brown fluff. She left a trail of it on her struggle back to the top. Her father was waiting to give her a hand up the last few feet.

"Well done," he said, and she nearly hugged him—but they were not a hugging kind of people, so instead she released her grip on his arm and walked away.

He stuck a cattail on either side of the glass, so it could be found again.

Jill, watching him, said, "I was thinking. If they weren't currently quarreling, how could they have gotten into a fight?"

"Old Jackson had a heck of a temper. Maybe Fred stopped and said something snarky about changing a tire in the snow, and Jackson got mad."

"I would think that if Fred stopped, it would be to help his friend."

"Maybe he did. Maybe Jackson made the snarky remark. Let's go, I can't feel my toes anymore."

They got back in the car and Jill started up the road again. "Fred said he didn't see Jackson's car on the road."

"I'm sure he did say that."

"He said he left a note for Jackson, but when he went to look at the door, the note was gone. I said maybe Jackson came along after he left for the dentist and took the note. He really liked that idea."

"How did he fasten the note to the door?"

Jill glanced over at him, surprised at such a trivial question. "With a tack, he said."

"So where's the tack? Was it still stuck in the door?"

Jill thought. "No, there wasn't a tack stuck on the door."

"So, did Jackson take it with the note?"

"That's an interesting question." She slowed and flipped her turn signal on. Glancing over her shoulder, she slowed some more, then pulled into an unplowed driveway. It had car tracks all over it, and by the way her car slid and bumped, there were deep ruts in the frozen mud under the snow—that was why it wasn't plowed.

They got out and Jill started for the door, but her father said, "Wait a minute." He turned his head until he was facing the wind, which was sweeping across the front of the little house, piling snow up in a corner of the porch, making little plumes like smoke rising from the tops of drifts out in the field beyond the house. He began walking around the little front yard. He bent over as he walked.

He'll never find it, thought Jill, and she went up on the porch to wait for him.

But he stooped beside a large bridal wreath bush, pulled off a heavy glove, and probed into the mass of thin stems and old, dead trapped leaves, coming up with an irregular rectangle of paper. It fluttered in the strong, steady wind, and he waited until he was up on the porch to take the loose end into his other hand and read it, nodding in satisfaction.

"May I see?" she asked. But he gave her a wink and tucked it into a pocket before gesturing at her to knock on the door.

★ ★ ★ ★

Fred saw them out there, of course. Jill and—by God, it was her dad, old Sigurd Cross! What the hell was that about? Sig went off across the yard, out of Fred's line of sight, but wasn't gone long. He wondered if Sig wasn't looking for the outhouse that used to grace the place. Fred gave a little shudder at the thought. The icy draft that used to greet his tender buttocks in the winter... .

A rap on the door brought him out of his musings. He opened it and there she was, holding up a little brown plastic cylinder.

"Dr. Lundini asked me to bring you your antibiotics," she said. "You left the prescription behind in his office. Walgreen's said they'd put it on your bill."

He held out his hand for the bottle. "Why, thank you," he said. "But you didn't need to make two trips in one day."

"Yes, I did, since it was my fault for forgetting to give you them the first time. You need to start taking them right away."

Sig spoke up. "Hello, Fred. Hell of a thing about Jackson."

Fred sighed. "Hell of a thing. Knew him since Hector was a pup. Well, come in, come in, you're letting all the heat out, standing there." He stepped back to give them room.

"What happened? I hear the car fell on him." Sig began unbuttoning his coat.

"Yeah, that's about it. He was changing a tire and the jack slid away."

"Huh." Sig rubbed the underside of his nose with a forefinger while he considered that. "I never heard of anyone getting under his car to change a tire."

Fred turned away, starting for the kitchen. "Me, neither. Excuse me, I'm gonna take one a these pills, since Dr. Lundini was so serious about it as to send Jill out here with them. Sit down, why don't you? Can I get you a cup of coffee?"

They made polite sounds of refusal, but he turned the heat up under the pot anyhow. They were both taking their coats off, so he knew they were just following the Scandinavian custom of refusing three times. He opened a cabinet and got out a glass, filled it at the sink, and made a couple of tries at opening the bottle before figuring out how to hold down the little plastic tab while twisting.

Then he got out a plate and put some fancy crackers—cheaper than cookies—on it and went to get down the thick stoneware mugs his daughter had given him last Christmas. He liked them, they kept the coffee warm a long time, and they reminded him of the kind of mugs you used to get in the café in town years back.

"What's keeping you?" said a voice, and he turned, startled. "Oh, I see." It was Sig. "No need for all of that, Fred, we're just stopping for a minute."

"I don't mind, I like a little company."

Sig came to the wooden table and picked up the plate and one of the mugs. "Well, all right then. You bring the other two and the coffee." He glanced around the kitchen like the nosy parker he always was. Fred was glad he was a neat and orderly person, the kitchen was clean, the only thing in the sink was the ballet glass he'd used to take a pill.

Oh, damn, the glass, one of a set, identical to the one he'd taken to town. Which was—where?

"Come on, then," said Fred, trying not to sound urgent, grabbing the pot and the other two mugs. Where had he left the glass of ice? He'd brought it out to the car and got out of the car—he had a terrifying notion that he'd left it where Jackson died. He'd go over there tomorrow and look for it. Though it was probably buried in blowing snow by now. For sure he hadn't seen it when he'd stopped on the way home. Not that he was looking for it.

But what if he hadn't seen it because the cops had already picked it up? There was its twin in the sink, and four more in the cabinet. Maybe he should throw away all his glasses and buy new ones. There was a Wal-Mart in St. Cloud, he could do it there anonymously.

"These are good crackers, Mr. Riggsbruk," said Jill, bringing him out of his plotting with a little start. He found himself standing on the other side of the coffee table from her, coffee pot in hand.

"Oh," he said. "Well, thank you. I like 'em." He did like them, especially with a good stinky cheese. "You want some cheese to go on them?" he asked.

"No, thank you, these are fine just by themselves."

Sig piped up. "I could use a little coffee, however."

"Huh? Oh, sure! You bet! Don't know where my head is, I'm all wore out from the tooth pulling, I guess." Fred poured coffee into the mugs. "It's from earlier," he noted. If it's too strong, I can make fresh."

"Fred, you can't have a wife too rich, a car too big, or coffee too strong," said Sig, repeating an old jest.

"Now that's for sure," said Fred, forcing a smile. He filled his own mug last, and sat down in the overstuffed chair whose sunken cushion just fit his behind.

He picked up a cracker and very gingerly bit into it, then put the cracker down on the table. Not yet, said his jaw. He gently probed the empty space where his tooth had been and winced. He took a sip of coffee to soak the fragments in his mouth into softness he could swallow.

"Fred," said Sig with an air of changing the subject, "did you hear from Jackson today? I mean, did he phone you to say he was coming to pick you up?"

"No," said Fred. He took a sip of coffee. "I wish he had, I would've told him I had to go to the dentist, it was an emergency. Because, y'see, I should've called him. I left a note on the door for him, but I should've called him."

"And he got the flat tire on his way back home," said Sig with a little nod. "He came and took the note, and left again, and had a flat."

Fred looked at Sig, then at Jill. They must've looked for it by now. And not found it. "Well," he said, "no. I mean, we thought that was what happened. The note was gone, so we thought Jackson must've come and took it."

"But he didn't?" asked Jill.

"No, the wind must've blown it away before he got out here. Because I found it."

"You did?" said Jill. "Where?"

"It was on the porch, in a little pile of snow over in a corner. It was mostly buried, I just saw a little corner of it sticking out."

"Do you still have it?" asked Jill.

"Sure. You want to see it?"

"Yes, I'd really like that."

He went to the little desk over by the front window and opened a drawer. He almost decided to pretend to rummage for it, but changed his mind and just picked the slip of paper up. He hadn't been able to remember exactly what he wrote the first time, but what did it matter? He'd torn another section out of the dictionary's blank page, and printed carefully, Jackson, can't make lunch today, have to go to dentist. Very bad tooth. Sorry. And signed it, Fred. He turned and brought the paper to Jill.

"See?" he said. "I told you I wrote a note."

"Well, now, that's interesting, Fred," said Sig. He stood up, and Fred took a step backward, remembering all of a sudden that Sig was a retired police detective.

"What do you mean?"

Sig reached into a pocket and pulled out a slip of paper. "How about this?"

He held out Fred's original note. If it had big teeth and was snarling at him he couldn't have been more dismayed. "Where'd you get that?" Then he remembered Sig walking around the yard. "That's what you were looking for!" he said.

"That's right," said Sig. "I found it in the bush by the driveway. You were right, the wind blew it away. Jackson didn't come by and get it."

"Well, that's what I said at first, but then Jill said he must a come and got it, and I agreed. But so what? Those fellas didn't believe I wrote a note, so I wrote another one. That was dumb, but so what?"

"It was dumb because it means you knew Jackson didn't come by for it. And how could you have known that, Fred? How could you have known that?"

K. J. Erickson

K. J. Erickson writes the Mars Bahr mystery series, set in Minneapolis. Third Person Singular was a Barry and Anthony finalist as the best first mystery published in 2001. The Dead Survivors received a Friends of American Writers prize for adult fiction published in 2002. The Last Witness (2003), and Alone At Night (2004), were both nominated for Minnesota Book Awards in the popular fiction category. Erickson was born in Chicago, grew up in South Dakota, and is a graduate of the University of Minnesota. Prior to becoming a full-time writer, she was vice president for risk management at the Federal Reserve Bank of Minneapolis.

Mickey's Last Mark

K. J. Erickson

Mickey Bosche was self-employed, working out of the Minneapolis-St.Paul International Airport.

He didn't go in to work every day, but he made it a point never to miss days before and after holidays. Bad weather days—when flights were delayed and travelers were stacked up in gate areas, at ticket counters, at the fast food restaurants that lined the concourses—well, he ran his butt off during bad weather.

His preferred clients were young mothers with babies and too much carry-on luggage. Tired businessmen who'd had a couple in the bar before boarding were prime marks. Elderly folks were either great or tough. Some of them had lost so much confidence in themselves that they held on to their purses and luggage like they were bearer bonds. You would've had to take a hack saw to their wrists to get anything off them.

Mickey had been in the business for going on fifteen years. Got into it accidentally, which, in his experience, was how most good things worked out.

He'd been an insurance adjuster, traveling the Upper Midwest, when he had a three-hour layover on a connecting flight at the Milwaukee airport. A guy sitting a seat over from Mickey in the gate area fell asleep, snoring steadily and shifting periodically on the plastic-molded seat. Third or fourth time he shifted, heaving his body downward and pulling at his suit jacket, his wallet fell out of the jacket pocket, landing on the empty seat between them.

Mickey stared at the wallet for a moment. His first impulse had been to pick it up, nudge the guy, and hand it back. Then he considered someone seeing him reach for the wallet before he had a chance to hand it back.

It wouldn't look good. Mickey glanced around. With more than two hours before his plane was scheduled to depart, and no flights leaving from the gate before his ride, the area was almost deserted.

Two rows over an elderly couple were faced in the opposite direction. Behind him a guy was reading the *Chicago Tribune*. There was no one at the podium.

His second impulse came in a flash that illuminated not just the moment at hand, but Mickey's past and his future.

He wanted to take the wallet. Not give it back, keep it. Not because he needed or wanted what was in the wallet, but because he was bored. Had been bored for most of his adult life.

In that moment, the wallet was a beacon of possibility. He was curious about what was in the wallet. That was how it started. As much as anything, it was curiosity that made him reach over, drop his magazine on top of the wallet, scoop the wallet into the magazine and stroll away from the gate area.

He couldn't remember the last time he'd had a rush like that.

The rush didn't have anything to do with money—until he'd locked himself into a stall in the men's room and folded open the wallet. There was over five hundred dollars cash in it.

At that moment, the rush was also about the money.

But never just the money. As much as being about the money, it had been, was, and always would be about how much more interesting Mickey's life was once he started working the airport. To do the grifting right took a lot of strategizing, and that was the part of the job that made his life interesting.

Right off he knew that his biggest issue was being noticed.

So he never worked a concourse more than once a week and he alternated between the Lindbergh Terminal and the Humphrey terminal. He spent time scoping out the concourses, the gate areas, figuring out where security cameras were positioned. He paid attention to where undercover guards were, looking for people in gate areas who never got on planes and who moved from gate to gate. He got so he recognized these people; and when he recognized them, he changed venues.

Mickey made investments in looking different without making himself look weird. That was the tricky part. Changing yourself without drawing attention. He had over two dozen coats and jackets, more pants and sports coats than he could count, and, as he liked to say to Bernie Hall, the guy who handled furs and jewelry for him, more shoes than all the gals on *Sex in the City* put together.

He had hats. Hats took real effort to get right. They could make a guy look suspicious, they could become easy points of identification. The right hat—the one that no one could describe when they were telling airport security about the guy who'd been standing next to them in line at the podium—well, a hat like that was very useful.

Hairpieces were another thing. He'd wear a hairpiece with a circa 1975 blue polyester suit, wide lapels, slightly belled trousers. A total look kind of deal. The idea was, he wasn't trying to pull off a hairpiece that didn't look like a hairpiece; what he was going for was a guy who looked like he'd wear a hairpiece. It was that kind of subtlety that was the mark of a professional.

Tattoos were the same kind of thing. He had sheets of wash-off tattoos he'd use with t-shirts in the summer, a black leather jacket in the winter. What he noticed about the tattoos was that they drew attention—but not to him. People might remember a guy with a coiled snake on his right arm, but they wouldn't remember anything else.

Then there were sunglasses. Mickey hardly ever used sunglasses. He viewed sunglasses as the mark of an amateur. If he had a look where sunglasses fit—like a Northwest flight to Honolulu in January, decked out in a flowered shirt and so on—well, maybe. As long as it fit in with what everybody else at the gate would be wearing. But even then, he preferred to low key it. Casual, but not showy. Nothing memorable.

The most important factor in not being noticed was the least obvious.

Confidence.

Confidence generated a better cover than any piece of clothing he could wear. This was something that took him a while to figure out. Early on he'd made the mistake of living too close to the edge. He spent what he got as he got it, convinced getting more was easy.

Then the Gulf War hit and he almost got put out of business. Airport security was all over the place. People didn't leave their luggage sitting around. And you had to have a fucking ticket to get on the concourses.

His overhead went through the roof at the same time that his revenues were dropping like a rock. And he had no cushion. If he didn't nail a loose wallet with a wad of cash, some high-limit plastic with plenty of unused credit on the line—or a jewelry case with some good stones—he was in serious trouble.

Worst of all, the pressure of worrying about money generated tension that affected his timing. And marks could feel the tension. It made them step away a bit when they felt his heat. Made them draw their stuff a little closer. Made them look at him, then look again. He was getting noticed.

There were only two good things Mickey had to say for the Gulf War. It ended quick and it taught him a lesson: he added a savings objective to his plan. Ten percent gross earnings went into the bank. Over two years, he saved enough to buy the duplex where he'd been renting the upstairs unit.

Five years after the Gulf War, he had a solid nest egg: T-bills and a diversified stock portfolio. He was a man with money in the bank. A solid citizen. And like any solid citizen, he felt confident about himself and his future. He didn't give off any sweaty vibes standing next to a mark. He moved into an area smoothly. He wasn't a man anyone thought about twice.

The longer Mickey worked the airport, the more he refined his skills. He spent time learning his merchandise. He subscribed to *Vogue, Vanity Fair, Town & Country,* and *GQ*. Kept a file on what was worth what. Kept up with new items coming on to the market that would be in demand. It wasn't just that this effort helped him identify the best marks. Just as important, it helped him avoid wasting time, energy and—most important—risk exposure on goods not worth getting.

He figured out which gates consistently produced good marks. Any international flight. Flights to Las Vegas, San Francisco, Miami, Honolulu—vacation destinations—were consistently good. People took their best stuff, carried cash, and brought jewelry when they were going on vacation. That, and they had a different attitude. Laid back, careless.

Best of all, if they could afford a flight to London or Honolulu, Mickey had no compunctions about making them a mark.

This was a subtle thing—being a grifter with ethics. Truth was, ethics were important to Mickey because ethics made him a better grifter. He loved the irony of that fact. He admired himself for figuring out that having ethics made him a better grifter. He was pretty sure there weren't many thieves around who'd figured out that not feeling like a thief was a real advantage.

Having ethics meant he chose marks that could afford to lose something. Hell, who would be better off learning a lesson by losing something.

Take your mother-with-toddler-marks. Mickey never took anything off a mother with kids unless they had expensive shoes, expensive purses, and a good sized ring. No way he was gonna rip off some pathetic broad who needed money to feed the kids. Of course, you had the same ethical issues with the old folks. Old folks, he looked for a general sense of entitlement that came with having made it to your seventies and not having any money worries.

In short, you had to pay attention to details to know who was and wasn't a fair mark. And paying attention to details was the name of Mickey's game.

Sometimes Mickey wondered how he'd feel if he got caught. 'Caught' as in did jail time.

He'd had close calls. Plenty of times when a mark had spotted what he was doing. Each time, Mickey had feigned confusion and backed off without the mark calling in security.

Then there was the one time he'd had a run-in with security. Talk about making lemonade out of lemons.

He'd been sitting next to a guy in a C concourse bar who was watching an NCAA game on the set over the bar. From the looks of him, the guy had been there a long time. At the half, he'd slid off the stool, steadied himself, then stopped, looking down at his alligator attaché case. He'd looked over at Mickey.

"You gonna be here awhile?"

Mickey knew better than to be too agreeable too quick.

"How long's awhile?"

"Long enough for me to unload a barrel of piss."

Mickey'd looked him up and down, taking his time, counting on the guy being too drunk to remember what Mickey looked like.

"Don't fall in," he said

The guy shot his right cuff out from under what looked like a cashmere blend pinstripe suit and glanced down at a Patek Philippe platinum watch with a black alligator band.

Slowly, he fumbled with the clasp on the watch, a simple task made difficult by alcohol. With the slow, considered movement of someone whose brain was operating on less than one cylinder, he placed the watch on the bar.

"Keep an eye on my case. I'll be gone five minutes. Tops." He tapped the face of the watch. "Buy you a drink when I get back." He slapped Mickey on the back, more to steady himself as he moved away than as a gesture of goodwill.

Then he staggered out of the bar, hesitated on the concourse, turning to the right. The wrong turn. He'd go a lot farther in that direction to find the bathroom than if he'd hung a left.

Mickey sat for a count of thirty, working hard at controlling his breathing. The Patek Philippe was one of those watches you needed a mechanical engineering degree to read. All kinds of numbers on a big black and white face, time zone divisions, military and numerical time readings. Kind of like the Lord's Prayer on the head of a pin.

To Mickey, a watch like this meant the guy had a big ego and a dick that was smaller than his brain—the brain not being rocket-science sized before it was soaked in alcohol. No other reason you'd spend thirty, forty thousand dollars to buy a watch. Much less spend that much on the watch and leave it in an airport bar with a complete stranger.

Here's something else Mickey had learned in his years of airport grifting.

He called it the Law of Related Values. A guy wearing a Patek Philippe watch would have an attaché case that was worth taking.

Mickey stood up slowly, paid his bill, palmed the Patek Philippe into his coat pocket, picked up the alligator attaché case, and walked out of the bar, leaving his own $39.95 black leatherette case under his bar stool.

He stopped briefly as he left the bar and walked onto the concourse, looking to the right to check for the guy. Nothing. Then Mickey turned left and, within a few steps, entered the men's bathroom.

Behind a locked stall door, he opened the brass locks on the case.

It just kept getting better. Cash. A lot of cash. A bottle of Obsession perfume. The guy was probably taking perfume home to the wife to make up for what a jerk he was, on the road or off.

One other thing. A plump, soft plastic bag of something white that Mickey was pretty sure was cocaine.

Back to ethics. Drugs were something that you came across now and again when you worked airports. Mickey didn't have anything to do with them. Not his line of work. But in this particular case, it gave him pause. There was so much of it. And everything he knew about the guy was that he'd have top grade dope. Mickey guessed the bag was worth $2,500, minimum. He even had half an idea about where he could boost it.

He thought about it. The watch alone was major. Most things you pick up in the airport you boost off for ten, twenty cents on the dollar. The watch he could get maybe forty cents on the dollar. So, conservatively, he was looking at twelve thousand on the watch. He thumbed the cash, paying attention to the denominations. Five grand, easy.

Mickey paused again. Considering the attaché case. Usually this would have been a no-brainer. First thing you do is get rid of the case. But this one was a beauty. Hand made. Hand fitted. Real alligator, calf-skin lined. Custom brass hardware. Not a scratch on it. Retail, it probably went for six, seven thousand. Mickey knew any number of people who'd give him a thousand for it. Too much to walk away from.

The whole package, with the coke, would probably net him—net him—twenty thousand. As he thought about it, he broke the seal and took a whiff of the Obsession. The effort that took jarred the attaché case, and as he lurched forward to keep the case from hitting the floor, the perfume spilled onto him and into the case.

Shit. He was going to smell like a whorehouse. The slip unnerved him. He'd deal with the case and the coke later. He just wanted to secure the watch and get out of the john before anyone else smelled the perfume.

The watch required special care. If there was one thing he wanted to make it home with, it was the watch. He unzipped his pants and strapped the watch around his dick. He held the strap tight for a few seconds, giving himself an erection, then buckled the watch on the last hole. If he'd been wearing boxers, it would have been too risky. But Mickey was a briefs man.

Afterwards, Mickey gave a lot of thought to what went wrong. Bottom line, he decided, it was greed. He should have ditched the case with the coke in it before he left the men's room.

Except it wasn't as simple as that. The way things worked out, having the case with the coke in it was what got him off.

Mickey was almost out of the C Concourse when he heard the words behind him.

"That's him. That's my case."

Mickey kept walking, feigning surprise as the drunk and a uniformed airport security guard came up on either side of him.

"You sonofabitch," the drunk said, grabbing hold of Mickey's shoulder.

"Sir," the guard said, "this gentleman says you've taken his brief case."

The drunk was breathless, addled.

Mickey said, "Excuse me—the case I'm carrying belongs to me…"

Mickey had no sooner spoken the words than he saw his salvation. He turned to the drunk. "I left your case at the bar, under a stool. You said you'd be right back, but I couldn't wait forever. If you can identify the contents of the case, I'd be happy to open it with the guard present…"

Mickey could see the drunk's brain synapses misfiring as he tried to sort out why Mickey's offer wasn't an option. Mickey may have looked calm, but underneath his suit, he was sweating with tension. His body heat was acting like a vaporizer on the spilled perfume.

The drunk smelled it. Then the light bulb went on. Both of them were seeing the soft, plump bag of cocaine at that moment. And all that cash.

The drunk looked down at the case. He was sobering up fast.

"No," he said. "I—I guess you're right. That isn't my case."

"Are you sure you don't want me to open it?" Mickey said, looking first at the drunk, then at the guard.

The guard rolled his eyes.

The drunk shook his head. "I'm okay with it—I apologize. Sorry for the confusion."

The guard said, "Sorry to bother you, sir."

When all was said and done, Mickey cleared just over $22,000. A record daily take for a single mark.

It was right around the time of his record mark that Mickey got another big break.

Airports started tightening up on smoking restrictions. The unintended consequence of that change was that airport security personnel spent almost as much time smoking in locked stairwells as they did on coffee breaks. What they didn't do was spend much time patrolling the smoke-free concourses.

In combination—his record mark and the absence of security personnel—led Mickey to be as confident as he'd ever been.

Here's another lesson Mickey learned. Good times don't last. If there was a harder way to learn that lesson than going through September 11, 2001, Mickey didn't know what it would be.

The airports shutting down was the least of his problems. After the planes went up again, airports were like wakes. Anybody who was flying was nervous as hell. They watched everybody. Old ladies with canes got the third degree. Then there were baggage restrictions. Nobody was bringing much of anything onto the concourses. What they did bring they kept track of. Hell, they even listened when the flight attendants gave their little spiels about how to fasten your seat belts.

Up until the end of the year, Mickey pretty much thought it was over. He was going to have to come up with a new career. Once again you needed a boarding pass to get on the concourses. To add insult to injury, the stock market went to hell. His nest egg lost seventy-five percent of its value between September and the first of the year.

But Americans. God love 'em. They just can't handle limitations of any kind, for any reason, for any length of time. By January 2002, people were traveling again, dragging all kinds of shit into airports, onto concourses, to their departure gates. They'd forget about their purses, laptops, carry on bags—whatever—while they ate fast food, read newspapers, and slept as they waited to board.

Other things changed after 9/11. But the damndest thing was, they changed in ways that worked to Mickey's advantage.

Security may have been tighter, but nobody was looking for Mickey. They were looking for terrorists. It was open season for any other kind of trouble. The other big change that worked to Mickey's advantage was the Internet. He didn't have to call up the airport or a travel agent and ask for their cheapest ticket to anywhere. He could find the cheapest ticket on line as well as a boarding pass that minimized his face time with airline staff.

So, here was another lesson Mickey learned: bad times don't last much longer than good times. And all the lessons he'd learned over the past fifteen years added up to one thing: Mickey was more confident than ever.

The last lesson Mickey learned was that there was such a thing as too much confidence.

It started simple. Bernie Hall's wife Sondra wanted a fur coat.

Mickey winced when Bernie asked him.

"Jeez, Bernie. Fur coats are a pain. Most of the time, they've got wear and tear. Initials sewn in the lining. A big headache for a guy to get out of the airport."

"I'm not gonna pay retail, Mickey. Hell, I'm not gonna pay wholesale. But I'll make it worth your while. You'll do okay on the deal, I promise. Bring me a nice piece of fur that'll fit Sondy, and I'll give you a fair price."

Mickey winced again. Bad enough to find a fur coat that was worth picking up, much less one sized to fit a particular person. That, and Bernie's idea of a fair price wasn't likely to be anybody else's idea of fair, least of all Mickey's. Bernie was your original cheap guy. Still, Mickey and Bernie had a long-standing, mutually beneficial business relationship. Good fences were hard to come by.

"I'll see what I can do," Mickey said.

For several weeks after that, Mickey carried a garment bag stuffed with plastic dry cleaning bags onto the concourses. It was a hassle. It annoyed him. He was just about to say, Hell with it, when he spotted the woman in the ankle length sable coat.

The perfect mark.

There was the sable coat. Perfect condition, a perfect fit for Sondy. And the woman was a total package: A Gucci sling purse with a brass chain. A beige Zac Posen pant suit. Marc Jacobs tuxedo pumps. Mickey's Law of Related Values was flashing neon: She's got it, go get it.

Here was the best part. Two brat kids that belonged to the mark. Fighting with each other. The boy, probably ten, eleven, throwing spit wads at the little girl who looked a year or two younger. The little girl was swinging her Barbie doll at her brother.

Mama, the perfect mark, was fed up. She swatted at one or the other, hissing at them in a low voice. They'd back off for moments, then try a different tack.

Mickey moved into the gate area, checking the board. They had another hour and a half before departure. No way mama was gonna stay in that coat for that long. Especially if the kids kept getting under her skin. She was hot and getting hotter.

Mickey had no sooner come to that conclusion than mama took the boy's shoulders in both her hands and moved him to her other side.

The girl slid down on the chair, her lower lip protruding. She was mad that her mama had deprived her of her antagonist. A kid who liked trouble. The worst kind. She sat forward, leaning around her mama to stick her tongue out at her brother.

Then she flopped back in her chair, pretending to be interested in her Barbie doll. She looked up for another target, meeting Mickey's eyes before he could look away.

Slowly, purposefully, she lifted the doll up, then dropped her backwards, spreading the doll's leg's in Mickey's direction.

"Mommy!" she said, grabbing at her mother's arm. "That man is looking at Barbie's pee pee."

Mama grabbed the kid's arm. "Tiffany, if I have to talk to you again about your behavior, I'm going to call Daddy on the cell phone…"

Then she stood up, sliding the sable off her shoulders, folding it inside out, and dropping it on the chair. "I'm going to the rest room. Jared, you stay with our things. Tiffany, you come with me."

"Don't want to," Tiffany said, sliding farther down on the chair.

Mama thought about it. "Can you behave yourself if I leave you for five minutes?"

Tiffany didn't answer, which mama took as a yes. Mama slung the Gucci strap over her shoulder and whipped past Mickey, leaving in her wake the unforgettable scent of Obsession perfume.

Damn. If this wasn't a good luck omen, Mickey didn't know what was.

Within seconds of his mama's departure, Jared reached over and pulled off one of Tiffany's patent leather Mary Jane's, then took off. Tiffany howled, dropping the Barbie and setting off in pursuit of Jared and her shoe.

This had the effect not only of taking the brats away from the sable coat, but of diverting the attention of everyone in the gate area.

Could it have worked out any better for Mickey?

He moved slowly but purposely, dropping the garment bag over the coat. He hesitated. Lying on the chair next to the coat was Tiffany's Barbie doll.

Mickey picked it up, snapped Barbie's head off, dropped the head into his coat pocket, and left the gate area with the sable coat under the garment bag.

Mickey had made it into the main terminal when he heard the clatter of mama's Marc Jacob's tuxedo pumps behind him. And Tiffany's whine: "He killed my Barbie!"

The security guard, who looked vaguely familiar, put a hand on Mickey's arm. "Sir—just a moment, please." The guard nodded at the garment bag over Mickey's arm. "There's some confusion about a missing fur, sir. If you could let us have a look in your bag, we should be able to resolve this quickly."

Mickey was prepared for this. Before he'd put the coat into the garment bag, he'd razored the label. And a major piece of luck. No initials embroidered on the silk lining.

He handed over the bag.

"Just on my way to Chicago," he said. "My sister inherited this coat from my mother who passed away couple months ago. My sister didn't want it mailed, so I'm bringing it to her."

"May I see your ticket, please," the guard said.

Mickey handed him his ticket. God. Was he ready for this or what?

Mama was mad. "It's got a Neiman Marcus label. So if there's a sable coat in there with a Neiman Marcus label, I hope you're not going to buy this crap about his dead mother…"

The guard held up the coat, looking for the label.

"At the collar," mama said.

The guard turned the collar inside out, looking at mama and shrugging. "Sorry, ma'am. But I'm not finding a label." He spread the coat, examining the lining. "No initials?"

"It's new," mama said, exasperated. "Look, maybe I'm not remembering right about the label. But we told you this is the guy who took the coat and, lo-and-behold—here he is with a sable coat in a garment bag. That can't be a coincidence…."

The guard stared at Mickey. Then he lifted the coat to his face, inhaled, and said, "Gotta say, Mister. The coat smells like the lady. Same scent."

"And he killed my Barbie," Tiffany said, taking a kick at Mickey with the foot that still had a shoe on it.

The guard was continuing to stare at Mickey in a way that made Mickey sweat. Then the guard said, "Sir, have you had other contacts with security here at the airport?"

Mickey remembered why the guard looked familiar. Same guy who'd stopped him when he'd had the Patek Philippe strapped to his dick. Mickey could see behind the guard's eyes. The scent of Obsession was making the same association for the guard that it had made for the drunk months earlier.

The guard said, "Sir, could I see some identification please."

"No problem." Mickey had left his fake ID in his pocket after going through security. He reached into his pocket and pulled it out.

Barbie's head came out with the ID, fell to the floor and rolled right up to Tiffany's socked foot.

It was then Mickey experienced a flash of illumination that was not unlike the moment fifteen years earlier when he'd picked up his first wallet.

His life was about to change.

Ellen Hart

After spending twelve years as a kitchen manager/chef at a large sorority at the University of Minnesota, it was either do the real thing, or commit murder on paper. Hence, Ellen Hart became a mystery writer. Her first novel, Hallowed Murder *was published in 1989, and since then this prolific writer has penned 19 mysteries in two different mystery series. The newest in her culinary mystery series,* No Reservations Required, *was released by Fawcett in June of 2005. An Intimate Ghost, the 12th in the Jane Lawless series, was nominated for the 2005 Lambda Literary Award, and is currently being turned into a screenplay by an independent film producer/ screenwriter in Hollywood.*

Her newest Jane Lawless mystery, The Iron Girl, *will be published in the fall of 2005. For the past eight years, Ellen has taught mystery writing at The Loft Literary Center in Minneapolis, the largest independent writing community in the nation. She is a five-time winner of the Lambda Literary Award for Best Lesbian Mystery, as well as a two-time winner of the Minnesota Book Award for Best Crime & Detective Fiction.* Entertainment Weekly *recently named her one of the 101 movers and shakers in the gay entertainment industry. Ellen lives in Minneapolis with her partner of 28 years.*

Norwegian Noir

Ellen Hart

You know that old poem that starts: "When I am an old woman, I shall wear purple."

Cora Runbeck wore plaid. In the summer, she preferred pastel plaids. Department store clerks always insisted she was an "autumn," and would nudge her over to the brown or orange dresses. Cora loathed brown and orange. At the height of a Minnesota summer, just as it was right now, Cora only wore pinks and blues and an occasional lemon yellow. She felt they went perfect with her little white socks and white shoes. And for formal occasions, she always had a clean pair of white gloves in her top dresser drawer. No properly brought-up Lutheran lady of a certain generation would think of going to church without her white gloves.

Cora had just celebrated her seventy-third birthday. She was a no nonsense Norwegian woman who'd grown up on a farm near Le Sueur. By the time she was ten, she was fixing the family meals, feeding chickens, milking cows, taking care of her three younger siblings, and nursing an ailing mother. That was during the war and times were tough. She understood work and she understood responsibility—and she had little time for people who didn't.

Cora had lived most of her life in Rose Hill, a small town in southern Minnesota. Her husband, Kirby, had died in a car explosion two years ago. The day he died, he'd asked her for a divorce. Cora had been stunned. Nobody in her family had ever divorced before. But then Kirby died and that was the end of that.

Kirby had been a lazy man. She'd married him because he was handsome and quiet, and because she was sick of being an indentured servant to her father at the farm. Unfortunately, she mistook Kirby's silence for great personal depth. When it became clear that it was only a mask, that his shallowness was matched only by his pathologically paranoid secretiveness, well, she stiffened her shoulders and gritted her teeth, and dug in for the long haul.

Cora had never really loved Kirby. After he was gone, she tried to miss him, but it just wasn't in her. She had a hard time squeezing out even a tear at the funeral. The best part of the day had been the meal at First Lutheran after the graveside ceremony. All her women friends had brought food, and they hovered around her, urging her to eat. She remembered one man commenting that he was astonished such a skinny little lady could eat so much fried chicken.

The same week Kirby died, Cora had entered her meat loaf recipe in the Minneapolis Times Register's recipe contest. Everyone always told her it was the best meat loaf they'd ever tasted. Cora was a modest woman—hated pridefulness—but she did admit to a certain pleasure in the compliments she got on her cooking. Amazing as it sounded, she'd won the contest and been treated to an all-expense paid visit to the Twin Cities. For Cora, this was a dream come true.

As a part of the deal, she was interviewed on a local morning TV show. Cora made such a splash that the producers invited her back, again and again. Eventually, she became a regular, selling her house in Rose Hill and moving to a downtown Minneapolis river condo. As she thought about it now, the year after Kirby had died had been like a magic carpet ride. The next invitation came from *A Prairie Home Companion.* Cora stood on stage and talked with Garrison Keillor for a few minutes, then accompanied him on several hymns. The entire audience had joined in on "Abide With Me." It had been a golden moment. As far as Cora was concerned, if the Lutheran church ever decided to institute sainthood, Garrison Keillor should be at the top of the list. He'd done so much to promote an understanding of the true nature of Scandinavian Lutherans. Cora felt as if he'd tapped into her essence.

A few weeks after her triumph with Garrison Keillor, Cora had flown to New York to appear on the *David Letterman Show.* People laughed uproariously at what she said. She wasn't entirely sure why, but she laughed, too, trying to be polite.

She appeared on Jay Leno, and Last Call with Carson Daly, where she met Phil Vassar and Adam Sandler. She hadn't been impressed by Mr. Sandler at all, but when Phil Vassar had invited her to sit on the piano bench next to him and then sung "I'll Take That As a Yes" directly to her, she knew she was on the road to hell and loving every minute of it. That guy was as hot as a July afternoon in a Le Sueur corn field! She'd never liked country music—or country anything, for that matter—but after that night, she'd gone out and bought his CDs. She realized when she got them home that she didn't have anything to play them on. So that led to an iPod, and then an iMac and computer lessons. Deep in her Lutheran soul, she knew that this rank consumerism was deeply wrong, but she couldn't seem to stop herself. She was kicking up her heels for the first time in her life!

Seven months after her first appearance on Letterman, Cora's agent was approached about a regular spot for Cora on Bill Mahr's show. But when that deal went south, Cora finally put on the breaks. She'd been corrupted by the money and the attention, that was a given. The worst infraction in the lexicon of Lutheran sins was "Getting the Big Head." From the start, she'd been worried about the Big Head issue. She tried desperately to maintain her humility, although at times it had been a struggle. She'd been on a roll for almost two years, but the truth was, she missed her old life, the weekly Lutheran Ladies Lunch at the Prairie Lights Cafe, Wednesday night bingo in the church basement, naps with her loving little cat, Winthrop. She missed morning coffee with her women friends, people who were in touch with time-honored Lutheran values—keeping a clean house, saving your money, preparing good, wholesome homemade food. She needed to reconnect with women who weren't swayed by big city silliness. She had finally recovered her senses, and yet something about returning to Rose Hill seemed too depressing for words.

Cora had been attending Christ Our Lord Lutheran since moving to Minneapolis. She didn't much care for the minister. He reminded her more of a politician in clerical garb than a real preacher. Cora liked her religion straight. She thought ministers should preach from the Bible on Sunday mornings, not offer a thinly disguised political plea in the form of a sermon. Why on earth did these men have such little faith in the intelligence of their congregations? Didn't they think they were listening? Ministers should preach from the Bible, draw their moral lessons from scripture, and let the people draw their own conclusions about how to apply them. Heavens, but some of these ministers were pushy!

One afternoon, while Cora was enjoying a piece of apple pie a la mode at Peter's Grill in downtown Minneapolis, a man she'd met at her church the week before stepped up to her booth and asked if she'd like some company. Cora saw no reason to say no. He ordered a cup of coffee, talking generally at first, then launched into what he was really interested in.

"What was Jay Leno really like?"

Her expression must have soured, because the man grew visibly embarrassed and quickly changed the subject. He asked her how she liked living in her river-front condo. Cora said she was thinking of moving, but hadn't quite decided yet just where. That's when the man launched into his paean to the suburb in which he lived. It appeared that the place was nothing short of utopia. Beautiful houses with bright shiny people living in them. Good Christians who took responsibility for their lives. Respectful children. Clean, quiet streets. He finished his comments by saying, "Well, Cora, if you save your money and live a good life, maybe one day you'll get to live in Burnsville, too."

Cora finally had a destination. A goal. Burnsville!

The next day she got on the horn to a real estate agent, and one month later she was the proud owner of a small two story brick house on Black Dog Lane.

That had been two months ago. It was now July. While Cora had been initially thrilled with the All-American look of her new neighborhood, she was beginning to detect certain cracks this side of paradise.

Around ten o'clock one evening, Cora had gone outside to turn off the sprinkler. On her way back up the steps to the front door, she'd glanced to her right and was shocked to see a man crouched in the bushes under her bedroom window. She stood in stunned silence as the man waved a golf club around and said he'd hit a ball into the bushes and was trying to find it. A moment later, a little creature of indeterminate origin scuttled out of the bush with the ball in its mouth.

The man introduced himself as Darwin Gustavsson. "I'm your neighbor. Two doors down." He pointed to a white aluminum-sided house.

Cora hadn't been born yesterday. She reserved judgment about his explanation, watching him extricate himself from the arborvitae. The porch light cast a yellow pallor over his pockmarked face. He was a tall, muscular man, with a chiseled jaw, pleasant enough face and a full head of white hair. He was definitely a geezer, but in Cora's opinion, a studly one.

"What is that thing?" asked Cora, pointing to the creature scuttling around her front yard with the golf ball in its teeth.

"Oh, that's my dog."

"It's a dog?" It looked like a large, fluffy centipede.

"A Yorkie."

"Something wrong with him?"

"He's got skin problems, lost the hair on his back."

Cora shuddered. She didn't like dogs.

"Name's Stonewall."

"Kind of a big name for such a little dog."

"Yeah, I didn't want him to get a complex about his size."

"I'm sure that was very kind of you."

He scratched the back of his neck, honoring her with a craggy smile. "Guess I'm that kind of guy."

"You always play golf at night?" asked Cora.

"Well, yah. I have to exercise Stonewall, don't I? He likes to chase golf balls. 'Course, sometimes they get lost."

Which gave this Mr. Gustavsson, alias Mr. Peeping Tom, a perfect excuse to get up close and personal with all the windows in the neighborhood.

Cora opened the door and was about to bid him goodnight when Gustavsson said:

"I know who you are."

That stopped her. "Pardon me?"

"I seen you on TV. You're that woman who won the meat loaf contest and got real famous. If you don't mind my saying so, I'm a huge fan of yours. I've been following your career right from the git go."

"You have?"

"Yes, ma'am. Sure have."

She straightened up. She liked his politeness. She noticed now that, except for the hair, he resembled Marshall Dillon on *Gunsmoke*.

She favored him with a demur smile. "Thank you."

"Maybe you'd like to have coffee sometime."

She wasn't sure what to say. "Well—"

"No pressure. But, see, I'd love to hear about all your exploits."

Cora sighed. People were always so impressed by celebrity. It was a cross she would have to bear. "I'll give it some thought."

"Well, ah, nice to finally meet you. Night," he said, hoisting the club over his shoulder and walking off. The centipede scuttled after him.

For the next few nights, Cora and Winthrop watched from an upstairs window. Gustavsson would appear in his front yard around ten P.M., tap a few balls for the dog to chase, then knock a long one into the bushes under Cora's bedroom window, or the bushes under a window at the next house over. Every night it was the same thing. He was obviously using the ball as a ploy to look in windows. On the fourth night, he didn't bother to hit the ball at all, just walked across Cora's yard until, three doors down, he disappeared from sight. Fifteen minutes later, he was back. He stood in her front yard, set the ball down, then knocked it back into his own yard. Stonewall slithered after it.

Cora had had enough. She felt a moral imperative to get the goods on this bozo, and when she did, she'd turn him over to the police.

On Saturday morning, three of Cora's new women friends arrived for coffee. She'd prepared two types of Kringla—a cherry pistachio and a raisin cream cheese. They weren't exactly traditional, but Cora was living on the edge these days. She wasn't in Rose Hill anymore.

"Well, ladies," said Cora, looking around at the gray heads. She'd met all of them at Christ Our Lord Lutheran in Minneapolis. Her very newest women friends at the Missouri Synod church in Burnsville were far too straight-laced for some of Cora's newfound activities. "Do we play first, or do we have coffee?"

"Play!" they all shouted in unison.

Cora led them down a hall to a room at the back of the house. After pressing the key into the padlock and removing the chain, she opened the door and flipped on the light. A large Royal Monarch pool table sat in the center of the floor. It was a Queen Anne style with red cloth and fringed leather pockets. Very grand. Cora had bought it on eBay. The women made quick work of divvying up the pool cues and then Frieda Johnson racked the balls and broke.

"I'd like to go to one of those three-day pool schools," said Frieda, moving around the table looking for her first shot.

"What would your husband say?" asked Honey Stiggersund, reaching for the chalk. Honey's bifocals rode low on her nose.

"He'd say, Hell, I'm goin' fishing!"

They all laughed. It wasn't funny, but this was the sort of thing that passed for humor in Minnesota.

While they played, Cora explained about her Peeping Tom neighbor, the Matt Dillon look-alike.

"Be careful, hon," said Enid Bjornstad. She was the one who always wore pink, frilly blouses. She'd just sunk the six ball in the corner pocket and was assessing a combination shot. "People are very odd these days. You never know when someone could get violent."

"But I can't just let him get away with it," said Cora.

"I think it's an empowering thing to do," said Honey. She stood behind Frieda, looking over her shoulder. Frieda turned and raised her eyebrow at Honey. "Empowering? You and your feminist jargon."

"You know what I mean. Go for it, Cora. Be fearless. I'm cheering for you—all the way."

"I do agree," said Enid. Enid was the only woman in the group who had ever smoked a cigar. It gave her a certain outlaw status they all secretly coveted. "We can't just sit back and allow evil to happen in the world. We have to do something about it."

Apparently, it was exactly what Cora needed to hear, because she felt fortified by righteousness now. She looked to her women friends for guidance, and they'd just given it. The only time her women friends had ever let her down was years ago. They'd augured against cataract surgery, which Cora needed badly. She'd finally gone and done it anyway and amazingly, her eyeball hadn't fallen out or exploded, as her friends said it surely would. But that was back in Rose Hill. Her Twin Cities friends were more worldly-wise.

It rained that night. Cora had picked out a bush across the street where she planned to hide and watch Gustavsson. She intended to document everything he did in five-minute increments. But the rain kept her inside, so she and Winthrop sat by the upstairs window and watched to see if the rain would put a damper on Gustavsson's golf game. Around ten, Gustavsson walked out to his car. He didn't seem to mind the rain, because he stood there, one hand on the hood, the other holding a cell phone to his ear.

Cora got an idea. She went downstairs and threw on her trench coat, then watched outside until he got in his station wagon. As he pulled away from the curb, she dashed through the rain to her red T-Bird, gunned the motor, and headed after him. She was curious where he might be going at this time of night.

The two cars sailed up Cliff Road until the station wagon hung a right onto 35W. Twenty minutes later Cora found herself following the station wagon down Central Avenue in northeast Minneapolis. This was truly the dark underbelly of The Cities, thought Cora. The Mean Streets. It could have been a scene straight out of *Law & Order*.

A few minutes later, Gustavsson pulled up in front of a business called "Tippi's." Cora darted her T-Bird for cover behind a huge SUV. She watched Gustavsson get out of his car and enter the front door.

That left Cora with a decision. Should she follow him inside, or just wait? If she didn't go in, she'd never know what he was up to. She gave it a couple more minutes. When he didn't come out, she made a snap decision. She slipped out of her car and crept slowly up to the storefront. Six small windows ran along the outside, but they were too high for her to see into. She figured it was a bar. She'd never actually been in a bar before, nor had she ever had the desire to darken the door of one, but this was research in an important cause, she had to keep that firmly in mind.

Screwing up her courage, Cora drew back the door and entered. She found the dimly lit room empty except for a young floozy with excessive eye makeup sitting on a stool behind a cracked wood counter. The young woman cradled a phone between her shoulder and her ear, her hand poised over a thick black book.

"MasterCard or Visa, babe?" She glanced at Cora and frowned. "Okay, I got you down. Later." As she hung up, her eyes dropped to Cora's white shoes and socks, then traveled up the trench coat to her face. "Help you?"

"Yes, you may," said Cora. "What sort of establishment is this?"

"Huh?"

"This is a business, right?"

"Yeah."

"What sort of business?"

"Well, ah,—" She sat up straight. "Therapeutic massage?"

"Is that a question?"

"Uhm, no?"

Cora looked around at the seedy wood paneling. Gustavsson was nowhere in sight. While she was deciding on her next question, a young guy with greasy long blond hair pushed through the door. He took one look at Cora, turned around and left.

"Lady, you can't stay in here. You're gonna hurt business."

"I can't imagine why." On a sudden whim, she added, "You know, I think I'd like a massage." She set her purse on the counter. "How much is it?"

The young woman's face scrunched up in confusion.

"Are you in pain, dear?"

"Uhm, I mean, aren't you a little old?"

Cora stiffened. "For what?"

The woman blinked. "Okaaaaay. But we only got women massage therapists."

"I prefer a woman."

Her eyebrow arched.

Cora was losing patience. "My money is as good as anyone else's, is that not correct?" A producer on the *David Letterman Show* had encouraged her to have a massage when she got back to her Manhattan hotel. Except, there hadn't been time. Cora tucked the idea away for another day. She looked upon it as a new experience. Now was as good a time as any.

"We, ah—" The young floozy seemed at a loss for words.

"If one of your therapists isn't free, I'd be happy to wait." She assumed that, at this time of night, not many therapists would be working. Gustavsson was obviously being attended to. If he came out and saw her sitting in one of the chairs, well, she'd just have to explain that he wasn't the only one who enjoyed an occasional late-night therapeutic massage.

"Look, lady, I think you should try somewhere else."

Cora cocked her head. "And why would I do that?"

"I think you got some kind of misunderstanding about what we do here. It's strictly hetero."

"Excuse me?"

"I'm not passing judgment or nothing." She gave Cora another penetrating stare. "Just...oh, hell. Go find yourself a copy of *Lavender Magazine*, okay? Maybe you can find something in there that will, you know, suit you better."

"I don't understand. What's 'Lavender'?"

The floozy narrowed one eye, folded her arms over her ample bosom. "You playin' with me, lady? 'Cause if you are--"

Cora felt that she was missing something important in this conversation, but she had no idea what it was. "Let me get this straight. You're telling me you won't allow me to purchase a massage here?"

"Tippi wouldn't allow it. She's kind of, you know. Vanilla."

Now Cora was completely lost. She picked her purse up off the counter, mustered up a withering glare, and left.

She drove home in the rain.

The next three nights were clear as a bell. Cora sat across the street in her pastel plaid sun dress, hidden behind a large honeysuckle, and took notes. Gustavsson seemed most interested in her bedroom window, and both windows on the house next door. She'd talked to her woman friends again, asking their opinion on whether this nightly vigil would be enough to interest the police in Gustavsson's activities. Enid, the cigar smoker and the most noir Norwegian Cora had ever known, said she thought Cora needed more direct evidence. Cora, who was working on her own Norske noir image, took the advice.

After some serious thought, Cora came up with a plan. Nobody could resist her meat loaf, right? She figured she'd use it as a Trojan Horse—or a battering ram. She needed to get into Gustavsson's house, see what she could find out.

On Saturday night, Cora knocked on Gustavsson's front door. She knew he was home because his car was outside. In her hands was a tray which not only held the meat loaf, but also a bowl of mashed potatoes, a bowl of gravy, a bowl of green beans, a loaf of fresh-baked bread, and a home-baked lemon meringue pie. Gustavsson would be putty in her hands.

He opened the door, sniffing the air, and gave her a big grin.

"Dinner?" he said, rubbing his hands together. "This is too cool!"

Once inside, Cora looked down and saw the fluffy centipede at her feet. It had a headless Barbie doll in its teeth and was shaking it back and forth, snarling and growling. Cora stepped around the little beast and followed Gustavsson to the back of the house.

An hour later, they were sitting at his kitchen table, finishing up their pie. Cora couldn't get over it. Except for his nighttime golf games, Gustavsson seemed like such a nice, normal, decent guy. The house was a little cluttered, and not very clean, but she'd expected worse. He told her he was a retired plumber, a working man, and that made him the salt of the earth, in her opinion. His wife had died many years ago and he'd never remarried. All during dinner he'd plied her with questions about her life during the past few years. He seemed genuinely interested in her as a person, as well as in her good fortune. After downing the last of his pie, he told her he was her biggest fan. Cora was touched. She finally got up the courage to ask if he was a church goer.

"Oh, yes. Absolutely"

She held her breath. "Are you...Lutheran?"

"Well, of course."

She smiled, feeling the tickle of romantic attraction. Except for the pockmarks on his face, Cora found him a highly attractive older gentleman. As they were letting their food settle, Gustavsson finally turned the conversation to something of import.

"That house next to yours," he said, wiping his mouth on a paper napkin, "I'm kind of worried about it."

"The house? Or the people living in it?"

"Both. See, the two people who own the place have been in India for the past two months. Their two kids, Justice and Jenny Wolcott, are living there by themselves."

"That's not a Scandinavian last name."

"No. I think it's English."

Cora narrowed her eyes. Not only had she not met them, she'd never even seen them. "How old are they?"

"Mid-twenties. They live in the basement."

"Well, they should be old enough to take care of themselves."

"That's not the problem."

Cora got up to pour them more coffee. "What is?"

"Do you promise to keep this to yourself until I can figure it out?"

She crossed her heart and held up her hand.

"See, Cora, I think they're cooking up Meth inside that house."

"Meth? You mean drugs?"

"Exactly."

"How could you possibly know that?"

"I been watching them. At night, mostly. The golf ball thing, it's just a ploy. That's why I was in your arborvitae the other night. I can see into their living room best from that angle. I'll lay you odds the lab's in the basement. I can smell it when they have the windows open."

"I haven't smelled anything."

"You gotta get real close."

"What does Meth smell like?"

"Cat piss, Cora. Or sometimes ammonia. And there's no cat in that house. Moreover, I see lots of empty chemical tubs in their garbage. Like I said, I wish I could get inside. They get lots of visitors after midnight, which is another tip-off."

"I'm always asleep by midnight."

He smiled at her. "Of course you are." Sipping his coffee, he continued, "Thing is, meth labs can be dangerous. The have a nasty habit of blowing up."

Cora's eyes blinked wide open. "I've had some experience with explosions, Darwin." And she didn't want another.

Gustavsson patted her hand. "You just let me take care of it, little lady. This is Burnsville. We don't want people like that living in our midst."

"Amen," said Cora, shuddering.

"I just wish I could get in that house."

She didn't say anything, but she would think on it and see what she could come up with.

On her way back to her house that night, she glanced into the Wolcott's front yard and noticed something small and light-colored lying in the grass. When she walked over and picked it up, she discovered that it was a soiled pink ballet slipper. She thought about it a second, and then whispered, "Gotcha."

The next afternoon, Cora rang the Wolcott's front doorbell. Nobody answered. She rang again, then knocked as hard as she could with her fist. This finally brought a response. The door swung back and a short, dark-haired young woman squinted out at her. "Yeah?" she said, giving Cora a suspicious look.

"I found this in your yard. Thought you might like it back. You must be a ballet dancer. I'm your neighbor next door. We haven't met."

Pushing the screen open, Jenny Wolcott took the slipper from Cora's hand.

The rush of air from the inside of the house nearly took Cora's breath away.

"Hey, Bean Brain," Jenny shouted back into the house, "here's that slipper you were looking for."

Justice appeared. He was shirtless, wearing baggy pajama bottoms, and holding a perfume atomizer. Both the Wolcott children were skinny as rails, and neither looked like they'd had a bath in weeks. Maybe months.

"What's that smell?" said Cora, waving fresh air in front of her face.

"Obsession," said Jenny, glancing at her brother. "I'm a...a...like a perfume maker. I make knockoffs and sell them for the real thing."

"Isn't that illegal?"

She shrugged. "I just made a new batch yesterday. You like Obsession?"

"I don't know."

Jenny looked down at the slipper. "God, look at that. You washed the thing."

"I couldn't give it back to you dirty," said Cora, a bit indignant.

Jenny glanced back at her brother. "Get her one of the bottles."

Apparently, Justice didn't talk. But he did do what his sister told him. He disappeared for a second and then came back with a small glass bottle filled with an amber-colored liquid. "Here," said Jenny, handing it to Cora. "Just a little thank you present. Hey, you ever try Channel #5?"

Cora shook her head.

Justice leaned down and picked up a large plastic container of Coke, drinking straight from the bottle. His sullenness equaled his manners.

"Well, as soon as we wash down the equipment in the basement," said Jenny, standing now on one foot, "I'm going to do another batch. Come back tomorrow and I'll give you a sample."

"You actually make perfume?"

"Yup. Keeps us in pizza and Coke." She laughed, tossing another look back at her silent, churlish brother.

Cora could tell that neither one of them was going to invite her in.

She took one last stab. "Is your brother a ballet dancer?"

Jenny laughed. "Hell, no. He's an artist. He bought a bunch of stuff at a garage sale a couple days ago to use in a sculpture. He must have dropped the slipper. It was driving him nuts, right Justy?"

Justice took another few gulps from the Coke bottle, wiped the back of his hand across his mouth, and grunted.

"Well," said Cora, backing away from the door. Maybe they weren't drug dealers, but they weren't exactly her idea of good neighbors either. "Nice meeting you."

"Yeah, likewise," said Jenny, closing the door a little too quickly.

Cora could hear the click of the bolt as she made her way back down the steps. She couldn't wait to talk to Darwin. He'd given her his phone number, but when she called him, he wasn't home. She left a message on his answering machine and then went upstairs to take a long, hot tub. She felt soiled by her interaction with the Wolcotts. Like all good Lutherans, she had faith that soap and water and a little elbow grease could fix almost anything.

Just after seven, as Cora was watching Emeril Live on the Food Channel, she got a call from Darwin. He invited her to come right over, said he'd make coffee.

Cora kissed Winthrop goodbye, then hustled across the lawn. Gustavsson was waiting for her at the door. He handed her a rose.

"What's this for?" she asked.

"Just felt like giving you a flower."

She blushed furiously.

"That's just the beginning, honey," he said, ushering her into the living room, his hand at her back.

She wasn't as pleased with the implied familiarity as she was by the flower. After all, they'd only just met.

Over coffee, Cora explained what she'd learned earlier in the afternoon. Darwin sat and watched her. To Cora, it didn't seem like he was really listening, but when she was done, he shook his head.

"Don't believe a word of it."

"You don't?"

"Hell, no."

The phone gave a sudden, jarring ring. "Lemme answer that, Cora. I'll just be a minute."

But he was more than a minute. Ten minutes into the conversation, with no letup in sight, Cora rose from the La-Z-Boy. She needed to use his bathroom. Moving down the hallway, she glanced into his bedroom. He hadn't made the bed. It made her stomach flip over. The next door was closed, so she felt it was a good bet that it was the bathroom.

Pushing the door open, she saw that she was wrong. She was about to back out when the wallpaper stopped her. She felt around on the wall until she found the light switch. Flipping it on, she saw that the three of the four walls of the room were papered with enlarged photographs. She could tell right away that most of them had been taken through a window. Curtains and blinds obscured some of the bodies, but all of them were of women and many of the women were nude.

Cora felt a sinking sizzle in the pit of her stomach. She should have trusted her instincts! Darwin Gustavsson was a Peeping Tom! And worse. As she looked closer, her mouth dropped open. One entire wall contained nothing but photographs of Cora. Cora in her backyard pruning the rose bush. Cora with the hood on her car up, working on the motor. Cora carrying in groceries. Cora in her living room watching TV with Winthrop. Cora in her bedroom, slipping into a bathrobe. And—heavens! She took a deep gulp. Cora walking into her bedroom after taking a bath, one shot with the towel around her, and the next after the towel had been removed.

"I'll kill him," she whispered, clenching her fists. Her mind went white with fury. All she could think about was digging Kirby's old shotgun out of her front closet, coming back, and blowing Gustavsson's head clean off. But that's when she heard the footsteps. She turned around to find Gustavsson standing in the hallway, holding a gun on her.

"I see you found my gallery," he said, smiling sweetly.

"This is disgusting!"

He seemed hurt. "Okay, maybe I shouldn't have taken the other pictures, but I thought you'd like the ones of you. I mean, like I told you, I'm your biggest fan. This is my homage to you, Cora. You're everything to me! I knew it the minute I saw you on Letterman. You complete me. That's why you moved to Burnsville. Right next to my house. It's freakin' Kismet!"

Cora almost gagged. But she had to play this carefully. "If I'm so important to you, why do you have that gun?"

He looked down at it. Shrugged. "I don't want you to leave until I can convince you how much you mean to me."

"Well, I, ah—" Before she could finish the sentence, an explosion ripped through the air, knocking both of them to the floor. Cora was momentarily dazed. Pulling herself up on a chair, she glanced around and saw that a bookshelf had been dislodged from the wall. Gustavsson was lying unconscious underneath it, books strewn all around him.

"Lord in heaven," she muttered, seeing that his beautiful thick white hair had been knocked sideways on his head. "A wig," she pronounced with great distaste, making her way through the rubble of books to the front door.

And that's when she saw it. The Wolcott's house was a smoking heap, the back of it blown clean off. Looked like Gustavsson was right about one thing. The Wolcott kids weren't cooking up perfume in their spare time.

Suddenly, Cora screamed "Winthrop!" She dashed back to her own house. Except for some pictures blown off the walls, it didn't look like it had been damaged. She found her cat in the bedroom closet hiding behind a pair of tall winter boots. "Come here, sweetheart," she said, scooping him up and cuddling him close. "Mama's so sorry. The big city's not for us, is it. We could have moved to any of the suburbs and it would have turned out the same. We need to get back to our roots, Winthrop." She'd been so worried about getting the Big Head that she failed to see the real issue: if she stayed around the Twin Cities too long, she might not have any head at all!

Still hugging Winthrop, Cora picked up the phone in the kitchen to call 911. As she reported the explosion and Gustavsson's injury, she could hear sirens heading her way. "Guess somebody else called the authorities. Well, then I've got another call to make." She checked the list on the side of her refrigerator, then tapped in the number of her real estate agent. As usual, he wasn't in. She decided to leave him a message.

"Mr. Saliers, this is Cora Runbeck. You sold me a house on Black Dog Lane a few months back. Here's the deal. I want to get rid of it pronto. Cheap. Oh, and when you list it, mention that the owner will throw in a pool table free of charge. That should get the ball rolling."

Three weeks later, after Cora had settled into a small house on the outskirts of Rose Hill, she heard from one of her women friends in the Twin Cities. Apparently, the Wolcott kids hadn't been in the home at the time of the explosion. They'd been arrested on a dozen different counts, one of them having to do with the meth lab in the basement. So, it was finally confirmed. Cora didn't like to think making perfume could be that dangerous.

But the most shocking revelation concerned another lie Darwin Gustavsson had told her. He wasn't a Lutheran after all. Frieda Johnson said she'd read in the newspaper that Mr. Gustavsson had attended the Unitarian Church in Burnsville.

Well, thought Cora, feeling a zing of satisfaction. If that didn't just say it all.

Carl Brookins

Before he became a mystery writer and reviewer, Brookins was a freelance photographer, a Public Television program director, a Cable TV administrator, and a counselor and faculty member at Metropolitan State University in Saint Paul, Minnesota. His reviews of mystery fiction, non-fiction articles, short stories and photographs, have appeared in many print and Internet publications, as well as on his own web site. He has written and produced local and regional television drama and educational programs, and he has led a monthly mystery reading group for Barnes and Noble Booksellers in Roseville.

An avid recreational sailor himself, Brookins writes the sailing adventure series featuring Michael Tanner and Mary Whitney. The first, Inner Passages, *was released in 2001,* A Superior Mystery *in 2003, and* Old Silver *in 2005. The first volume in a new series featuring a short private detective.* Sean Sean: The Case of the Greedy Lawyers *is scheduled for release in September, 2005.*

Brookins is a member of Mystery Writers of America and Sisters in Crime. He can frequently be found touring bookstores and libraries with his companions-in-crime, The Minnesota Crime Wave. He and his wife Jean, a retired publisher and editor, have two grown daughters. They live in Roseville, Minnesota.

A Winter's Tale

Carl Brookins

He stood in the center of the room, head cocked, bushy eyebrows raised into the deep furrows across his brow, listening. Damn, he thought, wind seems to be getting stronger. He walked to the window and scraped away the thickening layer of frost to peer outside. The landscape, what he could see of it, appeared to be lit from directly overhead with an odd, cold, yellowish light.

Very peculiar, he thought. In fifty years of living on the flat unforgiving Northern Minnesota prairie, he couldn't remember it ever looking quite like this. Today, there was no horizon. The only way he could tell whether he was looking at the snow or the sky was the faint texture of the snow that had drifted close around the base of the old wood-frame house. There wasn't any texture in the sky. Another blast of north wind trembled the house.

He went to the kitchen, the corner that faced northwest, that split the air clawing its way down the sides of the place. He took the cold steel handle of the counter pump and worked it vigorously for a few stokes until a gout of icy water spilled over the wide mouth and into the pail below. Good, he thought. The pipe's still not froze up. That'd happened one winter when there'd been a long cold period before much snow had fallen. The snow formed a blanket around the house and kept the wind out before the real cold of February came. Mostly. But there was a couple feet of frozen air between the floorboards and down into the topsoil. The rest of that winter he'd had to carry water from the well in the barn.

There was a window over the tiny kitchen counter. It faced southeast, toward town. Usually he could see wisps of smoke rising from the furnaces of townsfolk in Fertile, on days like this when there was no wind. He leaned forward and scraped at the frost on the single pane. It was thicker here than on the other window and he could feel the swirl of frigid air that leaked around the frame. His barn was directly ahead, about twenty yards away. He could barely see it on account of the icy sleet-snow stuck to the unpainted sides of the barn and the thickening snow cloud blowing almost horizontally across the land. Miles of it. While he watched, the light changed a little and when looking straight up, he saw pale blue sky overhead where the snow cloud breached. Damn, he thought again, if the clouds go we'll have some serious cold.

A loud pop caused him to glance back over his shoulder at the stove. Better check the wood box. The coal was already long gone. He scratched his chest through the gap in his long underwear where one button had disappeared last year. Or maybe the year before. S'pose I'll have to get dressed and feed the animals. He considered that. A formidable task. He remembered he hadn't been out to the barn yesterday. Was there enough feed in reach? The chickens had the run of the place. They'd tear open a bag of feed if they got hungry. He tried to remember how much Timothy hay he'd forked into the troughs for the two heifers and the three hogs that were resident. Hell, he couldn't remember. Seemed to be forgetting things more often these days. Well, wait a while, maybe the wind'll die towards night. Main thing was water. The well in the barn was a good one, but the leathers in the pump were old and must be rotting so pumping was a long arduous task. Come summer. . .

His thoughts drifted off. He shuffled in worn filthy slippers back to the stove. Against the wall, between the bed and the stove, was a big slant-topped box built into the corner between floor and wall. The sides were cold to the touch.

"How come the top is slanted?" Isabel'd asked.

"Keeps the top clear. When you need firewood you need to get in there," he'd told her. Now he pulled up on the hinged top and leaned in, felt the bony claw of cold wrap around his arm. The floor of the wood box reached all the way to the ground. There were only five or six split logs in the box. Enough, maybe, for half a day. He'd have to go out to the wood pile and get more. There was an odd whistle-moan as the wind tested the cracks and gaps in the outside wall of the wood box. When the man straightened up, he felt a tiny prick stick his belly and heard a ragged ripping sound. When he looked down, there was a three-inch tear in the front of his dingy underwear where he'd snagged it on a splinter. A tiny drop of blood appeared on his hairy belly. He rubbed it away and turned to open the stove door, chucking a log into the hot red center of the stove. He closed down the damper some in the sooty stovepipe. Then he sat on the bed and dragged a ratty blanket over his shoulders.

For a while he sat motionless, staring at nothing much, listening, somewhere in his mind, to the wind, to his jumbled memories, hearing the joints in the house crack and mutter as the growing cold squeezed down on the rafters and the roof boards, thought about nothing and everything.

His next conscious thoughts were more an awareness of change. His feet and ankles were numb from the bare floor. When he blew out his breath, he saw a tiny bloom of vapor in the air. Without moving his head, the man tracked eyes left to the stove. The fire within still guttered and snapped. Gettin' colder out, he thought. The clear space on the window glass across the room was already covered with a new layer of frost. The light from outside was weaker. Other than the sound of the fire, his world was icy still. Wind's dropped. Gotta get to the barn. Another rafter popped in answer.

He stood and dropped the blanket, heard the cracking sound in his knee joints. He dragged a mound of clothes off the foot of the bed, struggled into a ripped pair of jeans, hauled on thick discolored work socks. The red border around their tops was so dirty and stained as to be almost obliterated. Two flannel shirts were next. Then he stuffed his body into a pair of stained, formerly blue and white striped overalls. Laboriously, he shoved his feet into work boots and bent over to tie the frayed laces. He clumped to the door and, from a wooden peg driven head-high into the wall beside the door, took a long coat, a ratty, moth-eaten sheepskin that hung to his knees. The buttons had long since gone missing. An old leather belt kept it mostly closed. His mitts were also leather with thick linings, but they were hard to work in when they got stiff.

When he opened the door, the snow drift was already a third of the way up the frame. He kicked the drift away and pushed out into the snow. The wind had died, he realized, but the snow had come. Thick, silent, like a blanket of uncombed wool, snow fell from the lowering clouds. Already the tracks to the barn he'd made the day before, or the day before that, were obliterated. He plunged his hand into the hard snowdrift at his right side and fished out the slack line that ran from an eyebolt fixed to the side of the door out to a fence post ten yards away in the yard, then to another post, and then to a similar eyebolt beside the barn door. Alternately pulling on the line and pushing his weight through the snow drifts, he struggled to the barn. It took fifteen minutes of un-remitting effort and he was short of breath and sweating heavily by the time he was able to prize the door open and stumble into the tiny barn. It took nearly two hours to feed and water the animals, clumping around half frozen. He could see the breath-blooms from the animals' nostrils.

When he went outside things had changed again. It was darker and the wind had risen. The wind sounded and he thought he might have heard a similar sound from the train tracks running across the prairies of Dakota. He wasn't sure. Crunching through the snow in his tracks, the rope lifeline in his left hand, he struggled toward the unseen sanctuary of the glowing stove. It took twice as long as the trip to the barn. Once he stopped, wondering if he'd gone astray, but the rope was taut. still attached to the wall of the house.

Eventually he stumbled and fell against the door to the kitchen. Dropping the rope, he staggered right, sliding his left mitt against the wall of the house, dislodging snow that had stuck to the rough siding. Several steps away from the door, he fell over a long snow-covered pile of wood. He'd cut and hauled the logs several miles from the creek banks at the edge of his property. At the other end of the log pile was a hinged door over an opening which gave outside access to the wood box. Buried somewhere in the snow, he knew, was a splitting maul and probably the ax he hadn't been able to find since early November.

The wind drove the still-falling snow hard against his face and eyes, almost blinding him. He sucked in breath. It came in huge, gasping plunges, cold air burning down to the very bottom of his lungs. He was sweating and shivering at the same time. His toes were numb. It was all he could do to crack the ice and get the wood box top open. Without bothering to brush the snow off them, he threw armful after armful of logs into the box, not even stacking the wood. He knew he'd have to put more wood in the box again the next day, but he also knew he was wearing down from the cold, the wind and the snow. Throwing one last armful of logs into the box, he jammed the top down and took a huge chestful of air. It seared his lungs, and he gasped from the pain. The coughing started, hard, deep spasms that drove him to his knees. For long minutes he crouched there, head bowed, struggling to regain his life. Fingers and toes were long since robbed of any feeling. The insidious cold worked its way up to his knees and thighs. Huge shivers wracked the man's frame. He had to get inside to the stove. When he finally regained enough strength to stand, the snow on his shoulders and the bill of his cap was almost an inch thick.

Inside, he threw another log in the stove and opened the damper a little more. Even the sound of the fire was warming. Melting snow made random puddles of dirty water on the floor. He pumped a kettle full of water and set it on the stove, dragged off most of his clothes and fell onto the bed. Hours later, the dim daylight had gone altogether and the big kettle was sending a complacent plume of quiet steam into the thick damp atmosphere. He rolled off the bed and made a meal of thick soup and old coffee.

With the fire roaring and the stove beginning to show its characteristic reddish glow, he tromped to a tall bookcase in the corner and pulled down a ratty paperback, Burke's *Black Cherry Blues*. He'd read it before. He'd read all the scores of mysteries in the bookcase. Most more than once. He dragged the sagging padded chair closer to the fire and wrapped a blanket around him. For a quiet hour he read by the steady yellow light from a single kerosene lantern. Outside the wind rose again and pushed at the house, this puny impediment to its long sweep over the Dakota prairie.

When he raised his black eyes from the page, the light reflected shiny tracks of tears that ran down his cheeks and lost themselves in the tangled beard that covered most of his lower face. Why was he crying, he wondered? Isabel. He thought about Isabel more frequently these days, even though she'd been gone for three years. Why was that? In the near stillness of the night the man sobbed quietly. Insidious uncaring cold crept in from the corners of the room, curling around the well pipe and into the curtained back room.

Sometime the next day—still morning, he guessed it was, hard to tell with the snow drifted to the roof on three sides—the man dressed again in his layers of outer garments and pulled and pounded the ice off the door hinges so he could pull the door open. Chips of ice spattered his face and hands when he was finally able to force the thin wooden panel open with a ripping sound that startled him. A wall of packed white snow greeted his gaze, completely filling the opening. The white wall resisted his first, tentative poke with one mittened fist. He took up a long pole and began to thrust it into the snow, making a sieve of the drift. Eventually weakened, chunks of the drift fell away and he was able to push through the rest and step outside into a sunny, arctic, landscape. The brilliant sun, reflecting off the new snow out of a deep blue sky, hurt his eyes and gave him a headache. Squinching his eyelids almost shut, he dragged and hauled himself through the still air toward the barn.

Almost to the snowbound structure, he almost stumbled over faint impressions of another set of tracks leading toward the barn. When he fell against the barn door, he could see the scoop shovel that was always hanging by the door wasn't there anymore. Grumbling to himself, he pawed the snow and ice away from the door tracks and finally shoved it open enough to squeeze through the narrow opening. The man stood in the glare of the door, swaying, peering into the dark interior of the barn. Everything looked normal.

He went about his chores, noticing only that the animals seemed more restless than usual. Must be another storm comin', he mused. They always know ahead of time. Finishing up, he slammed the manure fork against a stanchion to dislodge the last bits of soggy straw and produced a sharp ringing sound. The animals were momentarily silent and that's when he heard a soft moan. It issued from a loose pile of straw in the far corner of one of the empty pens. When the man leaned over and poked the straw pile with the butt end of the manure fork, the pile yielded in an unusual manner. Now a distinctively human sound came forth and the pile stirred.

"Jesus H. Christ." the man exclaimed. He started at the sound of his own voice which he hadn't heard for several days.

"Jesus," he said again and leaned over to drag the straw off a crumpled, wet, dark body, still clearly alive.

Through still chattering teeth an hour later, the stranger stuttered, "My name's Gates. Ed Gates. Electronic supplies. I cover all of North Dakota and Northern Minnesota." He looked at the bearded man. "I sure thank you for finding me when you did. I was a gonner, sure as you know."

The bearded man shucked his coats and stomped his feet to relieve some of the tingling numbness. "Soup's about hot." His voice was scratchy and rusty. He turned his back on Gates and located a bowl into which he ladled thick steaming soup. He brought the bowl to the rude plank table and thunked it down. His thick fingers rattled across the narrow shelf above the range and he found a big spoon. He brought that to the table too.

Gates nodded and picked up the spoon, tried to control the trembling in his hand. Finally, after two tries when he spilled most of the soup back into the bowl trying to raise it to his blue-tinged lips, he gave up and bent over the bowl, sucking the soup directly into his mouth. There were chunks of potato and carrots and some kind of unidentifiable meat. Gates glanced up when the farmer sank slowly into the only other chair in the room, across the table, with another mis-matched bowl of steaming soup. He began to eat slowly, almost ponderously. "Good soup," Gates said gratefully. "What kind of meat is this?"

For a minute, he thought the other man hadn't heard him, then,

"Jus' meat."

"Well, sir, I'm mighty glad you found me when you did. You know, I never saw the house, nosir, must have stumbled right by it in the blizzard. Mighty grateful, yes sir."

He paused and looked at his host. The farmer didn't say anything, didn't even seem all that interested in his uninvited guest.

"I'm on my way to Crookston, you know. Didn't anticipate this snow storm. My car's out there on the highway somewhere." Gates waved at the walls. A rafter popped. "What was that?"

"Rafter," grunted the other man. "Cold does it."

"I got several customers expecting me. Is there any way you could maybe pull me out with your tractor?"

"No tractor. Nothin' to be done 'til the snow quits." He didn't mention the ancient pickup truck in the shed behind the barn. It had no chains anyway, so it was useless in this snow.

"Hell. Well, you got a phone, I suppose. I can call and tell 'em I'll be delayed."

"No phone. No electricity, neither."

Gates shook his head, then he smiled a little. "Well, hell, looks like we're stuck with each other for a while, hey? 'Til this storm blows itself out anyway. I'm Ed Gates," he said again, "and I do appreciate your helping me out here." He half rose and stuck a clammy hand out. The other man ignored it.

"Nothing to be done until the plows clear the highway and find your car. They'll prob'ly come up here an' clear the road some." The farmer knew they would. County plows had always done that, pushing a single track down the road only a hundred yards from the house. Sometimes, if he remembered to be out there, they'd take a few minutes and clear out the driveway and even a path to the barn. Then he'd shovel a track to the shed where he kept the truck. He only did that once a winter. Getting supplies in from Fertile, five miles away, was always a trial. He didn't like the way people stared at him and walked wide circles around him.

Two days later, it was still snowing off and on, more on than off. The man couldn't remember so much snow over a sustained period. He again wrapped himself in layers of clothing and prepared to wade out to the barn and take care of his stock. He hoped the plow would come by soon, he was tired of company. Gates with his restless manner, pacing, peering out the frosted windows, noisily sucking his teeth, and his tuneless whistling was grinding on his temper, never in the best of shape.

"Anything I can do to help?" Gates asked.

"Load the wood box. From outside. The wood pile is right by the box. You load the box from outside and we get it for the stove from inside." The big man pointed at the box behind the stove. Then he pulled open the door and went out into the cold winter afternoon. He decided he'd just spend more time in the barn, have a little quiet where the snuffling of the heifers and the grunts of the hogs had always soothed his soul.

When he finished his chores, he looked out the barn door toward the house. He could see Gates by the wood pile slowly bending and then tossing logs into the outside opening of the wood box. After a few minutes, Gates went back inside. The man looked at the featureless sky and the fitfully falling snow. He slogged a new path, through the drifts to the side of the house. The cold was insidious, sapping his strength. When he reached the window by the kitchen, he brushed the snow away and peered through the frosted pane. He saw Gates throw off his outer clothes, including the ragged coat he'd borrowed, ripping one sleeve as he did so.

Gates looked around. He scratched his head, shifting the cheap scratchy wig he wore. There were stacks of paperback books scattered in profusion around the room. He picked some up and looked at their titles. Outside, the man watched silently and felt the cold leaking into his boots. Melted snow dripped in and puddled around his toes. When Gates moved a pile of books in one corner, he knocked another pile off the low table shoved in the far corner opposite the stove. On the table was an untidy pile of old, yellowing newspapers. Gates picked up the top one. The farmer grunted. He knew what Gates was reading in the newspaper. He knew the stories by heart.

HENRY BACON FOUND MURDERED, ran the headline.

The faded newspaper, over thirty years old, was difficult to read, but Gates would figure out that somebody named Henry Bacon had been bludgeoned to death by his brother Hollister. The brother, only twenty, was judged mentally incompetent at the time. He'd been sent to a state institution.

He watched Gates examine another issue of the same paper. It reported that the surviving brother had now been pronounced cured and released. It was expected he'd return to the family farm just outside of town. There was another paragraph in the story that told that the girl over whom the boys had fought, one Isabel Johansen, was quoted as saying she was glad Hollister was finally free to live a normal life.

The final piece of newsprint Gates examined was only one page, carefully separated from the same paper and dated a year or so later. It reported that a young woman, Isabel Johansen, had not been seen for several days. Apparently she'd gone off to a dance in the next town to meet some of her friends. She hadn't shown up at the dance and never returned home.

Gates dropped the newspaper and restacked the books. His host watched him glance around. Gates looked at his watch and went to the door. He pulled it open, probably expecting to see the farmer coming across the yard, but there was nothing but white tracks through the snow, going from the house to the barn. There was almost nothing to see all the way to the horizon, except the vast expanse of white. Gates shut the door and went back to his prowling.

There was a patterned cloth, like a tablecloth, hanging on one wall of the room opposite the door. His reluctant host hadn't mentioned it and Gates hadn't noticed it before. But when he was outside loading the wood box, he must have seen the extension with the low shed roof hung on that wall of the place. Now, he walked toward it and pulled the cloth aside, revealing the tiny room behind it.

It was small, hardly bigger than a closet. The floor space was almost entirely taken up with a single metal-framed bed. On the bed there was a mound of bedding. There was no window, so it was dark in there. But the farmer could just make out when Gates leaned over the bed and pulled a corner of the bedding aside. The farmer flinched and pressed closer to the frosted glass. He saw Gates pull the bedding back and stare at an object on the bed. Then he snatched up a purse and pried it open. He watched Gates step back into the lighter main room, peering down at the purse. A tiny bottle appeared in Gates fingers. He peered at the label. The farmer knew what it was. Obsession. Some woman's perfume. Gates fingered out a small paper object, a driver's license. The farmer knew the name on the license. Isabel Johansen. Gates shuddered and dropped the purse. He must have bent over to pick it up because that's how he was, half crouched over when the door crashed open and Hollister Bacon slammed into the room.

"You ain't got no call to be pokin' in my things," he grunted. He raised one arm and pointed at Gates. He was surprised to discover he was holding a rusty ax.

The two men stared at each other. Outside, the wind began a rising wail as the blizzard returned to tighten its grip on the land. The wind's assault shivered the house and sent a swirl of snow across the room behind Bacon.

Gates licked his cracked lips and husked. "Oh, sorry. I . . . didn't mean to pry. I was just curious."

Bacon dropped the ax and it thudded to the floor. Then he kicked the door shut. Snow on the jam held it open a crack and more snow and arctic air continued to swirl in, dropping the temperature of the room. The wind made a low moaning sound, like the train whistle when the coal trains ran down the old Northern Pacific tracks through town. "Who are you, anyway?" he said. "What you doin' out here? That county road out there ain't the way to Crookston."

Gates collected the purse from the floor and shoved the license back in with trembling fingers. He closed the purse and backed toward the little room where he'd found it. "I told you, my name is Gates, Ed Gates. I'm real sorry. There's no call to get upset. I'll just put the purse back on the bed." He scrabbled at the cloth and shoved the purse behind it, never taking his eyes off Bacon. The sound of the wind rose higher and spicules of hard brittle snow rattled on the walls and windows.

For a long moment the two men just stared at each other. When another frigid blast pushed the door open farther, Bacon turned and began to kick at the snow-covered jam, trying to close the door. Out of the corner of his eye he saw Gates sidle across the room behind him. Bacon glanced over his shoulder once and then he put all his weight on the door and wedged it shut. He turned and went to the wood box, lifting the top and bending to pick out a log for the fire.

When he straightened, Gates was coming toward him with the rusty axe upraised.

Bacon flung up his hand with the log and parried the blow. He dodged to his left as the blade glanced off the log, tearing it from his cold hand and thunking into the wall of the room. "You murdering son of a bitch!" snarled Gates, yanking the rusty ax out of the wall and turning to face Bacon. Bacon pulled hard at the door, almost tearing it off its hinges. He fell back and Gates' second blow glanced off his shoulder and arm, tearing a long ugly gash. Blood spurted from the wound. He fell against the door, forcing it farther open. Snow and wind poured into the house. Dishes rattled on the shelf over the stove.

Gates next rush missed Bacon and carried him half way out the open door. With his good hand, Bacon grabbed the log he'd dropped and slammed Gates across his back and shoulders, driving him out into the yard. The blow knocked the wig right off Gates head. He watched Gates stagger to his knees and fling out a hand to grab the line from the house to the barn, lumbering into the snow-filled yard. Bacon's tracks from the barn to the side of the house were already filled in. The wind bent Gates over and he dropped the ax, trying to shield his face from the stinging ice blowing horizontally across the frozen prairie.

Bacon squinted and watched the other man slowly struggle toward the barn. Funny, he thought, I don't seem to be able to see things very good. He plucked a sharp knife from the table and cut the line where it was attached to the house, letting the wind whip it away. There was a momentary break in the snow and suddenly there was Gates, ten yards away, staring at him, and holding the severed life line.

"You bastard," he screamed at Bacon. "My name isn't Gates, it's Johansen. Isabel was my sister! I been workin' up to this for a long time! I'll get a pitchfork from the barn. Then I'm comin' for you." The storm asserted itself again and Gates-Johansen disappeared from view.

As Bacon stared into the wall of white his legs suddenly gave out and he sank to the floor in front of the open door. He looked at his throbbing arm, watched blood pooling in his lap. He knew he had to close the door but he couldn't make himself get up from the floor. More cold snow blew in, mixing with the blood. Bacon's head sank lower. A tiny smile lifted the corners of his bearded mouth, remembering. Johansen would never get to the barn. When he reached the second fence post in the middle of the yard, he'd find the rest of the line was cut. Bacon's last thought as his vision darkened and his chin touched his chest was that the wind would push Johansen away from the barn, and toward the fence line which was a quarter of a mile across the snow-laden, icy prairie. In the distance the moaning of the wind blended with the sound of a diesel engine struggling across the frozen prairie.

Lori Lake

Aquarian Lori L. Lake is a fifth cousin to Orville and Wilbur Wright, but she hates flying. She graduated from Lewis and Clark College in Oregon with a double major in English and Political Science and later earned a Master's Degree from Hamline University in Saint Paul in English and Liberal Studies. Lori teaches fiction writing at The Loft Literary Center in Minneapolis, and she often reviews books for various print and online journals.

Lori has been writing since her mid-twenties and saw her debut novel, Gun Shy, *finally published in 2001. Other recent books include* Ricochet in Time, Stepping Out, Under the Gun, Have Gun We'll Travel, *and* Different Dress. *Lori edited* The Milk of Human Kindness: Lesbian Authors Write About Mothers and Daughters, *which is a 2005 Lambda Literary Award finalist.*

Now living in Hastings, Lori's favorite song is a 1970s oldie, "Dancing in The Moonlight" by King Harvest, she supports the University of Minnesota Women's basketballers, and she really likes Duluth as a city. She is currently working on the first novel in a mainstream mystery series.

Take Me Out

by

Lori L. Lake

When is a crime also a sin, and when is that sin unforgivable? If you commit a crime and don't get caught, and only God knows what you've done, does that lessen the penalty phase at the Gates of St. Peter?

Kaye Brock had puzzled over such issues for most of her adulthood, and as she drove through icy streets to her housekeeping job, she wondered most about this: If you aren't sorry about what you have done, does it stay on your heavenly record, like the black cigarette residue left on a smoker's lungs? Surely this was a question for the priests, but it had been eight years, right after her senior year in high school, since she'd been to St. Bertold's Catholic Church, and she had no intention of returning to discuss her concerns. Still, she wondered.

On this gloomy, sub-zero morning, Kaye hustled out of her old Ford Taurus, pulling her coat tight around her. The skies threatened snow. Already the wind was bitter. As she walked toward the entrance to Seaton Senior Center, everything was etched in bright and bitter outlines. Dead plant stalks stood in stark relief against the stucco to the right of the handicap entrance. It was a barren, hopeless time for Kaye and had felt so for far too long. She sighed, and her moist breath created a swirling fog around her face.

Her glasses misted up upon entering the building. The eighty degree temperature difference between the outdoors and the huge meeting area through which she strolled caused her to break out in a light sweat as it had every morning since winter had descended.

Kaye passed the main office, careful to look away from the ever-present face behind the desk in the glassed-in area. The assistant administrator, Sheila Thornton, knew all about Kaye's sordid history and had never shared so much as one smile with her. It didn't seem fair to Kaye, especially since her crime had been a victimless one, and she had fully paid her debt to society. She'd served nearly four years of her seven year sentence, and the extent of her parole would soon be over. She'd returned home to find that the idea of debts being settled didn't matter to a surprisingly large number of people in town. Old school acquaintances looked away in the Target store. The servers in the café ignored her. Nobody spoke to her but gossip hounds and those new to Melville.

She reached Advanced Care and thumbed the door release. This was placed high enough that the residents, most of whom were in wheelchairs, could not reach it and make their escape into the world of the living.

Inside the hot and humid unit, the odors of a eucalyptus plant and industrial-strength pine-scented floor cleaner battled to cover up the underlying reek of urine and feces. When she'd first joined the AC staff, the smell had nearly overpowered her. She'd worked through those first shifts on the edge of nausea. But after a few weeks, she grew accustomed to the odor, and now it was merely an ever-present reminder of decay and sadness and loss. Not much different from prison.

Kaye shed her gloves, coat, and muffler, carrying them over her arm as she headed down the long hallway on the right. She was early and could afford to take her time, perhaps slip out back and sneak a smoke before her shift began.

"Hi, Kaye," one of the aides, Susie, said from behind the charge nurse's counter.

Kaye smiled at her, but before she could say anything, the ambulance bay opened and let in a gust of refreshing chilled air.

"Easy does it," a man said in a loud voice.

Kaye stopped at the charge nurse's tall counter and watched the attendants pull a gurney out of the wagon. One medic rolled it into the hallway while the other closed up the ambulance and quickly shut the extra-wide hospital door.

Nurse Judy and a hulking aide named Marcus moved down the hall and stopped on either side of the gurney. "Well, hello," the nurse said, in a baby voice. "Let's get you all warmed up and settled, sweetie pie."

The attendant came forward, holding out a clipboard to Judy. "Here's Gildecott for you. Sign off?"

"That's *Missus* Gildecott to you, young man." It took a moment for Kaye to realize that the imperious voice emanated from the stretcher. "Don't think I don't remember your abysmal manners from sophomore English!"

The man flushed bright red. He squinted and leaned down to look at the figure swathed in blankets. "Mrs.—Mrs.—"

"That's right, James McVie. I never forget a face. Never."

Wide-eyed, the medic reached across the gurney and took back his clipboard. "You folks have a great day."

He and the other medic rushed away so quickly that Kaye tensed. She looked down the hall, hoping they wouldn't run over any of the wheelchair occupants.

Judy said, "Well, then, Mrs. Gildecott, Susie and Marcus and I will get you settled."

"A most excellent idea. And I don't care for baby talk. This is not child care. I do hope they have brought me to an *adult* care facility."

"Oh, yes, ma'am!" Judy said.

Kaye stepped out of the way. Marcus released the lock on the gurney and gave it a gentle push. As the entourage rolled by, a pair of dark, bright eyes, glittering with anger, looked up at Kaye, holding her gaze as she passed. Mrs. Gildecott. Kaye's high school English teacher and the terror of Melville Secondary School. Kaye swallowed with difficulty. Suddenly she needed nicotine—badly. She clutched her coat tight against her and headed toward the back door, keyed the code, and stepped outdoors. Mrs. Gildecott was coming to live here? What a nightmare.

★ ★ ★ ★

Kaye stood stamping and sucking nervously on a Winston outside the back door of the AC Unit. Mrs. Gildecott. Jesus. She remembered sitting in mythology class, terrified that she would be called on. She liked to read about individual gods like Artemis, Apollo, Minerva, and Poseidon, but she couldn't keep track of who was related to who or whether they were Greek or Roman. Mostly she remembered keeping a low profile.

She recalled a time when Mrs. Gildecott waited in the hall before class one day, and Larry Knoche held court at the front desk near the door. Pointing at their textbook, he'd made off-color comments about Dido, queen of Carthage, calling her "Dildo" and laughing uproariously with his buddies. Next thing Kaye knew, tiny Mrs. Gildecott was behind Larry. The nearly six-foot kid shot up from his desk as though his chair had exploded. He was dragged to the door by one ear, thrown into the hall like day-old rubbish, and never seen again in mythology class.

Kaye remembered the thrill of terror and satisfaction she had felt. Larry Knoche was a popular kid with a mean streak. She hadn't been sorry to see him go and no one else complained, not even his buddies. In the four years she was at Melville High, Kaye learned that nobody crossed Mrs. G. If you didn't behave in her class, she threw you out. Simple as that.

And now she was at Seaton Center.

* * * *

The Center was far more than an old folks' home. The administrators spoke of it as a "campus," as though the place was an expensive institution for antique teenagers. At one end was the elevator entrance to a twelve-story high-rise. Ninety apartments thrust up from the Minnesota prairie to serve as Independent Living for couples and singles aged sixty and older. When the day came that occupants could no longer fend for themselves, they came down from their ivory tower and moved into a connected four-story facility. Assisted Living sported smaller rooms, but meals were provided as well as cleaning, laundry, medication dispensing, and round-the-clock monitoring.

When Kaye first applied to work at Seaton three years earlier, Sheila Thornton had made it clear that she would not be trusted in either of those facilities where people still kept sums of money, jewelry, and valuables. Never mind that Kaye no longer had any interest in theft. Apparently no statute of limitations existed with the Sheila Thorntons of the world, so Kaye was assigned to Advanced Care. No fancy "Living" name was attached to Seaton's AC section.

Apparently you literally came down in the world from the high-rise to the low-rise and then at last to the ground floor which was, quite simply, a nursing home. If euphemisms hadn't been so important to the families of the patients in the AC unit, Kaye thought it would be more aptly named Assisted Dying.

She pulled her unzipped coat tight, one arm crossed over her chest, and took a deep drag. During inclement weather, nobody used this back area. When the weather was nice, residents and staff were all over the gardened area. It was completely enclosed with no exit for confused patients to wander through. But the roses were long gone now, and the path leading to an eight-foot-tall wrought iron fence was iced over. Bushes and shrubbery in the flowerbeds were also shrouded with ice. In spring and summer, Kaye often came out to sit on the tiny white bench tucked in an alcove to the right of the door. Surrounded by roses, iris, and tiger lilies, she liked to watch the bees buzzing from flower to flower as the warmth of the sun bathed her face. Not today. She shivered as she took a final pull on the cigarette.

The glass door behind her jerked open, and a murder of crows, lined up along the gutter overhead, startled and flew upward, cawing raucously.

"Brock!" Marcus's light brown face squinted out into the breeze. "Another big shit attack from your favorite, Mr. Clancy." The door slammed shut, and the last intrepid crow took flight. A murder of crows, a gaggle of geese, a pride of lions—Kaye wondered what a bunch of elderly, wheelchair-bound people would be called. An exaltation of elderly? No, that was larks. Maybe a dejection—or desolation—of elders.

Kaye dropped the cigarette on the sidewalk, not even bothering to grind it out, and followed Marcus's football physique into the hothouse. She stopped at the housekeeping closet and prepared the mop and rolling bucket. Mr. Clancy had a serious bowel problem, and nearly every day she started out her shift cleaning up one of his "accidents." She rolled the bucket down the hallway, weaving her way around frail old ladies sitting in wheelchairs outside their rooms. She was constantly amazed at how Mrs. Adler and Mrs. Johanssen could sleep, their heads canted off at angles that made them look like someone had come along behind them and broken their necks. And Mrs. Polnicek always managed to fold forward like origami, her gray head resting on her knees and the knuckles of her skinny hands brushing the metal footrests of her chair. Just looking at her made Kaye's back hurt.

The morning passed slowly in a zen-like trance of mopping left, mopping right, wiping down surfaces, sweeping, vacuuming. Kaye slipped into a fog of numbness, humming old R.E.M. and Nirvana songs. The AC unit consisted of two long hallways connected at either end by short hallways. It was one big circle, and a few of the wheelchair occupants spent their days rolling 'round and 'round it. The lunchroom, various offices, rehab, storage centers, and nursing stations were situated down the middle, and the patient suites were all along the outside walls. Each room contained two or three residents. Kaye worked her way through the eighteen suites on the left side of the unit, then took her lunch break. Afterwards, she started in on the sun room and the eighteen rooms on the right. She hadn't gotten far when she came to the room occupied by Mrs. Gildecott.

The old woman lay at a slight incline on the small hospital bed. When Kaye had last seen her at Melville High, Mrs. Gildecott sported a cap of swirling silver hair, all of which was now snow-white. Her hands gripped the top of the coverlet, and her mouth was open slightly. Kaye started her cleaning in the open bathroom area just inside the door. The other three corners of the room were small bays for beds. The left rear bay was currently unoccupied, and Mrs. Gildecott lay in the front right bay separated from Mrs. Hoffmeier by a thin curtain. The two women's beds were head to head, close to the curtain. Kaye didn't understand why the nurses set them up like that. Three-quarters of the elderly people in the home snored like beached walruses. She thought it made more sense to put the heads of the beds as far away from one another as possible. But who was she to say? It wasn't like her opinion was respected.

Kaye didn't like to get to know any of the residents, other than by name. Too many of them died quickly, and the ones who lingered on just grew sicker as each day passed. The lucky few who were only temporarily placed for rehab came and went as their broken hips or pneumonias healed. The rest served life sentences of pain and confusion that Kaye didn't like to think about.

She sprayed harsh industrial-strength window cleaner on the mirror and expertly wiped it down. On the last sweep with the cloth, she caught sight of a movement behind her and met dark eyes, staring across the room.

Mrs. Gildecott cleared her throat. "Kaye Lynn Brock."

Kaye couldn't speak. Her heart thumped, and she reached back to steady herself on the sink's cold porcelain.

Mrs. Gildecott gazed out the window. "The snow is lovely. I surely wish you could take me out. I always loved sledding and a bonfire on a snowy night."

"Last I checked, ma'am, the temp was hovering at zero. You'll have to wait until spring."

"Yes, spring." She fastened her dark eyes on Kaye once more, seeming to look right through her. "You had an imaginative flair, but you couldn't spell to save your life."

Kaye swallowed. "Nope, and I still can't."

Mrs. Gildecott dug her elbows in on either side of her and inched herself up to a more upright position. She reached up a hand to smooth her hair. "I'm happy to report that many studies were done in the late 90s, and lack of spelling ability appears to be something with which you are born. No one considers it a moral failing any longer. Have you done anything in the interim—utilized any strategies, I mean—to overcome the problem?"

"Uh...not really. I have a dictionary." But I never use it, Kaye thought. In fact, I don't bother to write much of anything at all.

"Such a shame, dear. The stories you wrote were inspired. I expected you to go on and write for a newspaper or magazine."

Kaye frowned as she felt a rush of heat flood her face. Working in the writing field had never occurred to her. "I—I've had a different . . . well, that's not the direction I went."

Mrs. Gildecott nodded. "It's never too late to change course. Did you take any college classes after you left Melville High?"

Kaye took a deep breath. She never knew how forthcoming to be about her conviction, and obviously nearly eight years earlier Mrs. Gildecott hadn't followed the front page news of her arrest. "I worked for a short while in a bank when I got out of school, and

I've taken a few correspondence courses." She cleared her throat, purposely omitting the fact that the mail-order courses were all focused in the area of addiction and recovery, and they'd been underwritten by the Shakopee Women's Prison. "I've never gone back to further my education."

"Such a shame, a shame." The old woman closed her eyes and dozed off, leaving Kaye standing against the sink feeling not much better than she had when she'd come before the parole board three years earlier.

★ ★ ★ ★

The cold weather continued and Thanksgiving neared. As Kaye mopped the back hall near the laundry room, she tried to mentally prepare herself for the yearly holidays, hoping that maybe this would be the year that her family—her father and the families of her four older brothers and younger sister—would forgive her for her sins. Her mother had died of a heart attack just after Kaye went to prison, and without exception, the whole clan still blamed Kaye.

"Oh, shit," Marcus mumbled as he rushed out of Mrs. Swanson's room and nearly ran into Kaye.

"Whoa!" she said, reaching out to steady herself against the wall. "What's the matter?"

"Oh, good, Brock, it's you." He lowered his voice. "That old bag and her perfume! She just dropped and busted that whole friggin' bottle. It stinks to the rafters. Stinks so bad my eyes are watering."

"I'll take care of it."

"Thanks." He hustled off one way and she went the other, toward the housekeeping closet. She took a new bag of Tidy Cats kitty litter off the shelf and carried it back to Mrs. Swanson's room. No sooner had she stepped inside the room than the fragrance wafted up, overpowering and cloying. Mrs. Swanson sat in her wheelchair, tears running down her face. The egg-shaped bottle lay on the floor, amber liquid exploded out from it on all sides. The brown lid had bounced across the floor and lay by the windows.

"My only bottle. My last bottle. No more, no more," Mrs. Swanson whispered. Her wig was askew. She clenched her fists and pounded on the smooth plastic arms of her chair.

Kaye ripped open the corner of the kitty litter and went down on one knee to pour a generous amount on the perfume. Her eyes smarted, but once the noxious liquid was covered, Kaye knew the intense smell would gradually abate.

"You ruined it," Mrs. Swanson shrieked. "Ruined, ruined, ruined. Not pretty anymore."

Somebody skidded into the doorway. "Brock, what are you doing?"

Kaye turned to see Sheila Thornton standing behind her. Before she could answer, Nurse Judy came into the room, clucking her tongue. She leaned down and said soothing things in Mrs. Swanson's ear. The old woman's cries subsided, and Nurse Judy went on in a louder voice, "You come with me, sweetie pie. Come on now, and we'll let your room air out." She grabbed for the handles and maneuvered the wheelchair out of the room leaving Kaye and the administrator.

Kaye rose, rolling down the top of the kitty litter bag, and stepped around the other woman.

"Where do you think you're going? I asked you a question."

Kaye stopped and glanced into Sheila's baby-blue eyes. Her blond hair was beautifully coiffed into a high ponytail that was wrapped into a bun on top. Everything about her was elegant and classy, from her bone-thin physique to her smart high heels, designer jacket, skirt, and silk blouse. Kaye looked down at her own light blue uniform top and slacks. The knee of the pants now sported a perfume stain, and sometime during the day, she'd gotten a smear of something disgustingly tan on the sleeve of her smock.

"I had nothing to do with this accident," Kaye said and slipped past.

"If I find out differently, you'll be hearing from me."

Sheila's words followed Kaye down the hall as she lugged the litter bag back to the closet. When she returned to Mrs. Swanson's room with a broom and dustpan, Sheila was gone.

Later that night, in the comfort of her studio apartment, Kaye sat wondering why Sheila Thornton had it in for her. It wasn't like she'd ever touched the woman's purse or bank accounts, and she'd never been anything but polite to her. Kaye had walked into the housekeeping job with strikes against her, and she had no clue how they could be removed.

★ ★ ★ ★

Kaye pushed a dust mop down the hallway. At seven a.m. few residents were stirring, but Mrs. Crocker, bent over with a dowager's hump, slipped around the doorframe of her room like a wraith. "Help," she whispered. "Help me, someone. Help." One narrow, slippered foot slid forward a few inches, then the other, and she made her way by leaning a shoulder against the wall.

Moving the dust mop out of her way, Kaye strode quickly past the hollow-eyed woman.

"I need help," Mrs. Crocker said in a louder voice. "They've stolen everything."

Kaye left her for the aides and nurses. Mrs. Crocker regularly wandered the halls begging for help. She never stopped her pleas all day. When she tired, she headed for the nearest bed—regardless of whether it was occupied—and fell down into a dead sleep. If the elderly woman wasn't circling the premises, saying "Help" like a deranged peacock, she was in someone else's bed. Kaye wished she'd sleep a great deal more.

A wheelchair emerged from a room up ahead. Mrs. Hoff-meier, haggard and shriveled, sat in the chair, her eyes dull and sleepy as Nurse Judy pushed her. "Brock, I've cleaned up Mrs. Gildecott, but the floor needs mopping. I'm taking Mrs. Hoffmeier down to the sun room."

"I'll get right on it, Nurse. It'll be cleaned up before she gets back."

Kaye rolled the mop and bucket into Room 18. Mrs. Gildecott lay on her side, facing the wall. A pile of linens lay next to her bed. Kaye picked them up and took them out to the laundry barrel. When she returned to the room, Mrs. Gildecott was struggling to roll onto her back.

"Aren't you going to help me?"

"I'm a housekeeper, Mrs. G. I'm not allowed to help you." She grabbed the mop and put the head through the wringer. "You can alert someone with the call button."

"Never mind! It's not like anyone comes when the button is depressed—even repeatedly. You wouldn't be cleaning up that mess if they *had* come."

Kaye flicked the mop to the left, then to the right, in the practiced rhythm she had learned well in prison. Mrs. Gildecott struggled, eventually managing to get settled face up.

"Don't you want to know what's wrong with me?"

"I don't ask questions. I'm just the housekeeper."

"Oh, my. Now that's no attitude to have, dear. Surely you're more than that. You have a family? A husband?" Kaye shook her head. "Aspirations? Are you using this job as a stepping stone to other things?"

Kaye smiled and let out a snort.

"You find that amusing?"

"Not really." She dunked the mop head back in the bucket and then wrung it out again.

"You are a singularly incurious woman."

Kaye stopped and met the dark eyes surveying her. "All right, then. What are you in for?"

Mrs. Gildecott laughed. "You sound like a gangster, dear." She pitched her voice low and growled out, "What are you in for? You wanna float with the fishes? Make my day." When Kaye laughed, the old woman shook her head. "Just because I'm old doesn't mean I don't pay attention to what's happening around me. And you?"

Kaye smiled. "I don't ask questions. It's not my place. Somebody else is responsible for rounding up the usual suspects. The management has made it very clear that housekeepers are not to bother the residents." Dark eyes surveyed Kaye, and for a moment she felt vulnerable, as though Mrs. Gildecott could see right through her.

"In that case, Kaye, I shall just tell you. I've got the worst case of osteoporosis the doctors have ever seen. I fractured my pelvis last winter. I had fallen. When I saw the X-rays I was shocked at the images. My bones have turned to chalk, and there is no way to repair them or for me to recover the mobility that I've lost.

My cousin's son put me up for several months, but now he has developed renal disease and cannot meet my needs. So here I am. End of the line."

Gripping the mop handle with both hands, Kaye leaned forward. "I see. It's a horrible place to stay, you know."

"Actually, this is one of the finest facilities in the state. The rehabilitation department is top-notch, and the rating for patient care and administration is stellar." She paused. "But you're right. It's not so much the facility as it is the circumstances. No intelligent adult should ever be locked up—incontinent, alone, and lonely—in a place like this."

Kaye nodded. Seaton was not a place she ever wanted to be placed. She'd rather go over a cliff first. The image of Geena Davis and Susan Sarandon at the end of *Thelma and Louise* came to her, and she bit back a smile.

"I had seven good years of retirement, and then it went kaput."

Kaye frowned. "Seven?"

"I can hardly count last year, so yes, a mere seven."

"How old were you when you retired?" Kaye stopped abruptly and blushed. "I'm sorry. That was rude."

"Not at all. Your bluntness is refreshing after the distressing level of baby talk to which I'm daily subjected. I don't mind answering. I didn't quit teaching until I was 72."

"That's a lot of years."

"You mean that's a lot of years for one teacher to terrorize students devoid of any interest in the development, care, and feeding of the English language."

Kaye couldn't suppress her giggles. "Well, since you put it that way—"

"You graduated with my last full class. I returned the following September for three weeks to substitute for a teacher on maternity leave, and then that was it."

"You must have gone traveling after that."

"Why, yes. How did you guess?"

Kaye knew she was breaking all her own rules. She forged on anyway. "Did you go to Europe? Travel to Greece and Rome?"

"I did." Mrs. Gildecott's face took on a puzzled expression.

"You liked the myths so much, Mrs. G. I remember 'cause I took your mythology class. You even talked about the myths in sophomore composition."

"Ah, yes." She nodded and got a faraway look in her eyes. "I was gone for fourteen weeks. I saw all the sights and ate wonderful varieties of food. I folk-danced in Athens and toured the Parthenon and the Coliseum and every other lovely ruin, and I went on to France, Germany, Poland, the United Kingdom. I always wanted to go to Asia and Africa, too. I meant to return one day. Unfortunately, I never made it back overseas, and in my present predicament, I am unlikely to do so."

Kaye lifted the mop and dunked it into the sudsy water, suddenly overcome with the desire to flee. She rolled the mop bucket toward the door.

"Kaye?"

She didn't meet Mrs. Gildecott's eyes. "Yeah?"

"If I were to pay you for your trouble, would you consider doing a favor for me?"

"It depends on what it is."

"Always the cautious one."

Kaye paused in the doorway and peered out into the hall, waiting. Mrs. Crocker, the wraith, slithered past shrieking, "Help me! Help me! They're after me." Her high, piercing cry faded, and after a few seconds, Kaye turned back to Mrs. Gildecott.

"My dear, the selection of donated books here runs heavily toward light fiction and war books. If I gave you a list of topics, would you stop at the library and check out some books for me?" When Kaye didn't answer immediately, she said, "I would be glad to leave a deposit with you—in case any of the books were damaged or lost."

Rapid clicking of heels on the tiled floor startled Kaye, and she looked out to see Sheila Thornton steaming her way. With a hurried glance back, Kaye said, "I'll think about it," then rolled the mop bucket into the hall.

★　★　★　★

Kaye entered the Seaton Center juggling a heavy stack of books. She was glad it was Saturday and the weekend staff was on duty. Even better, Sheila Thornton was nowhere to be found.

The pile of books included *The Iliad*; *Three Plays* by Sophocles; *Till We Have Faces: A Myth Retold* by C.S. Lewis; travel guides to Turkey, Russia, and China; *Outdoor Survival Skills*; *Cold Weather Facts*; and *An Encyclopedia of Country Living*. Kaye thought this a strange combination, but if she were ever cooped up in bed, she'd likely want a variety, too. She had also checked out two additional books she thought Mrs. Gildecott might find interesting: Krakauer's *Into Thin Air* and the biography of aviator Beryl Markham.

When she reached room 18, Mrs. Gildecott said, "Kaye! I didn't expect to see you here today."

Kaye shrugged. "The library was open this morning, so I picked up the books on your list." She set them on the end of the bed and dragged a chair from Mrs. Hoffmeier's side over next to Mrs. Gildecott.

"I hope it was no trouble at the library." With a groan, she shifted forward and adjusted her bed's incline so that she was sitting nearly upright.

"Nope. I just told the guy I wanted science, philosophy, and travel literature. No problem. I wasn't sure what editions you wanted of anything, but here's what I got."

"Oh, I'm sure these will all be fine—just fine. Thank you." Mrs. Gildecott leaned forward and pointed. "If you'll get me my purse from that cabinet over there, I'll write you a check."

Kaye shook her head. "That's not necessary. I renewed my library card, and as long as we get them back in three weeks, it doesn't cost a thing."

"But for your time and trouble."

"It was really no trouble, and my time is worth next to nothing."

Mrs. Gildecott sighed and sank back. "I think it's high time you and I divulged some personal details. I'm not sure that our correctional system does a very good job with rehabilitation. Retribution, yes, but when it comes to restoring one to a level of esteem and faith—well, I think the system fails."

Kaye didn't respond. Once more she had the urge to flee the room.

"What did they do to you in there, Kaye?"

Kaye shifted so her elbows were on her knees and she was staring down at the floor. "How did you know?"

"Know what? That they did something to you?"

"No." She laced her fingers together and stared at them. "That I was in jail."

"I know where a lot of my students went, what they do for a living, if they have achieved successes or disappointments. I know Dennis Creighley became an alderman in Chicago, and Lisle Fredericks married that Hollywood action hero fellow. Did you know Mark Udall—he graduated a year or two ahead of you—was killed in Afghanistan? Such a waste. Missy Peterson writes scripts for one of those daytime shows. When I taught her proper grammar, I had no idea she would be subverting that knowledge for soap operas!"

Kaye laughed. "I haven't kept up with any of my classmates."

"Some of them aren't worth keeping up with, my dear, and some have disappeared. But I still get an occasional letter."

Kaye sat back in the hard chair and watched Mrs. Gildecott as she continued to speak of her students. Her eyes sparkled, and her haggard face was transformed to smiling and gleeful, a joy to behold. Mrs. G was nothing like the dragon-queen of high school days. She was someone Kaye wished she had known better long ago.

"—and so all that brings us back to the matter of you."

"What?"

"You. And what you choose to do with your life."

Was this to be the kind of speech Kaye's father delivered with regularity? She bit back disappointment and was reminded why she had rules about consorting with the patients. She tried not to be defensive with her answer. "I don't think you know anything about my life or my choices."

Mrs. Gildecott peered at her with such intensity that Kaye looked away. "There exists a wall inside you from which you recoil. You need to get around or over that wall, and then your life will feel worth living."

"You can tell all this by what—my mopping technique?" Kaye rose and grabbed the back of the chair, ready to return it to its spot near Mrs. Hoffmeier's window.

"There are far more ways to see into the heart of a human being than you can likely comprehend at the moment." Her eyes met Kaye's with conviction. "Please, sit down. I should like to hear about what goes on behind that wall."

As if in a trance, Kaye let go of the back of the chair, stepped around it, and sank into her seat.

"First, can you tell me how you managed to lift such a great sum of money? I suspect that took great cleverness—perhaps something with the checks or deposits? The newspapers never said, and I have always been most curious."

Kaye examined the open face before her. It showed no malice, no accusation. She cleared her throat and softly said, "It wasn't that hard. You'd be surprised how unsafe banks can be. I can assure you, though, that no one will ever let me work with money again."

"See? What did I tell you? You're too clever by the half, girl!"

★　★　★　★

In more than three years, Kaye had never made a friend at Seaton, but Mrs. Gildecott somehow accomplished what no one else had. Whenever Kaye entered room 18, the old woman was usually reading. The last two Saturdays, Kaye had returned books and checked out new requests, always about mythology, philosophy, and natural sciences.

On the Saturday before Christmas, she sat near the foot of Mrs. Gildecott's bed. "You seem so interested in science. Why is that?"

"To be honest, I never paid much attention to the topic, but I have developed a curiosity about certain aspects."

"Did you like that biography of Michelangelo?

"Yes, a great deal, but not nearly so much as the one about Beryl Markham. Did you know she was the first person to fly solo across the Atlantic from east to west? Not the first woman, the first *person*."

"There are a lot of things I don't know."

Mrs. Gildecott smiled. "Ah, but you have so many years ahead of you to think and study and learn. Did you like that novel about Joan of Arc?"

Kaye nodded. She had liked it a great deal more than she had expected. She'd gotten lost in the narrative, and when the book was finished, she felt bereft and craved more. "I wish there was more. I wish she hadn't had to die at the end. She was too young."

"Yes, any death, regardless of the age, is too young. I shall make a list of books you simply must read, dear. When I'm gone, I do hope you will continue your studies. You have a fine mind and ought to consider attending college sometime soon."

Kaye blushed. She couldn't afford it even if she could figure out a way to get in.

Mrs. Gildecott leaned forward, scrutinizing Kaye's face. "You think that because of your history they would not accept you, but you're wrong, Kaye. Start small and take a course at the community college. I would wager that you will find yourself to be good at it. You're thorough, as evidenced by your careful work here, and if you would come out from behind that wall and give it a chance, you would be surprised at what you could accomplish."

Mrs. Hoffmeier wheezed and let out a grunt. In a quavering voice, she called out, "Is there to be no peace for me ever? What do I have to do to get a little sleep around here?"

Kaye met Mrs. Gildecott's eyes, and both stifled laughter.

"Take me out, Kaye. Get me out of here."

"I don't want to hurt you. I'll call the aides."

"No." She threw the covers off, revealing a pair of pale pink cotton pants that did not go well with the emerald green top she wore. With a wince, she shifted her right leg until it slipped off the bed. Kaye rose and stood close, helping her to get seated on the edge of the bed with her knuckles white from gripping the mattress. "Just get that wheelchair, will you, dear?"

Kaye rolled it over and locked the wheels. She could tell that balancing on the edge was painful, so she hastily lifted the small woman and settled her in the chair. "Wow, you don't weigh much, Mrs. G."

Through gritted teeth she said, "I seem to be shrinking."

"Are you all right?" Kaye asked in a surge of panic. Maybe this wasn't a good idea after all. What if she fell?

"I'm fine." Her face had gone from relaxed and smiling to gaunt and gray.

"Let me get your feet set up." With a few quick motions she adjusted the metal foot supports. "There you go."

"I know this will sound like an unusual request, Kaye, but could you leave me here for a few moments?" She reached for the call cord, then looked back. "Please step out into the hall, and if no one is in sight, could you duck into some other room?"

"What?"

"Please? Please give me just a few minutes here to adjust. Let's say ten minutes."

"All right." Kaye assumed that Mrs. Gildecott had suddenly decided she needed to use the toilet, so she left the room and went down the hall to the staff lounge, keyed the code on the door, and slipped inside the empty room.

A four-foot-tall wreath with a plaid bow overwhelmed the wall near the door. Glitter had been spilled on the table in the middle of the room, and someone had decorated above the refrigerator and around the window with clots of hideous, multi-colored lights that blinked erratically. A gangly tree, festooned with tinsel and mismatched bulbs, stood over in the corner. One of the lights on the patient alert panel—one bulb for each of the thirty-six rooms—flashed. Room six. Mr. Rother with the Alzheimer's. By the time someone reached his room, he usually couldn't remember why he had called for assistance.

Kaye was glad she was going to be off work Christmas Eve. The annual staff Christmas party always took place then, and she was happy to miss it. She looked forward to spring. She planned to take a week off and go somewhere warm.

At the pop machine she bought a Pepsi, then sat on one of the two couches and thought about what Mrs. Gildecott had said. Should she consider taking some classes? Kaye liked the idea. Reading escape literature and watching Sci-Fi TV and marathons of *Law and Order* had long ago gotten old. In fact, her whole life felt old. Predictable. Boring. Useless.

She stood up and looked out the window into the ice and snow as she sipped the soda. Small bits of snow blew off the roof and formed a swirl in the gray light. Someone had shoveled the paths, and Kaye had the urge to go out for a smoke. But her cigarettes were in her coat, which hung in Mrs. Gildecott's closet, so she waited.

When enough time had passed, she took a last swig of Pepsi, tossed the can, and made her way back to room 18, almost running into the aide, Susie.

"Brock, what are you doing here?"

"Came by to see Mrs. Gildecott."

Susie lowered her voice. "She's improving. She managed to get herself into a wheelchair all on her own. I'm so happy for the sweet old dear. Maybe she'll get out of here soon!"

Kaye heard a squeak, and looked to the doorway. Mrs. Gildecott inched forward, her face white as if in pain, as she pushed the wheelchair wheels. She looked up and winced out a wan smile.

Susie reached down and patted Mrs. Gildecott's knee. "Good work, sweetie pie. I wish all the patients had your determination."

"I endeavor always for improvement. Kaye, are you ready for a stroll?"

"Sure. Let me help." She squeezed through the doorway and got behind the chair. "What was that all about?" she whispered into Mrs. Gildecott's ear.

"Shhh...I'll tell you in a bit. Take me out. Take me someplace where we can speak privately."

★ ★ ★ ★

On Monday morning, the day before Christmas Eve, Kaye stood in the housekeeping closet running water in the utility sink. Her hands shook. This was Day Three of Mrs. Gildecott's campaign, and Kaye was weakening.

Was what Mrs. Gildecott proposed a crime? A sin? How much trouble would Kaye get into, and would she be caught? When was a crime also a mortal sin? And was it forgivable or not?

She ran lukewarm water over her hands, then patted wet palms against heated cheeks. Her face was on fire. She reached for a towel in the stacks on the rack to the left and buried her face in it. Unexpectedly, tears sprang to her eyes. With Mrs. Gildecott gone, Seaton would be a bleak place—even bleaker than it had been before the elderly woman had come to stay—because now Kaye had a taste of companionship, understanding, and human kindness.

How could I expect her to stay on hold, immobile, in pain, waiting for her final demise? Why couldn't I move her to my place to take care of her?

Even as she considered that, Kaye realized that she not only lacked the resources, but she wasn't there for at least nine hours a day. *Dammit!* she thought bitterly. *Why did I let myself get involved?*

Decisions about what Mrs. Gildecott proposed weren't to be lightly made, and she wished she had someone—anyone—to talk to. But the one person with insight who was trustworthy was Mrs. Gildecott, and Kaye already knew how she would answer. She wiped her eyes with the towel and fought back the tears.

"Brock." Kaye jerked around to see Marcus looming in the doorway. "Any chance you could work swing shift for me on Christmas Eve?" She stared at him, not answering. "It's double time. I originally switched shifts with Carlos on swing, and now my wife tells me her family has changed our Christmas celebration from the 25th to the 24th. Come on, will ya? I gotta know now. You want the extra hours?"

"Double time?" she squeaked out.

"Yeah. Look, I know it's last minute and all, but I'd really appreciate it if you could cover for me. I'll pay you back somehow in the future."

"Okay."

"You'll do it?"

"Sure."

He grinned, his big teeth wolfish in the dim light. "I owe you, Brock. I'll let Thornton know." He moved away from the doorway.

Was the world conspiring against her? Was this a sign?

★　★　★　★

"All the books are there on the shelf, Kaye." Mrs. Gildecott pointed toward the half-empty closet. "If you return them within in the next two weeks, you'll have them in on time." Kaye accepted this information wordlessly. Mrs. Gildecott lay on her back, pillows propping her up, one book cradled in her hands. She wore a gold and brown paisley brocade vest over a lightweight black turtleneck.

"You look . . . happy, Mrs. G."

"I am. Today I slip the surly bonds of earth, and I am relieved and joyous." She reached out and took Kaye's hand in her firm grip. "Do you think I'm a lunatic?"

"Not like in high school." The words slipped out, and Mrs. Gildecott burst into a delighted laugh that tinkled in the room, echoing over Kaye's head like celestial music. "I didn't mean that."

"I know just what you meant, Kaye, and you need not worry that I would misinterpret your honesty. It's wonderfully refreshing. Here, listen." She picked up the book in her lap. "One of the nurses lent me this book, and I was struck by this line: 'Suffering is not the border on the outer edges of one's life, but the cloth itself, elegantly stitched on one side, crude and miserably sewn on the other.' Isn't that lovely?"

"What does it mean?"

"What do you think it means?"

"Suffering is both good and bad?"

"Well…yes, but I think it's even more than that. Life is shot through with suffering, but you can decide if you want to focus on the elegant side or the crude, miserably sewn side. Either way, both are there for each person."

Kaye still wasn't sure she understood. "Who wrote that?"

"Alice Hoffman in her novel *Blue Diary*. Here, you should read the book." She set it on the bed's coverlet. "I believe you would enjoy it." She reached under her covers and took out a steno pad. "This is quite messy, but I've written pages and pages of authors and topics you simply must investigate. Study hard. I'll be checking on you."

Kaye fought to keep from crying. She glanced over her shoulder. Seeing and hearing no one coming, she bent over the tiny woman and gently took her in her arms. Now she couldn't hold back the tears. When she let go, Mrs. Gildecott smiled.

"Now, now, dear, no tears." She took Kaye's hand. "Every time you think of me, you must know that it is then I'll be looking in on you."

Kaye's heart beat with such force that she could feel it in her arms and legs. For a brief moment, she felt light-headed. "Oh, Mrs. G. I don't know. Are you sure you want to do this?"

Mrs. Gildecott's laugh was rich and full-bodied. "I'm certain. And just remember, you're not out from behind those prison walls in your mind until you decide that you're truly free. It's up to you." She winked and offered the steno pad. "Go on, take it. And I believe you have something for me?"

In a dull voice, Kaye said, "Three six nine three."

"Thank you. Your friendship has been a joy, Kaye. Now go on with your work. I'll see you when everyone is at the Christmas party. Here's lookin' at you, kid."

★ ★ ★ ★

Kaye mopped the area around the charge nurse's desk. All afternoon she had been careful to stick close to one aide or another.

Sheila Thornton passed her, pausing to turn and say, "You've certainly been glum all day, Brock. What's the matter—your Christmas tree burn up?"

Kaye stared at the woman. Her exterior was so attractive, so lovely, but the interior was rotten clear through. Why did it have to be this way? Why did good people find themselves in terrible situations without any recourse, without any escape, while nasty people like Sheila Thornton were allowed comfort and beauty and happiness?

When she didn't get a response from Kaye, the administrator made a tsk-tsk sound, and walked away. Kaye stared at her back and was suddenly consumed with anger.

The sounds of laughter spilled out of the staff lounge as Thornton opened the door. Kaye stared at the clock over the charge nurse's station. Oh, my. It's after six now—time for the Christmas party.

She pushed the rolling bucket aside, cut through the nurse's station, and hustled down to room 18. Mrs. Gildecott lay in her brocade vest, looking slightly alarmed. "I thought you weren't coming." The clock on her wall read twelve minutes after six.

"Your clock is a little fast." Kaye hesitated, her heart thumping.

"You're worrying again." Mutely, Kaye nodded. "Stop it. You'll not be responsible for my escape."

"Yes, I will."

Mrs. Gildecott laughed. "This is no place for an intelligent person. If one still has her wits about her, she can find out anything she needs to know by guile, and the information I've given my attorney will indicate that. Come now. Help me." As Mrs. Gildecott swept the covers off, Kaye maneuvered the wheelchair over and lifted her into it. "Thank you, dear. Try your very best to give me at least an hour head start. Run now. You must not be seen."

At the door Kaye looked back. Mrs. Gildecott raised a hand. "Enjoy life, dear. Enjoy!"

Heart beating fast, Kaye charged out the door, wove her way between three sleeping occupants in wheelchairs, and made it to the charge nurse's counter. She heard footsteps and the low murmur of voices. Panicked, she realized her mop and bucket were on the other side, in the other hall. She ducked down behind the counter, grabbed a waste basket, and strolled out just as the chief administrator and two administrative assistants reached the counter.

"Hey, there, it's party time," the administrator said. "You're joining us, right?"

"Yes, sir."

"Leave the trash for later and come along."

She set down the metal basket and followed them to the staff lounge where she found the other housekeepers, all the nurses and aides, and several staff who weren't even on duty today.

"Merry Christmas!" someone yelled. A CD player clicked on, and the song, "It's Beginning To Look A Lot Like Christmas," played, the voice happy and smooth. Nurse Judy pressed a mug filled with hot apple cider into Kaye's hand, and she eased her way over next to one of the couches and leaned against the wall.

For the next thirty minutes, awards were given out, people laughed and joked, and everyone helped themselves to plates of holiday sweets.

Kaye stood glued to the wall, her heart in her throat. When the light for room six flashed, one of the swing shift aides hauled himself up from the couch on the far wall. "Guess I'll go check on Mr. Rother. Probably forgot where he put his teeth again."

While he was gone, the light for room 21 flashed. Someone else went to check on that. People came and went, and after a time, Kaye's stress had run so high for so long that she slipped into a sort of dull torpor, unaware of what was happening around her. When she tried to look out the window to the back garden, it was so dark that she could see only the reflection of the party.

"Brock."

She came alert with a shock. "What?"

One of the aides said, "Mr. Vander just called your name."

Someone else muttered, "She may be dense, but she's always here."

Mr. Vander strode across the room and handed Kaye a slip of paper. "Thanks for your reliability. You never missed a day all year."

"You're welcome, sir." She looked down at the Target gift certificate in her hands. Ten dollars. Ten bucks to come to this joyless place where nobody even called her by her first name. She looked around the room. Everybody's last name was stitched into their uniforms, but they were all on first name terms. Only she belonged to a lesser order, the Last Name People.

After a time, the party broke up. Kaye set her mug of untouched cider in the sink and followed Nurse Judy out to the charge nurse's station. Five women hung around there chatting. Kaye picked up her mop and stood nearby, saying nothing, but nodding and listening. She glanced at the clock. Seven p.m.

★   ★   ★   ★

Kaye stood in the housekeeping closet where she'd spent considerable time all evening removing cans and bags and containers from the shelves, dusting, and wiping down surfaces. The closet was now a disorganized mess. She wasn't sure if rearranging the kitty litter would serve as a good alibi.

At twenty minutes to nine the first shout went up. She stepped into the hallway clutching a dirty cotton rag. Nurse Bradley, who usually worked graveyard, rushed toward her. "Have you seen the resident in room 18—Mrs. Gildecott?"

Kaye shook her head and watched him stride past and head around the corner toward the staff lounge. She returned to the closet and surveyed the wreckage, her hands trembling. At the sink, she ran warm water over her fingers and waited.

The administrators had left long ago, so Kaye was surprised to hear Sheila Thornton's voice in the hallway. "I want every room, every closet, every inch of this entire campus searched. Now!" The voice grew louder, calling out instructions. High heels clicked to a stop in the doorway, and Kaye turned, glad that the housekeeping closet was dim.

"Brock, what do you know about this?"

"About what?"

"Where's Esther Gildecott?"

Kaye shrugged. "How should I know?"

Thornton hesitated in the doorway, examining Kaye, then whirled abruptly and moved off. Moments later, Kaye heard the deep bass of one of the male aides calling for help. She followed his shouts toward the back of the facility.

The glass door to the garden was ajar. Gusts of wintry wind blew crystals of snow into the hall. Kaye stepped out and stopped. Her eyes followed parallel lines dug in the snow to the wheelchair glinting silver in the night. Mrs. Gildecott had managed to half turn it and sat in profile near the bare arbor, her elbows on the chair's arms and her palms up as if meditating. Her head was tipped back slightly, her face toward the heavens, with a wisp of a smile gracing ghostly white features.

"Shit!" the aide said. "She's frozen solid!" He grabbed at the wheelchair and dragged it, his big feet leaving footprints in the carpet of snow.

People pushed past Kaye, shouting, calling out orders. She heard a siren in the distance. Tears poured down her face.

★　★　★　★

For the first time since her childhood, Kaye had the desire to go to church, to step inside the confessional, and be absolved of her guilt. Were her actions a crime? She was complicit in the death of another human being. How could she ever come to terms with that?

She didn't work Christmas Day and called in sick for the two days following. She stayed up late, smoking, pacing, crying.

On the third day, she went to work. She learned that both Sheila Thornton and Vander, the chief administrator, had been reassigned to jobs elsewhere in the nursing home network. The police were still nosing around, asking questions, but it appeared that the cause of death would be determined as suicide. The garden door was now boarded over. Nice of them to lock the barn after the horse is through, Kaye thought. At noon there was a memorial service for Mrs. Gildecott, but she couldn't bring herself to attend.

When she arrived home that night, in her mailbox was a letter written in a shaky hand.

> *Dear Kaye,*
>
> *Knowing your propensity for self-blame, I arranged to have my solicitor send this letter to you after my passing. Thank you for all the kindnesses you showed me. You made my final days a joy in ways you might never know, and I am eternally grateful.*
>
> *I am released now from my prison. Please remember that, as Wittgenstein said, "A man will be imprisoned in a room with a door that's unlocked and opens inwards, as long as it does not occur to him to pull rather than push." You've been pushing far too long. Move on, dear, or I shall haunt you from the grave!*
>
> *In one year, my solicitor will be contacting you. In the meantime, I hope that you will get out of that horrid job and prepare for a new and better life. Consider this a Voice from the grave—or from the Great Unknown—spurring you on to better things. You deserve it, Kaye. Your parole is soon over, and it's time to start living.*
>
> *Love Always,*
> *Esther Gildecott*
>
> *P.S. Do not forget to return the library books. And please—visit Greece and Italy some day and think of me.*

Kaye wondered if Mrs. Gildecott had suffered. Was there pain? How long did it take? How much courage did it take to do what Mrs. G had done? She still wondered if her part in Mrs. G's death was a crime. But how could it be a sin to do something like that?

"Could I ever be that brave?" she asked aloud. At what point did the balance tip between wanting to live and needing to die?

Kaye had no idea how to answer these questions, but she did know that continuing to live a joyless, hermetically sealed life was no longer an option. Even in death, Mrs. Gildecott had urged her to live. Maybe it was time for her to do that after all.

"Thank you, Mrs. G," she whispered as she carefully folded up the letter and returned it to the envelope.

Deborah Woodworth

A southern Ohio childhood, near the abandoned sites of several Shaker communities, and a Sociology of Religion Ph.D. inspired Deborah Woodworth to create a Shaker mystery series set in Depression-era Kentucky. Sister Rose Callahan, eldress of a dwindling Shaker village, does the sleuthing, often with the energetic assistance of her young friend, Gennie Malone, an orphan brought up by the Shakers. Publishers Weekly called the Sister Rose mysteries "a first-rate series; warmhearted, richly detailed, and completely enthralling." The books have received acclaim for their accurate portrayal of Shaker life, and in 2000, Woodworth was the keynote speaker at the annual Friends of the Shakers meeting at the last remaining Shaker community, Sabbathday Lake, in Maine. Killing Gifts, the fifth book in the series, won a 2002 Barry Award for Best Paperback Original. The award is sponsored by Deadly Pleasures Mystery Magazine *and voted on by readers. Woodworth is also the author of two biographies for children—* Compassion: The Story of Clara Barton *and* Determination: The Story of Jackie Robinson. *She has recently completed the first book in a new mystery series, set in the 1950s, and is at work on a seventh Shaker mystery.*

Waltz of the Loons

Deborah Woodworth

"Well, you're a horse of a different kettle of fish, aren't you, little fella?" Police Chief Jens Johansson's late wife Klara had often used that phrase whenever she encountered something unexpected. Jens had never been sure what it meant, but he'd found himself using it since her death. It was like having her back again for a moment.

In fact, what Jens found early on a Minnesota March morning was neither a horse nor a fish, but a filthy mutt sitting in the pool of light at the locked front door of the Loon River Police Station. The dog looked like a mix of chocolate Labrador and about four different terriers, at least from what Jens could discern under the mud caking the creature's dark fur. He looked to be about forty pounds, with wiry brown fur and a floppy-eared face, now tilted endearingly.

"What's that you have there, son?" Jens asked, keeping it conversational and friendly as he held out his hand toward the frilly pinkish object the dog held in its teeth. Jens knelt down and felt his knees crack. The dog wagged its tail but held on tight as Jens tried to remove the toy. He gave up. No point arguing with four terriers.

"Might as well come in and warm your paws, Mutt." The name fit. Anyway, it would do for now. As police chief of Loon River, Jens' job included returning lost animals to their owners, but he didn't recognize this one. Might take some asking around—maybe a bath before anyone would recognize the dog. Jens unlocked the station door and Mutt pranced right in like it was his winter palace. He followed Jens into the chief's office, where he sniffed around and seemed to approve of the arrangements. Without further fuss, the dog dropped his toy at Jens' feet and made for the visitor's chair and a nap.

Mutt's antics made Jens smile, something he hadn't done much of in the almost two months since his wife's death from pancreatic cancer. Came on so fast it took the family's breath away, along with Klara's life. Last spring she was strong and beautiful, only forty-eight and looking forward to their little empty next. By New Year's she was gone. Those months had added what felt like a decade to Jens' fifty years and subtracted ten pounds from his spare six-foot frame.

Jens picked up the dog's toy and recognized it at once. His daughter, now a junior at the University of Minnesota, had received one very similar for Christmas when she was about eight. Ballerina Barbie, as he recalled. The doll had come dressed in a frothy pink tutu and tights, with shiny pink toe shoes strapped to her feet. She'd had sleek blond hair pulled back in a bun and tied with a frothy pink ribbon. Jens had to rely on his memory for the hair because this particular Ballerina Barbie was minus her head. A razor-sharp instrument had cleanly severed the swan-like neck. What remained of the doll was dirt-stained and punctured by canine teeth. One toe shoe was missing. Turning her over, Jens noticed some marks on her plastic skin, beginning in the middle of her back just below where the shoulder blades would be, if she'd had them. With his finger, Jens lowered the stretchy fabric of the tutu bodice. Someone had used a blue ballpoint pen to draw a heart shape with a knife through it and little blue dots, probably meant to be blood. Jens let the fabric snap back into place and looked up to find the dog watching him.

"You hungry, Mutt?"

The dog bounded over to Jens and gazed up with liquid brown eyes.

"I'll take that as a yes." Ever since Klara's death, it had been Jens' habit to pack himself a thermos of instant coffee and some turkey rolled in lefse and go to work early, while the station was quiet. He poured himself a cup, took one bite of the sandwich, and gave the rest to Mutt, who swallowed it more or less whole.

It took a lot of effort for Jens to talk to people these days. Around mid-morning, once the breakfast crowd had cleared out, he'd tramp over to the Silence of the Loons Café—so named by its proprietor, Viveka, because the town didn't have even one of Minnesota's ten thousand lakes, just that puny creek they called a river. Hence, no ducks, no geese—and no loons. Jens still enjoyed talking with Vivy. She knew everyone and everything that happened in town, so he could keep up through her. Also, she'd been Klara's best friend and had come to the Twin Cities to spend time with Klara at the end. He didn't have to explain anything to Vivy, and if he laughed about something, she wouldn't tell him he wasn't grieving properly.

Jens decided to break his self-imposed isolation. He had a dog to return to its owner, and Vivy would be the best place to start.

"Come on, Mutt," Jens said, bundling himself into his down jacket. "Let's go get us some food and information." Having heard the word "food," Mutt was already heading for the front door. As an afterthought, Jens slid the doll into a plastic bag and stowed it in one of the deep pockets of his down parka. He might be a small-town cop, but he knew to hang onto things until he was sure they didn't mean anything important.

★   ★   ★   ★

"Couldn't you at least have washed the beast before bringing it in here?" Vivy frowned at Mutt and then at Jens. "Hang on, then, I'll get a brush." Vivy was a tall woman in her early fifties, with generous curves growing more generous with each passing year. She'd say what was on her mind, no matter whether her listener wanted to hear it, but everyone in town had cried on her shoulder at some time or other. She had a listening sort of face, that's what Klara had always said. Vivy reappeared with an old hairbrush and handed it to Jens. "Here, make him presentable. You want food?"

"Steak and eggs," Jens said. "Double the steak and make it rare."

"He better not get sick in here, Jens Johansson, or you're in deep—"

"He promises he won't." Jens began to brush with vigor.

"—dog poop." Vivy passed Jens' order to a waitress and sat down across the table from him. She watched as the dog happily submitted to vigorous brushing. "So," she said, "what are you doing with Lord Furfull, and why is he such a mess?"

"You know this dog?"

"Sure, you would, too, if you came in at breakfast time like a normal person. He belongs to that new undertaker lady, Angela Borgina. She's usually in here every morning with his lordship. Orders Eggbeaters for him. Imagine." Vivy grabbed a piece of toast off Jens' plate as it arrived. "Here you go, Furfull, if you keep this down you can have some steak."

"I've been calling him Mutt."

"Good choice." Vivy nodded her approval.

"I've met Angela, of course," Jens said. "I don't know her very well, though, since Klara wanted to be buried with her family in Grand Marais. Haven't seen Angela around lately. When's the last time she was in here?"

Vivy selected a second piece of toast and slathered it with strawberry jam while she thought. "Must be about two days, not counting today, which would make three. She had the dog with her then and he looked just fine, or as fine as he ever looks. She didn't say anything to me about leaving town, though she does that a lot."

The gossipy edge to Vivy's voice intrigued Jens. "Where does she go, any idea?"

"Down to the Cities," Vivy said. At least, that's what Jens thought he heard, since Vivy's mouth was full of toast. After swallowing, she continued with more clarity. "She never says whether it's Minneapolis or St. Paul, just that she's going to a convention. Some undertakering convention, I guess."

"I believe it's called mortuary science," Jens said, before he could stop himself.

Vivy shrugged. "Whatever, it sounds suspicious to me."

"Why?" Jens asked quickly, to catch her before she filled her mouth with more toast.

Vivy looked Jens straight in the eye. "You've got to wonder," she said, "how many mort-iary science conventions a girl can take." Vivy finished off her toast and eyed the second portion of steak on Jens' plate, which he speared with his fork and fed to a grateful dog.

"Any idea what Angela might really be doing in the Twin Cities?" Jens asked.

"My guess, she's got herself a lover. He's probably married or something. Anyway, she wouldn't want him to come here because everyone would know about it, and then she couldn't flirt with all the Loon River men and get them to do her 'heavy lifting' for her, if you get my drift." Having lost the steak, Vivy said, "Gonna get me some eggs and bacon. Stick around." Klara used to say, always fondly, that gossiping fueled Vivy's appetite.

Jens sipped his coffee and set about digesting his breakfast and Vivy's information, but audible muttering from the next table over interrupted his thoughts.

"Huh," the voice said. "Married lover.... Thinks she's too good. . . ."

Jens didn't have to turn his head to recognize Thor, a logger who lived just south of Loon River. Thor was a good six foot three, all bulging muscle, and he seemed averse to bathing. All this plus the perpetual tirade he directed at the air around him kept most folks, even other loggers, away from him. His daily breakfast at the café seemed to be his only social outlet.

Thor always consumed a double portion of the Logger's Breakfast, and he kept right on talking while he chewed. Jens could understand about every fifth word, but it was enough to make him pick up his coffee cup and move to Thor's table. Vivy arrived with her bacon and eggs and, without turning up her nose, joined the two men. Mutt roused himself enough to move his nap to Jens' side.

Thor gaped in surprise, several slices of half-chewed bacon in his mouth.

"Don't forget to swallow," Vivy advised him.

To keep the conversation more private, Jens leaned his forearms on the table. Unfortunately, this position also brought his nose closer to Thor. "You know our new undertaker well?"

Thor shrugged and shoveled hash browns into his mouth.

"Come on, Thor," Vivy said. "Now isn't the time to start being quiet."

Even mountain men obeyed Vivy. "Yeah, sure," Thor said. "Little slut. Been here four months and gone every weekend. Every goddam weekend. Fifteen goddam weekends." He pointed his fork at Jens. "I kept count."

"Doesn't sound as if you like her much," Jens said.

Thor got his mouth around a chunk of steak.

"When's the last time you saw her?"

Thor stuffed his partially chewed steak in one cheek and said, "Don't recall."

"I heard you helped her move some furniture just last Wednesday," Vivy said. "Must not have been all you'd hoped for."

Some pink appeared above Thor's thick black beard. Without another word, he scraped back his chair, paid his bill, and left the café.

"I'll find out what happened," Vivy said, as she renewed her attack on breakfast.

Jens pondered the effect Loon River's new undertaker seemed to have on men. After a while, his mind wandered back to Mutt's situation.

"Vivy, does Angela usually let her dog run around free while she's out of town?"

"That's the odd thing," Vivy said. "She's always been real careful of Mutt here. Always leaves him with Melvin, you know Melvin, he lives just a mile out of town. He's not so good with people, but he loves dogs, and he's got lots of land for a dog to run around in. Also, he's sweet on Angela, any fool can see that. She encourages him, too, probably so she can get free work and dog sitting out of him."

Jens thought, *So that's two men sweet on her.*

Jens had one of his feelings. Melvin had his problems, but he'd never mistreat a dog. If Melvin had been in charge of Mutt and the dog had run off, it would have been Melvin standing by the police station door.

An alarming thought hit Jens. "Has Melvin been in to get his thermos of coffee this morning?"

He'd asked the question so urgently that Vivy nearly choked. She took a gulp of water and answered, "Sure, just like usual. Real early, on his way to work. I hear he's fixing up the Peterson's barn these days."

"How'd he seem?"

"Same as always. Weird," Vivy said. With some effort, she pushed back her chair. "Well, Kiddo, the kitchen will fall apart without me. You need any more food?"

"Toast would be nice."

"I'll send some out. And more coffee."

Jens wasn't inclined to chat with his neighbors just then. Not because he didn't enjoy a good rambling conversation about the recent sloppy snowstorm or the cost of farm equipment or how the Cities were getting all the money for roads—No, Jens needed to mull. Something was wrong.

A talk with Melvin couldn't hurt. Like everyone else in town, Jens knew Melvin on the surface; nobody much wanted to get to know him any better than that. Melvin was in his mid fifties, a few years older than Jens, and had grown up in Loon River. Much of what Jens knew about him had come from Vivy, through Klara. Jens wasn't sure how much was true. Melvin rarely spoke more than a word or two, and only if necessary. Folks felt uncomfortable with him because he never met their eyes, just looked down and to the side all the time. Klara said a few girls had liked him in high school because he seemed shy and brooding, but he'd never dated anyone, maybe because his parents had been deeply religious. Every Sunday, the three of them had piled into their rusty old Chevie truck and gone to some country church with a lot of words in its name. The church wasn't Catholic, and if it was Lutheran then it was a kind of Lutheran the folks of Loon River didn't recognize.

Melvin had been close to his mom. Klara once remarked that Melvin's mother, Catherine, had "never quite grown up." She had treated Melvin more as a playmate than a son. It had broken Catherine's heart when Melvin was drafted right out of high school and sent off to Viet Nam. She died while he was still serving—died of worry, Klara had said. Her husband followed soon after, and Melvin returned to an empty house. He'd gotten angrier and stranger after that. As a young police officer, Jens had broken up a few fights between Melvin and some of the younger fellows who'd spoken out against the war.

After a while, Melvin seemed to settle down and find a life for himself. He was a genius at fixing just about anything. Jens had hired him on occasion and found him hardworking, competent, and almost devoid of conversation. Even Klara had been unable to wrest more than a word or two out of him. They'd always felt relieved when he'd left. There was something menacing in Melvin's brooding presence, like having a volcano waking up under your roof.

A whimper from Mutt brought Jens back to the café, now filled with morning customers. He glanced up to see Loon River's mayor heading his way. Alrik's pudgy body radiated righteous indignation. He was probably outraged because a rock had hit his windshield, and he'd demand that Jens nail the perpetrator. Jens wasn't sure which irritated him more, the pettiness of Alrik's complaints or the high whiny voice in which he delivered them.

Before Alrik was halfway across the café, Vivy appeared in front of him and, with a few words and a gentle arm, guided him back toward his table, where his wife Trude sat rigid and stone-faced. Not for the first time, Jens wondered how such a silly man had snagged such a wealthy and intelligent woman; Trude ran the town's social calendar with flawless efficiency. Alrik reputedly made a bundle with some kind of online company. He was generous with money, which kept getting him elected mayor. The rumor was Trude ran the business. Heck, Trude probably ran the Mayor's Office, too.

It struck Jens that no one had come up to his table to chat the whole time he'd been ruminating. Vivy had been running interference for him. If he started moping around and feeling sorry for himself, she'd give him a kick in the behind, but she wouldn't let anyone else do it. Having cajoled Alrik back to his table, Vivy turned around, and Jens smiled his thanks to her. With a slight movement of his head, he beckoned Vivy back to his table.

"You still hungry?" Vivy asked as she lowered herself into a chair. Mutt thumped his tail at her, and she said to him, "You've had enough, young man."

"I've got one more question for you, Vivy. You said that Angela Borgina flirts with the men in town. Is there anyone she seems especially interested in?"

"Let me think." Vivy leaned back and her chair creaked. "Mostly I'd say she's just flexing her muscles, if you get my meaning.

She isn't much to look at, too small and skinny, but she's got good posture and a way about her. When she walks across the room, the men stare and the women glare. She's got that long dark hair, leaves it loose so it floats while she walks. She knows what she's doing." With a throaty chuckle, Vivy leaned in toward Jens. "A month or so ago, Angela caused a scene right here in my café." Vivy sounded entertained rather than scandalized. "She tried her flirty act on Alrik. He turned beet red, and that wife of his—well, I thought Trude was going to knock Angela on her backside, the way she jumped up and put herself between Angela and Alrik."

Since Trude was nearly six feet tall, with Valkyrian proportions, Jens could imagine how she might have threatened Angela, who was about a foot shorter and maybe a hundred pounds.

"I've got to hand it to Angela, though," Vivy said. "She just swirled around and sashayed out of here like she'd won. Maybe she did." Vivy cocked her head at Jens. "You worried something's happened to Angela?"

"She's probably fine, having a shopping spree in Minneapolis or something," Jens said. "You know me, always looking for a mystery story."

Vivy turned a critical eye on Mutt, who nuzzled her hand. "Funny, though. . . . Angela dotes on this dog. Hard to believe she wouldn't have left him with Melvin, like usual."

"Maybe she did." Jens rose to his feet and so did Mutt. "I'll just check on things. Don't worry—and don't go spreading rumors, either."

"Who, me?"

★   ★   ★   ★

With a freshly bathed Mutt by his side, Jens headed back out to his truck. Two days earlier, a squall had dumped five inches of snow, which now had a hard crust from surface melting and refreezing. With each step, Jens' boots crunched and sank a few inches, and Mutt had enough weight to create lightly sunken paw prints. Jens felt his heart warm up for the first time since Klara's death. He told himself not to get attached; Mutt belonged to Angela, who might even now be returning home.

After calling and getting her answering machine, Jens drove to the outskirts of town, where Angela Borgina had renovated an old farmhouse for her funeral business. Angela lived upstairs. *Must have cost a bundle,* Jens thought, as he pulled up the driveway. *Wonder where she got the money.*

Mutt bounded out of the truck and ran to the front door, where he sat expectantly. Jens tried the door. "Sorry, fella, locked up tight." Mutt put his head on his front paws and whimpered.

The curtains were open, so Jens peered inside. Nothing looked disturbed or suspicious—no half-completed embalmings or tossed furniture. The back door and all the windows were securely locked, as well. As he walked around the house and property, Jens noticed that Mutt's paw prints were everywhere, peppering the snow and even appearing on some of the windows. Mutt had tried hard to get into his house. Jens peeked in the garage window, where Angela's brand-new hearse was parked. Her little red Mazda Miata was gone. There were no tire tracks in the snow, so the Miata had been gone for at least two days.

Mutt had wandered off somewhere. Jens gave a sharp whistle and called out, "Come on, Mutt, come on, boy, where are you?" Mutt came racing out of the evergreen woods that marked the beginning of Melvin's property. The dog was clutching something furry in his mouth. At first it looked like a rabbit, but as Mutt drew closer, Jens saw a long pink ribbon dragging in the snow. Luckily, Mutt's Labrador side was in control; he dropped his find at Jens' feet and waited.

Jens squatted in the snow and examined the object, without touching it. What he'd thought was fur was actually hair. Human hair, tied in a bun with a pink ribbon, just like he remembered from his daughter's Ballerina Barbie. Only this was human-sized. Jens had his gloves on, so he carefully lifted an edge of the hair; with relief, he saw it was a wig. He pulled a plastic bag out of a coat pocket and slipped the wig into it.

"Where'd you find this, boy?"

Mutt barked and did a little dance in the snow.

"Okay, let's head over to Melvin's place."

The dog was way ahead of Jens before he'd taken more than a couple of steps. Once in the woods, he called out to Mutt, but this time there was no sudden appearance. Jens stood still and listened. Over the swishing of bird wings, he heard a scratching sound somewhere off to his left. He walked through snow-covered undergrowth following the sound until it suddenly stopped. The next sound he heard made his blood pound dangerously through his heart—it was the haunting howl of an animal in pain.

Jens ran toward the cry and found Mutt sitting in a hole he'd dug in the snow. He seemed to be guarding another pink object. Jens edged toward the dog, soothing him with gentle phrases. Mutt let him approach, his howl fading to a whimper. He dropped to the ground with his head on his paws as Jens reached out to pet him. Once he knew Mutt wouldn't attack, Jens examined the find—a ripped and dirty pink ballet shoe. The satin over the wooden toe was shredded vertically, as if the wearer had been dragged. Rusty spots marred one of the ribbons used to secure the shoe to the dancer's ankle.

"This belongs to your mistress, doesn't it, boy? Do you have anything else to show me?" Mutt looked up at Jens with dark, baleful eyes, but he didn't move. "Okay, let's get you back in the truck. You can take a nap while I do some exploring. I think it's better if you stay out of it this time."

Mutt followed willingly to the relative warmth of the truck cab, and Jens locked him in before heading back to the funeral home. At the door, he pulled a small file from a coat pocket and picked the lock. The ground-floor funeral home portion of the house was clean and neat, right down to the pamphlets on Angela's desk. Her answering machine flashed three messages, all from Monday and Tuesday. One message was his, and the other two were inquiring about her services. Funny, though—both callers gave phone numbers with Twin Cities area codes.

Angela's upstairs living area was less neat. The bed was sloppily made and the bathroom could have used a mop. Jens noticed the absence of a toothbrush, toothpaste, and hairbrush.

By the time he'd toured the entire building, Jens was convinced that Angela had left for the weekend and had expected to be back at work on Monday.

Leaving Mutt sleeping in the truck cab, Jens headed through the woods to Melvin's place. The wig and the ballet shoe had been on his property; Jens couldn't let that pass. When he emerged from the woods, Jens stopped a moment and looked over Melvin's yard and house. The snow was more or less untouched, except for neat paths dug from the front door to the garage, which was open and empty. As Jens walked through the snow toward the path, he saw prints from birds and rabbits and indentations from deer hoofs, but nothing that looked like dog paws. Wherever Mutt had been since the storm, it hadn't been here.

Melvin's house was the only one in town that Jens had never been inside. Melvin wasn't what you'd call social. He conducted his business at customers' homes or at the café, and he'd never, as far as Jens knew, invited a single person to visit him at his home. Jens had always assumed the house would be a shambles, given Melvin was a lifelong bachelor and strange to boot. Whatever Jens had expected, it sure wasn't this. The living room was the neatest room he'd ever seen—not a speck of dust or a pillow out of alignment. Even the windows were clean. The furniture was plain and there wasn't much of it, but everything was organized with an eye for function and comfort. Jens became aware that his boots were dripping melted snow on the shiny wood floor. He removed them and left them on a rug placed by the door. If Melvin came in and found them, so be it.

The thought of Melvin returning got Jens moving. In stocking feet, he went from room to room on the ground floor, searching for any sign of Angela. Every room was equally clean and neat, so he climbed the staircase to the second floor. Two rooms turned out to be bedrooms with a shared bath. Again, he found nothing. The third door was closed; he expected it to be locked, but the knob turned easily in his hand. Unlike all other rooms in the house, this one was dark. The curtains were drawn shut, and there wasn't so much as a nightlight. Jens flicked on the light.

"Whoa, Nellie," Jens whispered as he gazed around the room. He stepped inside, onto white carpet, recently vacuumed. The walls, ceiling, and furnishings were various shades of pink. All this was merely background to the main attraction—dozens and dozens of dolls. Dolls covered every surface in the room. They seemed to be organized by type, such as baby dolls on the bed and international dolls on the dresser. On a round pink table in the center of the room, a grouping of ballerina dolls occupied the place of honor. From the variety of costumes, Jens guessed the dolls were dressed for different ballets, but they were arranged as if dancing together. In the center of the table stood an empty platform with a wire contraption on it. Jens had a strong hunch which doll it was meant to hold. He turned out the light and backed into the hallway, closing the door.

Back in his truck, Jens pulled out of sight and radioed one of his part-time officers for back up. Erik could be counted on to be quiet and discreet. Jens had missed lunch, so he rummaged in the glove compartment for the chocolate he always kept on hand. Mutt perked right up when he heard the crackle of candy bar paper. "Sorry, son," Jens said. "Wouldn't be good for you. I'll get you another steak when this is all done."

His watch said 3:00 p.m., but the darkening sky made it seem like dusk. Big wet snowflakes began to plop on his windshield. Jens settled back and mulled over the collection of clues he and Mutt had discovered. His gut told him the clues related to Angela Borgina's absence, though they sure wouldn't convince a judge and jury. Not without a body. He didn't want to draw attention to his presence by turning on his cab light, so he dug a flashlight out of the glove box and examined the wig and ballet shoe as best he could. Inside the wig, he found something that might help—a number of long dark hairs. He left them untouched and carefully slid the wig back into its plastic evidence bag.

When Erik arrived with sandwiches and coffee, Jens locked Mutt in the back of the squad car, along with a ham sandwich. Jens climbed in front with Erik. "Did you tell anyone where you were going?" Jens asked.

"Nope."

Darkness was coming on fast, along with the snow. Erik clicked the ignition key halfway so he could use the windshield wipers, but otherwise he remained silent while Jens pondered. Right around 6:00 p.m., headlights turned into Melvin's driveway and stopped in front of the house. The living room light flicked on, followed by an upstairs light. "I don't want to alarm him," Jens said. "You know Melvin, he's unpredictable. No telling what the war really did to him. Probably got guns, too. Take it as easy as possible, but be on your guard." Erik nodded, his head a silhouette against the snow.

As they reached the front door, Melvin's back disappeared into the kitchen. Jens motioned Erik to knock and watched through the window as Melvin reappeared, a beer bottle in his hand. Unaware he was being watched, Melvin's face showed surprise and fear. Jens pulled away from the window.

"Who is it?" Melvin shouted.

In a rare expenditure of words, Erik said, "Hey Melvin, it's me, Erik. Open up, man, it's really coming down out here."

The door opened a fraction of an inch. It was enough. Erik pushed through and had Melvin in an arm hold before the beer bottle hit the floor. Melvin started to struggle, but the fight went out of him quickly. With his free hand, Erik brought out his handcuffs.

"Don't put those on," Jens said. "Not yet, anyway."

Erik looked a question at him but put his handcuffs away.

"Let's go in the kitchen and have a talk," Jens said. When they'd settled at the kitchen table, Jens reached in his pockets and retrieved the wig, the ballet shoe, and the headless Ballerina Barbie. He placed them side by side in front of Melvin, whose eyes filled with tears. He reached for the doll, but Erik grabbed his wrist.

"That doll belongs to you, doesn't it, Melvin?" Jens asked.

"Belonged to my mom. It was her favorite."

"How about the wig and the shoe?"

Melvin shook his head.

"They belong to Angela, don't they?"

Fresh tears spilled down Melvin's rough cheeks.

"What happened to Angela?"

For the first time ever, Melvin lifted his face and looked directly at Jens. He had dark blue eyes; Jens wondered if anyone in town knew that. "Her name was right," Melvin said. "She was an angel."

"You said 'was.' Is Angela dead?"

Melvin gave a slow, sad nod. Then he took a deep breath and let out a wail that made Jens jump and Erik reach for his gun. "I did the best I could," Melvin said, between sobs. "I tried, I really did." His body grew rigid as his eyes dried and flamed with anger. "It was a land mine. A land mine can do that, blow a guy's head right off. She had a bomb under her dress, and I didn't see it coming. I couldn't do anything."

Jens and Erik exchanged confused glances. "Are you saying Angela was wearing a bomb and it killed her?" Jens asked.

"Whoever killed her. Whatever killed her. They all died that way."

"He's pretending to be crazy," Erik said, "so he won't be blamed."

"I *am* responsible. I should have known, should have stopped it. I should pay, not her. Not her. She was an angel. I gave her back her head, that was the best I could do."

"Oh my god," Erik whispered.

Jens tried to keep his voice even. "Melvin, are you saying you cut off Angela's head?"

"She was perfect, I'd never disfigure her." He reached his hand out to Jens as if pleading for understanding. "I tried to put it back on. Only it got blown up, I couldn't find it, so I had to use the doll's head. My mom's favorite, and just like Angela, so it was the very best I could do."

Erik opened his mouth to speak, but Jens shook his head at him. "Melvin," Jens said kindly, "that was very generous of you. I don't think anyone could have done better."

Melvin looked across at him like a hopeful child.

"Tell me," Jens continued, "why was Angela like the doll?"

Melvin smiled. Another first. "She was a ballet dancer. I saw her in Minneapolis once, dressed in a pink dancing outfit, just like my mom's doll. She was so beautiful and so graceful."

"Where in Minneapolis did you see Angela?"

Melvin lowered his gaze. "On Hennepin Avenue. I was. . . visiting."

That would explain Angela's source of money, Jens thought. She was probably a call girl on the side, maybe specializing in costumed services. Had Melvin's loneliness driven him to seek the same services, as a customer? If so, his religious upbringing might have filled him with enough guilt and confusion to believe he had to kill Angela to save her.

"Where is Angela's body, Melvin?"

"She's home," Melvin said. "I took her back there, tried to clean her scratches and the dirt from the undergrowth. I couldn't find her head, so I put the doll's head on her neck, and I drew her tattoo on the doll's back, so they'd be the same." He sounded calm to the point of insanity.

"I'm sorry, but we'll have to take you in, Melvin."

Melvin held out his wrists for the handcuffs. "I don't care what happens to me."

Klara had always said that Jens did things by hunches more than by the book. It was a hunch that had Jens living on minimal sleep and roaming around town. He'd left Erik in temporary charge of the station and announced he was taking some time off. No one seemed to question his intentions.

Angela Borgina's head hadn't been found, and another foot of snow had been dumped on Loon River since her murder, so no one was looking very hard. The legal wheels were rolling over poor, ruined Melvin, who sat nearly catatonic in his cell. Feeling safe from a psychotic killer, the café buzzed happily with the latest developments in the investigation.

Melvin was quite willing to be punished for Angela's death, but he wouldn't say he'd killed her; that bothered Jens. So Jens left Mutt safe at home and went out each night in his truck. He watched over his town—watched, waited, and mulled. The investigation into Angela's past had revealed some juicy tidbits. She had indeed worked as a call girl for select and well-heeled customers. Their names were never recorded, but a neighbor reported that some visited Angela's apartment on a regular basis. One such gentleman sounded very much like Loon River's esteemed mayor. There was no proof, and Alrik had threatened to sue the entire justice system if his reputation were sullied, but he remained on Jens' mental suspect list.

Vivy had tapped the deepest levels of Loon River gossip and discovered that Thor had been seen pounding on the funeral home door and yelling "slut." The witness was afraid of Thor and hadn't mentioned the incident to anyone until Vivy cajoled it out of her. Several jealous Loon River wives had been heard to express hopes for Angela's tortured death, as well. Jens had been keeping an eye on all of them.

About two weeks after Melvin's arrest, Jens was parked on the south edge of town when a dark sedan, probably a late model Chevrolet, rolled past him into town. Jens knew he'd hit pay dirt when the car slowed to a crawl and turned out its headlights. He waited until the car had almost disappeared before turning on his truck's ignition. Also slowly and without lights, Jens followed the car's brake lights, staying about a block behind. When the car stopped at the woods between the funeral home and Melvin's empty house, Jens parked and followed on foot.

There was no moon that night, but Jens finally sited the figure, bundled in a bulky coat, in an area where a couple of large oaks had fallen years earlier. Holding his revolver in one hand and an unlit flashlight in the other, he watched as the dark figure brushed snow off one high stump, shoveled out layer after layer of dirt, then reached inside and lifted out a round, wrapped object.

"Found what you were looking for?" Jens leveled his gun at the figure, flipped on his flashlight, and pointed it into his eyes. Her eyes, as it turned out. "Hello, Trude. I'd hold real still, if I was you." He edged toward her. She tried to avoid the flashlight by holding her bundle in front of her face. "Put it down, Trude, for god's sake. You'll give yourself nightmares."

Trude seemed to remember what she was holding and quickly put it back in the tree trunk. "Look," she said, "I didn't. . . . I mean, it wasn't me."

"Are you claiming that Alrik killed Angela?"

"Yes."

Jens lowered his gun. "Trude, if Alrik was involved with Angela in Minneapolis and you knew about it, you're the one with the motive. Especially if she moved to Loon River to be with him."

Trude gave her opinion of Jens' theory with a disdainful "Ha! Alrik is so incompetent. I didn't care if he had other women, as long as he was discreet, but the fool had to take up with a prostitute, for heaven's sake. She was paying her way through school—mortuary science, she told him—and he actually felt good about paying her for sex. The idiot. Then to make matters disastrous, he convinced her to come to Loon River and take over the funeral home. He thought of it as an act of charity. It never occurred to him that his sweet Angela would threaten to reveal his secret unless he paid her off, over and over. And do you know what Alrik broke down and cried over? Angela didn't want to sleep with him anymore, once she could get money out of him with blackmail." Trude snorted in derision.

"Mind you," Trude added, "I didn't know any of this until a few days ago when Alrik confessed." Trude released a huge sigh. "He cut off her head, you know, because he thought it would look like a serial killer or something. Even he usually thinks more clearly than that. I told him he was safe as long as everyone thought Melvin was crazy, but he was obsessed with getting rid of that head. I already had to get rid of her car for him, so it would look like she went off to the Twin Cities, like she did every weekend. I knew he'd try to get rid of that damned head and just mess it up, like he always does, so I said I'd do it."

"Were you really going to dispose of Angela's head?"

Trude didn't answer, and Jens tightened his grip on his revolver, just in case. He had one more hunch, and this one was based on knowing Trude for years. Alrik was mayor, but his wife was always the one who ran things. Jens was willing to bet she had a plan.

"What were you going to do, Trude, hide the head in Melvin's backyard? Maybe plant some of Angela's belongings there, too— make it look like Melvin was collecting souvenirs like a serial killer?"

Even in the dark, Jens could see Trude straighten her spine and square her shoulders. "You've got what you wanted," she said. "I'm not answering any more questions without my lawyer."

By dawn, both Alrik and Trude were in custody, and Jens left the details to Erik. The Silence of the Loons Café would have to do without him, too. He intended to sleep and sleep—at least until Mutt woke him up for a walk. It had been a long time since he'd looked forward to being in his own home, and he had a mighty fine dog to thank for it. He could almost believe that Klara had sent Mutt to wait for him at the police station. It would be just like her.

Kerri Miller

Kerri Miller is the host of Mid-Morning on Minnesota Public Radio. She spent 15 years as a television journalist covering politics in the Twin Cities, where she was the principal political reporter for KARE-TV. She lives in Wisconsin with her husband.

Kerri has a degree in English Literature from Saint Bonaventure University in the New York community of the same name. Her first novel, Dead Air, a mystery featuring a hard-working political television reporter, was published in 2002. Miller is currently hard at work on another thriller in the same genre.

Confidential Sources

Kerri Miller

They brought the mattress out at dusk, tipping it on its side to wedge it through the door. I remember hearing one of the crime scene techs curse as his knuckles scraped the doorframe. I knew they'd waited until the sun went down to remove it, hoping the early-winter darkness would conceal the worst of it. But the crimson bruises and deep gouges left by the serrated blade were vivid in the camera lights, as the photographers shot it for the ten o'clock news.

I was standing a few feet away, my mood as acrid as the taste of the cigarette that lingered on my tongue. I wiggled my numb toes, wishing I had on boots instead of my favorite navy blue Keds. But then I hadn't expected to be exiled to the front lawn for twelve hours.

I was on the outside looking in and it ticked me off.

You see, for the last two months, I'd been embedded, like those wartime reporters, but my beat wasn't the battleground. I was on the inside of the city's vaunted homicide division, covering its two brightest stars; a pair of investigators with a case clearance rate that even prompted the mayor to sit up and take notice. The fact that they were women attracted a lot of attention and gave my story a great hook.

But it had been a hard sell. The detectives were wary when I first pitched my idea of a magazine profile. They were still taking some not-so-good-natured flak for the *Cagney & Lacey* angle a local TV reporter had done last spring. I'd finally worn them down with persistent phone calls and a favor I'd called in at the last minute from their lieutenant. He owed me for a couple of puff pieces I'd written when I'd covered the cop beat for the *City Herald*.

In the end, I think it was Detective Westerholt who talked her partner into it. Westerholt was ambitious, had her eye on the chief's job when he retired in a few years and then, perhaps, a run for public office. Val Monroe didn't like the celebrity or the scrutiny that their jobs brought them, but she said later that she gave in because it was what Westerholt wanted.

Our agreement, hashed out over a couple of beers in a downtown bar, gave me a backstage pass to the unit. I'd be there when Monroe and Westerholt caught their cases, when the crimes were fresh and impenetrable. I'd be there when they entered the scene and examined the spatters and prints and debris. I would eavesdrop on interrogations and watch as they joined clues with witnesses to solve the case.

In return, I'd write the kind of sweeping piece you often see after a political campaign, when the reporter has been on the trail for months, observing the candidate and collecting anecdotes for the election post-mortem. They liked the idea of that, especially Westerholt. But they made me promise one thing.

I couldn't publish any of the off-the-record details of their homicide cases until they'd been resolved in court or I'd gotten the okay from the detectives. I readily agreed to that, figuring I'd cross that bridge when I came to it. I just wanted the story.

We toasted our arrangement with a fresh round but I drove home that night thinking it was a good thing the detectives hadn't probed too deeply into my background. Two years before, newly assigned to the courts beat for a national newspaper, I'd written a story about testimony that had been given behind the sealed doors of a grand jury room. When the indictment went south, the infuriated prosecutor threatened me with prison time if I didn't give up my source. I caved. The source went to prison, instead, for leaking confidential information, but I was forced to resign when my boss discovered I'd knuckled under.

In our exit interview, my editor urged me to reflect on what I'd done. Think of the important exposés, he'd said, that would've never been published if some of journalism's greatest reporters had succumbed to intimidation. I'd quickly packed my things and slipped out of the newsroom as he told my colleagues that I was homesick and wanted to return to the city in which I'd grown up.

It had taken me a long time to get back on my feet. I'd saved little money and had returned with few prospects. I was living in a single room in an old Victorian on the north end of the city and avoiding most of my friends, when I finally got my first freelance assignment from a magazine editor who remembered my byline in the national paper. When I pitched her the story on the homicide cops, she said it might make the cover if it was good enough.

So, the morning after our meeting at the bar, I took a seat in the corner of the bullpen, the open area where the homicide squad worked, and began creating a portrait of my two subjects. Joanne Westerholt intrigued me. She was a born-again Christian with a rock-hard faith that resided in one of the most unyielding, compassionless hearts I'd ever encountered. I often heard her murmur at crime scenes, where violence was the consequence of hopelessness or despair, "Well, God doesn't give us what we can't handle."

I realized early on that her stoicism didn't hide a gentle nature steeled against the grotesqueries of the job. She was joyless, in the way the truly pious sometimes are, and implacable. I secretly thought she resembled those grim-faced pioneer women who knew their reward wasn't coming in this life. And it made her a damn good detective.

She didn't prop photos of a murdered child on her desk, as some of the other detectives did. She didn't keep in touch with the victims, as her partner did. She didn't need the motivation. Every case, every perpetrator, got the same unrelenting regard.

I liked Val Monroe better. She was divorced and raising a boy by herself. I'd overheard a couple of cops say that her husband had disappeared when their son was diagnosed with cerebral palsy. I'd also heard she was a recovering alcoholic. She rarely talked about herself but I caught a revealing glimpse of her personality the first time I watched her interrogate a suspect.

He was a young Hispanic man, with shiny black hair and the dead eyes of a glue-sniffer. They'd picked him up on suspicion of smothering his girlfriend's two-year-old. He was denying it, even though he'd been the only adult with the child while the girlfriend had been working her convenience-store job.

I'd expected Monroe to go in hard, like they did on TV, hammering him with the evidence: a neighbor's statement that he'd been screaming at the kid to shut up and a hand print on the child's flesh that matched his own. But she hadn't.

Watching from behind the two-way mirror, I'd jotted notes as Monroe had sat down close to the guy, and flipped picture after picture of the child on the autopsy slab in front of the bastard, like she was dealing cards. When he wouldn't look, she hung them on the grimy walls. When that didn't work, she said, "A couple days ago, while you were still hiding out at your cousin's, I sent this one to your mother." His face had gone still. Monroe nodded. "Yep, sent it all the way down there to San Antone, 'Berto. Overnighted it so I knew she'd get it." She'd leaned back in her chair. "They say she was still holding on to it when the paramedics got there."

While the confession was being typed up, I asked Monroe if the perp's mother had died. She'd shrugged, an odd smile on her lips. I suspected then that it had all been a lie. I'd wish much later that I'd remembered that.

I ground out my last cigarette in the snow and stood on tiptoes, trying to peer past the crime scene tape, and through a small opening in the drawn curtains. A television reporter was practicing his lines for a ten o'clock live shot and I could hear him saying something about the "grisly bloodstains" on the bed. I shoved my hands in my pockets and glared at the front door.

Monroe's cell phone had rung earlier that day as we were having lunch in a Mexican place on the east side. I'd been quizzing her about her short career as a cellist for a small orchestra, thinking about how I'd weave it into my story, when she'd yanked the phone out of her pocket and answered it with a clipped, "Monroe here."

On the way to the scene, Monroe told her partner what she knew as I listened from the backseat, taking jittery notes.

"The perp chased her to her bedroom ... tried to stab her with a butcher's knife right through the mattress. She bled out on the way to the hospital. Guys on the scene say she tried to protect her daughter by telling her to hide ... perp found her and slashed her too."

"The kid make it?" The half of Westerholt's face I could see from the backseat was expressionless, but her hands were wrapped tightly around the steering wheel.

Monroe shrugged. We'd ridden the rest of the way in silence. When we pulled up in front of a three-story Colonial with a dark green door, I'd yanked the press pass I wore on a chain around my neck from beneath my coat and tried to follow the two homicide detectives inside. But the young officer at the door put an arm across the entranceway saying, "Sorry. Chief says no press inside."

"We have an agreement. Check with the chief." I could see Monroe and Westerholt being briefed in the foyer of the house by another detective. They hadn't noticed I'd been stopped.

The officer shifted and his gun holster creaked in the cold. "Chief says you don't come in on this one. Everyone has to wait behind the tape."

It didn't take me long to figure out why. A curious neighbor who'd come out of her house to watch the goings-on told me that the victim was the estranged wife of Congressman Mitch Reilly's eldest son. The two had separated, very publicly, last summer, and she'd moved in to the neighborhood a few months later. The neighbor said she was a pleasant woman who kept to herself. Neighbors always said that to reporters, even if the guy next door was a serial killer.

"Ever see the ex-husband around," I asked, lighting a cigarette with a cheap Bic Monroe had lent me. I'd quit smoking right after college—and started again the day I'd gone to the coroner's lab with them to watch an autopsy and couldn't get the smell out of the back of my throat.

"Just once." The neighbor narrowed her eyes and stared pointedly at my cigarette. I held it against my thigh. Swirls of smoke slid under the hem of my coat. "Someone said he joined the Peace Corps or something. Mighta' been what caused the divorce."

She'd eventually drifted back to her house and I'd been joined in the front yard by the rest of the media rabble. I'd chatted with some old pals, being purposefully vague about my move back to town and my current assignment, and listened in as two blonde television reporters complained about not getting enough face time on the news. At one point, I'd heard a grizzled photographer close a deal on his cell phone with someone who wanted to buy a couple of guns he had for sale. I wondered if his boss knew about his side job.

Fifteen minutes after the late newscast was over, the television crews were gone and the newspaper reporters were back in their bureaus filing their stories for tomorrow's editions. I waved them off and returned to my vigil. My feet felt clunky, like they were encased in blocks of ice and I'd been using my sleeve for a persistent post-nasal drip. But I wasn't leaving. I had to get inside.

At ten minutes after midnight, Westerholt finally shouted from the front door, "Lucy! Come on in." She was silhouetted in amber light from the hallway. As I stepped onto the porch steps, I spotted the imprints of someone's shoes in the thin crust of snow just below the large bay window. One of the techs had used bright spray paint to draw a circle around them. They looked like they could've been size sevens, my size, perhaps just a little bigger.

I made a mental note of it and entered the house, shivering from the sudden warmth. All of the lights were on and a cluster of crime scene technicians and police officers stood talking in a small room off the foyer.

Westerholt said, "I brought you in 'cause a deal's a deal." She gave me a quick grin. "And I was feeling kind of sorry for you."

And because this could be a career-making case and you want it all in the story, I thought. I blinked in the bright light of the chandelier suspended over our heads and brought my pad out of my pocket. "Thanks."

"As long as you remember the terms of our agreement. Nothing off-the-record gets written until and unless we say it's okay. When we catch the bad guy we don't want anything going wrong."

I nodded, unbuttoning my coat and removing my gloves, the ones with the fingertips cut off to make it easier to write. "Who found the bodies?"

"House painter hired to paint the living room. Says the front door was open and he finally went in when no one answered the doorbell."

"He a suspect?"

She gave me a sideways look. "Follow me and watch where you walk."

I trailed her down the hall and past the cluster of techs and officers. She called out, "She's with me." I saw one of them shake his head and give me a hard stare before going back to the conversation.

We entered the kitchen, a spacious room with granite countertops and a stainless steel refrigerator. I could see smudges of fingerprint dust everywhere. Westerholt pointed to an open drawer. "We think that's where the murder weapon came from." I jotted that down. "What kind of a knife was it?"

She frowned. "I think Monroe said it was made in Japan. Maximum…Maxam… yeah, that's it. Maxam Steel. It was serrated and had a notch on the topside of the blade."

That was the kind of detail prosecutors loved to tell juries.

"Where'd you find it?"

"Upstairs, In the kid's room. The handle was clean. No fingerprints."

I glanced up but she'd turned away and was heading back down the hall. Did that mean the killer had worn gloves or had wiped his prints off before leaving? Why hadn't he taken it with him?

We went up a wide staircase and I was careful not to touch either of the banisters. At the top of the stairs we turned right and after a short distance came to what I guessed was the mother's room. We stood in the doorway and Westerholt said, "This is where the perp cornered her and cut her a few times before she tried to slide in between the mattress and the box spring. She must've thought the padding would protect her," Westerholt said, shrugging, clearly puzzled by the victim's actions. "The killer tried to stab her through it but when the knife wouldn't penetrate the mattress, the suspect shoved it aside and stabbed her again. We think the victim slipped away but the killer caught her and threw her back on the mattress, where she was stabbed again and died."

Several large splashes of eggplant-dark blood stained the naked surface of the box spring and I sketched them quickly in my notepad. I'd been doing sketches like this since I'd covered my first crime scene. It brought the details back more keenly when I sat down to write the story. Once an editor had used a couple of sketches to accompany my story, but mostly they were there to jog my memory. I had old notebooks full of sketches I'd never need but hadn't discarded.

I let my gaze travel around the disheveled room, drawing and jotting notes on what I observed. Just as juries liked the odd or bizarre item in the narrative of a crime, so too did readers. I saw a book about meditation open to page 133 on the nightstand and a compact disc sitting atop a portable player. The CD case had a scene of a lake on the cover with a bird rising out of the water. The title was *Silence of the Loons*. I wondered if the victim had had trouble sleeping.

I scanned the room again and noticed the jumble of debris atop the victim's vanity, cosmetics and silver-backed brushes, hair clips and combs, and a large glass bottle of Obsession perfume lying on its side, the amber liquid quivering as Detective Monroe walked into the room. She was carrying a large plastic bag with something pink inside. She looked exhausted, her eyes rimmed red and bloodshot.

She glanced at me and said, "Hey, Lucy. Pretty cold out there, huh?" I nodded, more interested in what she was holding than in small talk. "What's that?" "Evidence." She turned to her partner, holding the bag up. "Victim's sister says she'd hung onto her ballet slippers all this time. Souvenirs from her years as a dancer with the Houston Ballet."

As I looked more closely, I could see the pink satin material of the slipper, slightly soiled where it was drawn to the sole, and the small pink bow on top. I pointed at the bag with my pencil. "Was the victim wearing that when she was attacked?"

Westerholt and Monroe exchanged glances. Monroe tipped her head as if to say, you tell her. Westerholt studied my face, her eyes hard. "Not the victim," she said, finally. "The suspect." She stilled, watching me.

I blinked. "The suspect was wearing pink ballet slippers when he killed her?"

They said nothing, waiting as a teacher would for a pupil to solve a complicated math problem. I stared at the bag. And then I understood. I looked between them. "The suspect is a woman? A woman tried to stab her through the mattress and went after the child?"

I let the sequence of what had happened in this house run through my head but this time the knife-wielding pursuer was female, the kidskin soles on the slippers silent as she chased the victim up the stairs and cornered her in the bedroom. "Do you know who it is?"

"Remember this is all off—"

I held up my hand. "I remember."

Monroe spoke up. "We think it's the kid's former nanny. We're told by some of the family members that she's the reason the Reillys were getting a divorce."

"The nanny? Why—" I stared at Monroe and she gave an awkward shrug, as if to cut off any speculation about a motive. I swallowed, my mouth suddenly dry. "A neighbor told me that the husband went into the Peace Corps."

Westerholt nodded. "We haven't confirmed it yet but his father says he was sent to Sri Lanka. We're trying to reach him."

"So you think the nanny and the Congressman's son were having an affair?"

Westerholt turned to Monroe, who said, "Not sure. We're still putting it together."

I gestured to the slipper. "Where'd you find it?"

Monroe said, "Under the little girl's bed. We think it came off as she chased the child around the room."

I swallowed. "Why would the nanny have been wearing Mrs. Reilly's ballet slippers?"

Westerholt sighed. "There's evidence that she spent quite a bit of time in the house before Mrs. Reilly and her daughter came home. We think she may've come in through the back door, which wasn't locked, right after Mrs. Reilly took her daughter to school. It appears that the daughter had a doctor's appointment around 10:45 and they were back home by noon. We think the suspect was hiding in the house somewhere when they came back."

"Do you know what the nanny was doing while she was alone in the house?"

Monroe glanced down at her notes. "Looks like everything from watching videos to hanging out in Mrs. Reilly's bedroom."

I imagined the woman trying on her former employer's clothes, spraying perfume on her throat, perhaps making herself a snack in the kitchen while she waited. I remembered the fingerprint dust. "So you found her prints in the kitchen? Even though the knife was clean."

Westerholt said, "There are a lot of different prints in the kitchen. The techs are working on that."

Monroe cut in, "The victim's sister said the nanny had brought a birthday present over for the little girl a couple of weeks ago, so her fingerprints may have already been in the house."

I made a few notes. "Can I see the little girl's room?"

Another silent exchange and then Monroe motioned for me to follow her. Westerholt said she'd meet us in a few minutes by the front door.

The child's room was painted a sunny yellow with pale blue clouds floating across the ceiling. Stuffed animals lay on the floor as if they'd been pulled off of the shelves and I noticed a yellow-painted nightstand had been upended and was tipped on its face. The closet door stood ajar, crime tape strung across the opening. As I walked toward it I said, "This is where the little girl was hiding?"

Monroe replied, "Unh huh."

I peered in and drew back immediately. There was a headless Barbie doll on the floor, its torso clad in a green frothy dress. I imagined the terror-stricken child cowering in the dark as she heard the screams and violent sounds coming from her mother's room down the hall. Maybe she'd scrabbled around the floor of the closet, discovering, and then clutching the discarded toy. Maybe she was holding it when the door was flung open as the nanny found her hidey-hole.

I straightened, feeling light-headed for a moment, and forced myself to make a quick sketch. Monroe was watching me and I said, "Just want to get it right when I finally write about it."

She nodded and then looked at her watch.

"One more minute," I said.

I circled the room, on the lookout for any telling details. I peered into the attached bathroom to find more painted clouds and a gaggle of rubber toys perched on the edge of the bathtub. Monroe followed me and I wondered if the wide-eyed ducks and teddy-bear soap reminded her of home.

I lingered for a moment, aware that something seemed out of place, but I couldn't see what it was. There was no sign of any violence in the small room, just a pink brush and a hand mirror on the counter, a small blue bathrobe hanging on a hook on the back of the door, and a four-by-six photograph of the little girl with her mother taped to the mirror over the sink.

I studied the faces in the picture. The child appeared to be around seven years old in the photo, her dark hair held back by pink barrettes, her smile a bit tentative as if the photographer had had to coax her. Mrs. Reilly was petite and pretty, with a light brown pageboy and a shy gaze. She was holding her daughter's hand tightly.

I drew a quick sketch, detailing the placement of the sink, tub and toilet. I drew the bathrobe and rubber toys and even the photograph on the mirror. I checked the sketch several times against the scene, unsure why I had the feeling that something was wrong.

"We've gotta get back downtown to write up our reports, Luce. Anything else you want to see?"

I hesitated. "Something is..." I scanned the bathroom again and finally shrugged, unable to articulate what I meant. She switched off the bathroom light and I followed her down the stairs, where we found Westerholt waiting. As we pulled out of the driveway, Monroe's phone rang. She spoke for less than a minute and shut it off. Staring straight ahead through the windshield she said, "The kid died an hour ago."

They brought the nanny in for questioning just after dawn. I was struck instantly by the close resemblance she bore to the deceased Mrs. Reilly. Standing behind the two-way glass that looked into the interrogation room, I noted the smooth bell of brunette hair, the wide dark eyes, the petite frame. I also made a note of the crease that a bunched-up pillowcase had left on her cheek. She'd apparently been sleeping soundly when officers had pounded on her apartment door.

Westerholt established the date, time of day and names of the people in the room for the tape. She verified that the former nanny had waived counsel and then she began.

"Ms, Verrett, where were you yesterday morning between seven and noon?"

"What is this about? Is my brother in some kind of trouble again?"

"Could you just tell us where you were?"

Her delicate brows drew together, "I was in my apartment studying for an exam I have next Tuesday." She smiled tentatively. "I'm training to become a dental hygienist."

"Did you see anyone, talk to anyone?"

She thought for a moment. "No. I had breakfast and then studied for the next several hours. I showered and left for my class around 1:30."

She was blinking rapidly and I could see that she was beginning to realize there was nothing casual about being awakened before dawn to be questioned by the police. I wondered what they'd told her at her front door.

Westerholt said, "Ms. Verrett, how long did your affair with Carlton Reilly go on?"

She drew back, recoiling as her wide gaze skittered around the room. Her lips were parted and she was breathing through her mouth. "I..,we...what's happened to Carl?"

"Please answer the question, Ms. Verrett."

She put a slender hand to her forehead. "We had a—relationship for more than a year. It ended last spring."

"When Abigail Reilly found out what was going on? Is that right?"

"Why are you asking me these things? Where is Carl?"

Westerholt ignored her. "And you were angry about what happened afterwards, weren't you? You thought that Mr. Reilly was going to divorce his wife and marry you, correct?"

Westerholt had moved out of her chair and was perched on the corner of the table, looking down at Candace Verrett. Monroe was writing something on a yellow legal pad.

The ex-nanny shifted in her chair, a hand cupped against her temple as if she was in pain. "He said he wanted to be free of her. That we could be together... and since Mary Elizabeth liked me so much, we could be a family."

"The little girl was quite fond of you, wasn't she?"

"She's a wonderful child."

I made a note of the present tense.

"What did you think Carlton Reilly meant when he said he wanted to 'be free' of his wife?"

She went still, her head tipping backwards, her face tilted up to Westerholt's expressionless gaze. It would've made a terrific photograph that needed no caption. I tried to make a swift drawing of it but couldn't quite capture the guarded look on Candace Verrett's face. She rose from her chair and said, "What's going on here? Is Abby hurt? Did something happen to Mary? Tell me!"

"Please sit down, Candace." It was the first time Monroe had spoken. She opened a large brown envelope and pushed a packet of folded letters toward the trembling woman. "Mr. Reilly has been writing to you since he joined the Peace Corps, hasn't he?"

"Where did you get those?" She reached out for the letters but Monroe kept them just out of reach. "You've been in my apartment?"

Westerholt slid a paper in front of her. "We obtained a warrant from a judge to search your apartment, Ms. Verrett."

"Why? Why would you go into my apartment? What have I done?"

"Please just answer the question, Ms. Verrett."

She licked her lips and glanced between the two detectives. "Yes, Carl has been writing to me. So what?"

She was showing the spark of defiance I'd seen when the people being questioned realized the cops had more cards up their sleeves.

"So this." Monroe opened a letter and scooted it across the table. Candace Verrett caught it and held it in a shaking hand. "The middle of the letter."

She read it to herself, and from behind the glass, I could see her mouth soften.

Monroe said, "Doesn't Mr. Reilly tell you in that letter that you must stop worrying about how badly his wife treated him and their daughter? That you must be patient and—quote unquote—not do anything rash. Isn't that what it says, Candace?"

She held the paper against her breast, her face flushed. "Abigail Reilly was cruel and petty and selfish. That's why he was divorcing her. Everyone knew it."

Westerholt interrupted and I realized they were engaged in the classic good cop-bad cop interrogation but that they were switching roles to confuse her. "I thought she kicked him out because she discovered your affair."

"But he was getting ready to split up with her. He-he hated her."

"You hated her! Isn't that right?" Monroe threw another letter on the table, this one written on ivory vellum stationery. "That's what you said in this letter you were writing to Carl. 'I've hated her from the very beginning.' That's what you wrote, Candace." Hot color flooded the other woman's face. "You read my letter? How dare you!" Westerholt reached under the table and drew out the bag with the ballet slipper in it.

She slid it to the center of the table. "You stole Abby Reilly's ballet slippers, didn't you?

We found one of them in your apartment."

The former nanny stared at the bag, her face draining of color. "I-I..."

"Ms. Verrett, I want you to hear something." Westerholt nodded and Monroe put a small tape recorder on the table and pressed play. A man's voice, strained and distant, came out of the small speaker. I pressed against the two-way mirror to catch all of the words.

"I knew that she was obsessed with Abby. She asked me to buy her the same scarves and jewelry that I'd given my wife. She even talked about doing... harm to my wife."

Candace Verrett started, the sensitive microphone in the room picking up her drawn in breath. "Carlton?" she whispered, sliding one outstretched arm, the palms turned outward, toward the whirring recorder. I was stunned that they'd tracked Carlton Reilly down so quickly.

The voice on the tape continued, "I warned her not to act too hastily," there was a harsh sob and a moment of silence, and then, "but I'm afraid she's done something irrevocable."

Monroe clicked the recorder off and, with a swift gesture, handed her partner a large piece of paper. When Westerholt slapped it down in front of Candace Verrett, she screamed, "Oh no! Oh, please, no!" and covered her eyes. When I saw what it was, I had to put a hand to the glass to steady myself.

An 8-by-10 photograph of a young girl's face, her skin waxen, framed by wispy dark hair, her upper chest a mass of blood. Candace Verrett sobbed, "Oh my God!"

Monroe leaned forward, her fingers resting lightly on the picture. "Just tell us how it happened, Candace. I know you cared for Mary and you'd want her to rest in peace."

But Candace Verrett bent over and vomited so violently the liquid streamed across the table, covering the photograph, and dripping to the floor. The two detectives leapt away, Monroe uttering a muffled curse. Candace Verrett's eyes were squeezed tightly shut and she was trembling as if in the grip of hypothermia.

Monroe opened the door and called out for some paper towels and disinfectant. When she closed the door again, she said, "Candace Verrett, I am placing you under arrest for the murders of Abigail and Mary Elizabeth Reilly. You have the right..." The rest of her words were drowned out by the ear-splitting screams of their prime suspect.

My account of how a nanny plotted to kill the estranged wife of her former lover and the child she'd once cared for, made the cover of the magazine and turned Westerholt and Monroe into media stars. The story was chock full of exclusives. I'd written of the bloodstained box spring and the tattered ballet slipper, discovered at the scene of the crime; I'd lifted passages from the letters that Carlton Reilly had written to his mistress, pleas that she wait for him and passionate assertions that he still loved her.

And I described, in the kind of vivid detail known only to someone who was there, what Candace Verrett had said and done when presented with the consequences of her actions.

Westerholt and Monroe gave their benediction to all of it because, forty-eight hours after that pre-dawn interrogation, the case was solved and closed.

Sometime after midnight on the night following her arrest, Candace Verrett awakened in the jail infirmary, and using the edge of a plastic spoon, scored her thin wrists over and over, until she finally broke through the skin and opened a vein. She'd lost so much blood that she'd slipped into a coma before anyone found her. She'd died the next day.

My editor was ecstatic. I had the inside track on one of the biggest news stories of the year. I was urged to do television interviews about the case, but I deferred to Monroe and Westerholt, who were persuaded to sit down with Matt Lauer for a Dateline Exclusive. Nevertheless, my phone began to ring with offers.

I ended up taking a couple of them but a friend had suggested an intriguing idea. Why not do what so many other journalists had done when they possessed an exclusive and write a book. Really delve into Candace Verrett's background. Find out why Abby Reilly had kept her ballet slippers all these years. Perhaps Carlton Reilly would be ready to talk about the tragedy. I pitched the idea to an agent, who sold it to a respected publishing house.

As I began my research, I decided I needed one last visit to the Reilly home before it was sold. I prevailed on Val Monroe, recently promoted to lieutenant, to open the house up for me. She put me off several times but finally agreed. Joanne Westerholt was in California, the new deputy chief in San Francisco, but Monroe said her former partner had her eye on a job with Homeland Security in Washington.

We were in the midst of a late-winter thaw the day I returned to the house. I'd arranged to meet Monroe there at noon but when I pulled up I saw a young man in uniform standing on the porch. I got out of the car and he walked across the soggy lawn to meet me. "The lieutenant couldn't make it. She said she had a family emergency."

I wondered if something had happened to her son. We stepped up on the shallow porch and he broke the tape that still sealed the front door. "I have a package for you in the car when we're finished."

I noticed the sour smell as we stood in the foyer, like a clothes hamper that hasn't been opened in a while. I knew Congressman

Reilly had had the house sealed since the night of the murders, afraid that if he put it on the market it would only attract voyeurs.

The officer looked around, glancing up at the dusty chandelier. I remembered its brilliance that night, as clusters of cops conferred in lowered voices, one of them shaking his head when he saw me.

We followed the same path I had that night—except I was leading this time—down the hall to the kitchen, where I noticed the smudges still on the surface of the stainless steel refrigerator. The drawer that had held the murder weapon was still open. There was mud on the tiled floor.

I consulted the notes I'd made that night and added a few more. "I think I'm ready to go upstairs."

We walked back down the hall and ascended the wide staircase, pausing halfway up so that I could get a birds-eye view. We turned right at the top and walked down a short corridor before entering Abigail Reilly's bedroom. The officer lingered in the doorway as I stood in the center of the room.

The bloodstained box spring had been removed but that was all. The perfume bottle of Obsession still lay on its side on the vanity and I remembered seeing the cream-colored towel that was draped across a chaise in the corner. A bizarre thought crossed my mind when my gaze fell on Abigail's silver hand mirror. If I wiped off the dust and peered into the glass, would I see images of the violence that had occurred in this room?

The patrolman cleared his throat and glanced at his watch, exactly as Westerholt had done on that night three-and-a-half months ago. I looked around again and then nodded, going back out into the hallway. We walked past the stairs and went into the child's room.

A broad cone of winter sunlight splashed the bed, brightening the yellow daisies on the quilt. I looked around, pencil poised over my pad, remembering the unease I'd felt here that night. Had it just been the thought of the little girl cowering in the closet with that broken toy?

I opened my sketches and notes from that night. Nothing looked as if it had been moved. At the bottom of one of the pages, I'd described the bath toys and teddy bear soap in the child's bathroom and on the next page was the sketch I'd drawn. The young officer retreated to the doorway as I crossed the room and pushed the bathroom door open, pausing in the doorway. He cleared his throat.

I murmured, "This will just take a minute." I looked around, recalling the sensation I'd had that night that something was out of place. I studied the sketch I'd made.

And that's when I saw it.

I'd drawn the toilet seat up, the way a man would use a commode. That's why it had nagged at me. Why would the seat be raised in a little girl's bathroom? Females just didn't do that. How many times had I fumbled my way to the bathroom in the dark in the old house I'd shared with a male college friend only to plop down on icy porcelain because he hadn't put the seat down?

Now it was down, but I'd bet my entire book advance that the crime scene video I'd requested from the department would show the toilet the way I'd drawn it that night. With the seat up.

I felt an almost percussive wave of realization, as if the barometer had dropped suddenly. If I were right, it would mean that a man could've killed Abigail and Mary Reilly. That the focus on the nanny was wrong from the very beginning. And that someone had figured it out and come back to tamper with the crime scene.

"Are you all right, Miss?"

I turned to the young officer, blinking as if I'd been staring at the sun. I cleared my throat. "Did you say that lieutenant Monroe gave you a package for me?"

"Yes, ma'am. It's in the car."

"Would you mind going to get it?"

He frowned, clearly reluctant to leave me alone in the house.

"And if you have any water in the car, I'd appreciate it. I'm feeling a bit dizzy."

He nodded and I heard him taking the stairs two at a time. I sank down on the daisy quilt and stared at the sketch I'd drawn that night. If the murderer wasn't Candace Verrett, then who had killed Abby Reilly and her daughter?

By the time the officer returned with the package and a bottle of water I'd begun to figure it out. I sipped the water and opened the large envelope, drawing out the videotape of the crime scene I'd requested along with a slim stack of papers. I set the tape aside and spread the papers on the bed.

The first sheet was a lab analysis of someone's DNA. The sample, the report said, was urine that had been collected from the underside of a toilet seat during a homicide investigation. I flipped to the next paper. It was a rap sheet, detailing prior arrests and convictions for burglary, possession of child pornography and one count of child molestation. The name at the top was Bradley Thomas Anderson.

The sheet beneath that one was a photocopy of a newspaper clipping. It was a brief account of how one Bradley Anderson had fallen from a ladder last Monday while patching and painting a wall inside the city's ornate cathedral. He'd been dead on arrival at the hospital. He was survived, the clipping said, by one sister.

My fingers trembled as I put the cap back on the water and set it down on the carpet. The officer was watching me, his hands propped on his gun belt, his expression curious. "Feeling better?"

I nodded and gathered the papers together to slide them back into the envelope. But they jarred against something hard at the bottom. When I tipped the envelope over, Valerie Monroe's badge and police identification fell out.

I drew a deep breath, turning the metal badge over in my hand and remembering Monroe at her desk in the bullpen, talking to someone on the phone, as she reached out to straighten a framed photograph of her son. I recalled her colleagues saying her boy needed help with even the most intimate of tasks.

I wondered how long she'd known. And where she'd gone. And what she'd been thinking that morning as she'd slipped into the chill dusk of the church and waited for just the right moment.

David Housewright

Born, raised and educated in St. Paul, Minnesota, David House-
*wright is a reformed newspaper reporter (*Minneapolis Tribune,
Albert Lea Evening Tribune, Grand Forks Herald*) and ad*
man (his client list includes Federal Express, Miller Beer, Hormel
Foods and Chilly Willie Frozen Soft Drink). His novel Pen-
ance *earned the 1996 Edgar Award for Best First Novel from the*
Mystery Writers of America as well as a Shamus nomination from
the Private Eye Writers of America. Practice to Deceive *won the*
1998 Minnesota Book Award. His other novels include Dearly
Departed, A Hard Ticket Home, *and* Tin City.

Housewright's short stories have appeared in publications
as diverse as Ellery Queen's Mystery Magazine *and* True
Romance. *He has taught novel-writing courses at the University*
of Minnesota and Loft Literary Center in Minneapolis and was
chairman of the committees that awarded the 1999 Edgar Award
for Best Paperback Original and the 2002 Shamus Award for
best First Private Eye Novel. He currently lives in St. Paul with
his wife, the poet and theater critic Renee Valois, and his son and
daughter.

A Domestic Matter

David Housewright

I answered the phone at my desk in the city room of the *Minneapolis Star Tribune*.

"I'm in trouble," Jack said. He didn't bother to say "hello," or to identify himself, but then it wasn't necessary. We grew up together, went to school together, played on the same hockey teams since we were pee wees—it might have been a month since I spoke to him last, yet he could've just stepped outside for a smoke for all the difference it made.

"What now?" I said.

"My wife wants to kill me."

"Tell her if she needs any help to give me a call."

"I mean it, Danny…" He was one of the few people who still called me that. To everyone else I was Dan or Daniel or Thorn or to the occasional bartender, Mr. Thorn. "She wants me dead."

"Why should she be any different than the rest of us?"

"Dammit, Danny, I'm not kidding. Do I sound like I'm kidding? Tess is going to kill me."

"Why?"

"Because she found out I've been cheating on her."

"Oops."

"She found out and now she's, she's—you can tell just by looking at her that she wants to rip my heart out."

"Jeezuz, Jack. You've been married for fifteen years. How did you think she'd feel?"

"You know the way she's been. When you came up for the holidays, Tess could barely stand to be in the same room with either of us, always finding an excuse to be somewhere else."

"Don't remind me."

"Well, nothing's changed. We don't talk, we don't have sex—the love is gone, Danny."

"And you decided to cheat on her."

"I didn't decide to cheat. It's just—I met this girl. This woman. I was jogging and she was jogging and how many people do you know up here in Fertile, Minnesota who go jogging? Especially in the winter."

"You're the last of a dying breed."

"We don't even have sex that often. Mostly we just talk. We talk about everything. We talk about the things that Tess and I used to talk about."

"I'm sure that's a lot of comfort to your wife."

"She wants to kill me."

"Hell, Jack. I want to kill you."

"Danny, you're not listening. Tess took out a half-million-dollar insurance policy on my life without telling me. She gets another $150,000 if I'm murdered."

"Are you serious?"

"Hell yes, I'm serious. What do you think I've been trying to tell you?"

I pulled out a tan-covered Reporter's Notebook. This wasn't a story I intended to write, but I had learned long ago—take lots of notes.

"Tell me everything, Jack. From the beginning."

★ ★ ★ ★

Three days and a lot of frantic long distance calls later, I was in Fertile, Minnesota, population 887, home of the Fertile-Beltrami Falcons. You can find it about 275 miles northwest of the Twin Cities on Highway 32, which came as a surprise to me. Until a couple of years ago, I didn't know you could take Highway 32 to the ends of the earth. I learned different when I helped Jack and Tess move. She was a hospital administrator at Bridges Medical, a 49-bed facility just down the road in Ada, where they needed someone to run the place. He was a day-trader and figured he could earn a living anywhere he could plug in his PC.

It was late March. Light snow had just begun to fall when I pulled off the main drag and parked in front of Eats 'N' Antiques on Mill Street. I told the woman who ran the place that instead of the curios she displayed in her glass counters, I had come for a cup of joe and a slice of blueberry pie which my good friend Jack Edelson said was the very best in Minnesota.

The woman actually blushed, something you don't often see these days, and said, "That Mr. Edelson."

She served my coffee at a window table, but I told her I'd hold off on the pie until Jack arrived. The woman glanced at the electric clock on the wall. It was quarter-to-ten, about the time Jack usually came in for his daily fix. Fifteen minutes later she refilled my coffee mug and said, "I don't know where that boy could be." At 10:15 she served me a slice of pie that made me question Jack's taste and a third cup of coffee. By 10:30 the woman was pacing. You might have thought she was Jack's worried mother. I was starting to become anxious myself.

At 10:40 I said, "I bet Jack is at home waiting for me. Maybe he thought we'd meet there and then go out for pie."

The woman looked at me like I had just tracked mud into her kitchen.

"Don't you think you should find out?" she told me.

Snow continued to fall but it was nearly 35 degrees and the flakes melted on contact with my windshield as I drove west on Summit Avenue. I had my wipers going but they couldn't do anything about the hard gray sky or the dark, dreary woods. Jack and Tess had a place overlooking the Sand Hill River. To reach it I had to turn off the blacktop and follow a sand and gravel driveway that meandered nearly a quarter mile through the forest—Tess would rather go around a tree than cut it down. At the end of the driveway I found all the bright lights I could want—red, blue and white. They flickered silently from the bars on top of the Polk County Sheriff Department cruisers that blocked my way. I counted them—one, two, three. I had been a reporter long enough to know that three cop cars meant serious trouble.

I parked my car and dashed the rest of the way to the house, slipping and sliding in the melting snow, but not falling. The garage door was open and Jack's SUV and Tess' Audi were parked inside—Jack's golf clubs were leaning against the wall. I could have reached the back door through the garage, but went to the front instead. I pounded on the door. A deputy opened it like it was a great inconvenience to him.

"Who are you?" he wanted to know. His nametag read B. Hermundson.

"Danny?" Tess was sitting on a sofa beyond him next to a female deputy. "Danny," she called again.

I brushed past the deputy as Tess left the sofa and rushed straight into my arms. "Oh. Danny," she moaned, her face pressed hard against my chest. I embraced her even as a deputy with chevrons on his sleeve shook his head—a message to Deputy Hermundson at the door I guessed.

"Tess, what's happened?" I said. "Where's Jack?"

"I don't know. Last night... He... Danny, Jack has disappeared."

She felt my body tense, felt my arms release her shoulders. Her eyes found mine.

"Danny?"

"What do you mean, 'Jack has disappeared.'"

"He wasn't here when I came home last night. I haven't seen him since I went to work Monday morning."

I stepped away from her, moving backward until I bumped into the deputy.

"Tess, what did you do?"

"What do you mean?"

"Sir." The sergeant slid past Tess. "Sir, could you identify yourself."

"Daniel Thorn. I'm a reporter with the *Minneapolis Star Tribune.*"

"Why are you here, sir?"

"Jack Edelson is my friend. My best friend. He asked me to meet him at ten this morning at the Eats 'N' Antiques. I came here when he didn't show."

"Why did he want to meet you?"

"He was afraid."

"Afraid of what?"

"He said his wife was plotting to kill him."

"What?" Tess moved between the sergeant and myself. "What did you say?"

"Jack said you were plotting to kill him because you discovered he was having an affair. He said you took out a half-million-dollar life insurance policy on him."

I didn't think it was possible for a woman to hit a man as hard as Tess hit me. She caught me just to the left of the point of my chin and snapped my head back so violently I thought my neck was broken. I left my feet and flew against the door—I would have fallen if the Deputy Hermundson hadn't braced me by the shoulders.

The sergeant didn't seem to mind. He gently guided Tess by the elbow back to the sofa.

"Is it true, Mrs. Edelson, what your friend says?" the sergeant asked.

"He's not my friend. And of course it's not true. I would never hurt my husband. Never. You have to…"

The sergeant squatted next to Tess and patted her knee. "It's okay," he said. He glanced over his shoulder at me.

"I only know what Jack told me," I said.

"Mrs. Edelson, is your husband having an affair?" The sergeant asked the question with as much sympathy as he could muster. It sounded like a slap in the face just the same.

"Absolutely not. How dare you?" Tess glared at me. "Jack loves me."

"Mrs. Edelson…"

"He does."

"Mrs. Edelson, I need you to do something for me. A favor. I need you to go upstairs and go through your husband's belongings. His razor. His toothbrush. Clothes he might wear. A suitcase he might pack. I need to know…"

"This is ridiculous."

"When you called, you said your husband might have been

kidnapped. That's why we dispatched three units. I need to be sure that he didn't leave of his own free will before we investigate further."

Tess glared at me some more. She leaped so quickly to her feet that the sergeant fell backwards. "Fine," she said and rushed upstairs. The sergeant and I followed.

Tess went first to the bathroom where she opened and slammed a cabinet door and threw a toothbrush cup that shattered in her bathtub. She went to a bureau in her bedroom, opened one drawer, then the next, then the next; starting at the bottom and working upward like a burglar. Finally, she yanked open a closet door, rifled the jackets and slacks and dress shirts hanging inside and kicked something on the floor.

"It's true," she said. She closed the closet door and rested her forehead against it. "Oh God, it's true. My husband left me."

Tess slowly sank into a puddle on the floor, her voice singing an aria of anguish and pain that the sergeant couldn't silence with all the "there, theres" in the world.

All in all, I thought it was a fine job of acting.

It took awhile before Tess was calm enough to answer questions. She was again sitting on her sofa surrounded by the deputies. The female deputy—her nametag read C. Moore—kept repeating "It'll be all right." I don't think she believed it.

"Who was Jack having an affair with?" I asked. I already knew the answer, but I wanted her to say it.

"Leave me alone, Danny, can't you?"

"No, I can't. Who was he having an affair with?"

"That's enough, buddy," said the sergeant.

"You're thinking Jack ran off with his girl," I told the sergeant. "You think this is just a domestic matter and the police shouldn't be involved. If that's true, then why is Jack's SUV parked inside the garage?"

From the expression on his face, the sergeant thought that was a good question.

"Mrs. Edelson, I need to know," he said. "Who was Mr. Edelson involved with?"

Tess stared at him for a long time while her face registered the five steps of the grieving process from denial to acceptance. Finally, she exhaled slowly and said, "Jodi Bakken."

Tess spoke the name so softly I could barely hear it. The sergeant heard just fine. He stood straight and crossed his arms over his chest, a classic defensive posture.

"Who?" asked the sergeant.

"Jodi Bakken, all right?" Tess answered, choking out the words. I had the distinct impression that she would have been a lot happier if Jack had been kidnapped.

"Are you sure?" he wanted to know.

Tess nodded.

"Do you know her?" I asked the sergeant.

"She's married to one of our deputies."

I followed the sergeant outside; told him I wanted to be there when he interviewed Jodi Bakken. He didn't like the idea and I had to give him the old indignant reporter routine—"What do you have to hide?" A Twin Cities cop probably would have blown me off. The sergeant didn't have much experience with the press and I convinced him that terrible things would happen if he left me out of the loop. Finally, he agreed, only he told me I had to take my own car. "I ain't running no taxi service for muckrakers," he said. Before we left I made him tell me about Deputy Bakken.

"Professionally, he's very good at his job," the sergeant said. "He's one of the few deputies we have who's willing to do knock and talks."

"Knock and talks?"

"About 75 percent of Minnesota's meth labs are outstate. People cook their crank out here because it's easier to get farm fertilizer and other ingredients, because distant neighbors are less likely to smell the odor, and because there are plenty of places to dump the waste—a pound of crank yields about seven-eight pounds of hazardous waste. The problem is so big and there are so few of us—a dozen patrol officers and one investigator—that whenever we hear about a lab, we'll do a knock and talk. We'll show up at the suspect's door and warn them to shut down, leave or prepare to be arrested. It usually works. These people are so paranoid, it's easy to drive them out."

"Deputy Bakken is good at these knocks and talks?" I asked.

"He's fearless. See, these people, these meth users, they're unpredictable and completely dangerous. Yeah, you can drive a lot of them out with a stern lecture. The rest—their aggression is far above and beyond any other drug users. There are more guns, more explosives, more violence. Most of us don't want to deal with them. Deputy Bakken, he just goes up there and does his thing. Mostly he goes alone."

"Alone?"

"I know what you're thinking. Maybe Bakken says and does things that maybe he shouldn't. But because of him we have control of our meth problem. There are still dealers our here, still labs, I'm sure of it, but you don't see it like you do in other counties."

"You said professionally Bakken's good at his job," I reminded the sergeant. "What about personally?"

"Off the record?"

"Sure."

"Personally, he's an asshole."

Deputy Bakken lived in a double-wide trailer in a large clearing deep in the woods on the other side of two railroad tracks. It was a nice looking trailer, well kept up, with a wooden deck leading to the front door. But there was an unsightly pit of dirt and ash and melted snow about a dozen steps in front of the wooden steps where someone, probably Bakken, recently had a large fire. The sergeant parked in the driveway and I parked directly behind him. An old, single-car garage stood at the top of the driveway with a window in the door. In front of the garage was another Polk County Sheriff Department cruiser. The country supplied a cruiser to its deputies and encouraged them to use it. "Everyone's on call 24-7," the sergeant said.

I went to the garage and peeked through the window. Inside was an old Buick Regal. I told the sergeant and he said, "Jodi's." We followed the shoveled path from the driveway to the wooden deck. Deputy Bakken answered our knock almost immediately.

"Sarge, what are you doing here?" Bakken asked. He gave me a hard look, but didn't ask for an introduction.

"Truth is, Deputy, we came to speak with Jodi. Is she in?"

The sergeant moved to step through the doorway. Bakken blocked his path.

"Jodi? What do you need to talk to her for? Have people been sayin' somethin'? Has she been sayin' somethin'? I got a right to know."

Bakken spoke quickly and used his hands to punctuate every other word. I thought he was acting as paranoid as the crank heads he dealt with. The sergeant didn't seem to notice.

"It's about Jack Edelson," the sergeant said.

"The stock guy? What about him?"

"You know him?" I asked.

"I've seen him around."

"He's gone missing," the sergeant said.

"What's that got to do with Jodi?"

"We're hoping Jodi might be able to help us."

"Why would Jodi be able to help you with that? What's going on here? What's this about?"

"Where is your wife, Deputy Bakken?" I asked.

"Who are you?"

"Is she here?"

"No, she's not here."

"Where is Jodi?" the sergeant asked.

"Visiting her sister Joanne in Fargo."

"Joanne what?" I asked.

"Joanne Farmer. Who are you?"

"Is that her car in the garage?" I asked.

"What of it?"

"When did Jodi leave?" the sergeant asked.

"Yesterday morning."

The sergeant set his hand on Bakken's shoulder. "We need to talk," he said. The deputy brushed the hand away.

"Talk about what?"

The sergeant gestured at me to get lost. I told him, "I'll meet you at Eats 'N' Antiques." As he nudged his deputy back inside the trailer, I moved off the deck and casually walked over packed snow to the fire pit. A chunk of pale plastic caught my eye and I retrieved it from the ashes. It was the body of a Barbie doll, the head torn off. I tossed it back into the pit, moved to Bakken's cruiser and leaned against it while I studied the trailer. After a few moments to build up my courage, I slipped around to the driver's side, opened the door, and used the lever below the seat to pop the trunk. A few minutes later I was backing my own car out of the driveway.

I drove about 150 yards to a crossroads, hung a left and parked, hoping the sergeant wouldn't notice the car when he left. I abandoned the vehicle and made my way on foot through the woods back to the edge of the clearing overlooking Bakken's trailer. I was just in time. Before I had a chance to settle in, Bakken and the sergeant emerged from the trailer, stood and chatted for a few minutes on the wooden deck. They shook hands and the sergeant went to his cruiser. Bakken watched him drive off from the deck.

I gave it a slow count after the sergeant was out of sight. At twenty-seven seconds, Bakken leapt from the deck and dashed into his garage. He came out a moment later carrying a small spade, ran behind the trailer and disappeared into the woods, moving fast. I noted the time on my watch. Less than fifteen minutes later he returned, walking casually and smiling, the spade slung over his shoulder. He returned the shovel to the garage before disappearing back into the trailer. I circled to my right, keeping out of sight, until I cut his trail. A double set of footprints in the fresh snow—they weren't difficult to follow.

It was an hour before I was able to join the sergeant at Eats 'N' Antiques. He was walking out as I was walking in.

"I waited for you," he told me, his mood foul.

"I'm sorry," I said. "There was something I had to do."

"Bakken is all broke up about his wife. I hope you're satisfied."

"Not really, but then it takes a lot to satisfy me."

"Jodi Bakken and Jack Edelson running off together isn't a criminal matter," the sergeant said. "I don't see how it makes much of a newspaper story, either."

"If that's what happened."

"You know something I don't?"

"Did you talk to the sister—Joanne Farmer?"

"No. Why should I?"

"Because she has an interesting story to tell."

I retrieved my cell phone from my pocket, hit the re-dial button. A moment later, Joanne Farmer answered. I had spoken to her during my drive from Bakken's place to Eats 'N' Antiques.

"Ms. Farmer, this is Daniel Thorn. Could you please tell the sergeant everything you told me?" I handed the sergeant the cell. He asked the woman the same questions I had and while I couldn't hear her voice, I knew what her answers would be.

She told the sergeant that Jodi had not come to visit her, that a visit had not been planned and that she was worried about her.

"When was the last time you spoke to Jodi?" the sergeant asked.

"Three days ago, the last time that creep beat on her."

"Bakken beat her?"

"He's been abusing her for years. Last time he burnt her collection of Barbie's."

"What happened?"

"Who knows? Maybe he didn't like the way Jodi grilled his steak. Maybe his beer wasn't cold enough. Maybe he has serious self-esteem issues and whenever he doesn't get the respect he thinks he deserves from the people he works with, from the people on the street, he takes it out on Jodi. Only this time he not only beat her, he destroyed her collection of Barbie dolls—Jodi's been collecting Barbies since she was a little girl. She loved those dolls. Sergeant, my sister is a beautiful woman both inside and out. She deserves a lot better than getting beat on by that, that creep."

"I understand."

"Do you? Than you can do me a favor. If my sister ran off with some guy who treats her decent, don't find her."

After he finished his conversation, the sergeant returned the cell and I deactivated it.

"Come with me," he said.

The sergeant drove us to Bridges Medical in Ada. The admitting nurse confirmed what Joanne Farmer had told us— Bakken regularly abused his wife. Jodi had been treated for major contusions, sprains and a few fractures over a three-year period.

"Why didn't you call the police?" the sergeant asked.

"Deputy Bakken *is* the police," the nurse replied. "Besides, as hard as we tried to make her say it, Mrs. Bakken refused to admit she had been abused. She insisted her injuries were the result of an accident. Forty percent of the women we treat in emergency rooms are sent there by husbands and boyfriends and it's always an accident."

"That's probably why Bakken acted all paranoid before," the sergeant said when we were back in the cruiser. "He thought someone, maybe Jodi, had dimed him out."

"Unless he has some other reason to be upset by a visit from the cops," I told him.

"What are you getting at?"

"You know what I'm getting at."

"First Mrs. Edelson killed her husband, now Deputy Bakken killed his wife."

"Yes."

"Like most reporters I've met, you have a vivid imagination."

"Think so?"

We were on Highway 32, following the railroad tracks as we drove south to Fertile. Without warning, the sergeant pulled off the highway onto the shoulder and halted. He rolled down his window. The snow had stopped and the sky was clearing. Cool, crisp air filled the car.

"What do we know?" he asked.

"You tell me," I said.

"It looks to me like two lovers ran off together, deserting their spouses. The only reason I'm sitting here now is because there's the suggestion that Mrs. Edelson was plotting to kill her husband and Jodi's husband has a history of abusing her—which are two darn good motives for taking off, don't you think?"

"Bakken lied when he said Jodi went to visit her sister in Fargo."

"Not necessarily. That could've been what Jodi told him before she left and he believed it."

"Except her car is still in the garage. So is Jack's."

"Meaning what?"

"How did Jodi and Jack leave Fertile? Do you have airline service here? Buses? Amtrak?"

The sergeant shook his head. In the distance we could hear the mournful whine of a railroad whistle.

"Do you think they hopped a freight?" I asked.

"Maybe they had help."

"Maybe they never left."

"We need a little more evidence before we start saying that."

"If this was the Twin Cities, the cops would be all over it—the beautiful wife of an abusive police officer disappears, are you kidding? Forget the local media. CNN, Fox News, every tabloid in the country would be in your face demanding to know what the hell you're doing about it."

"This isn't the Twin Cities," the sergeant said.

"What's it going to take for you to bring Bakken in for questioning? To get a warrant to search his place? A dead body on the street corner?"

Apparently, that was exactly what it was going to take. The sergeant made noises about issuing a missing persons bulletin, monitoring credit card usage, contacting the Social Security Administration, even placing a notice in the American Hotel Association monthly newsletter, but what it amounted to was this: the Polk County Sheriff's Department did not have jurisdiction to look for two lovers on the lam from their spouses. Unless it uncovered physical evidence that a crime was committed, it was inclined to look the other way.

Like many a poor gambler, I had overplayed my hand.

Then I got lucky.

The Winnebago blew up.

From what we were able to piece together later, every month a Hispanic and his Dakota partner would drive from Mason City in Iowa, to La Crosse and Eau Claire in Wisconsin, up to Duluth in Minnesota, across to Grand Forks and Fargo in North Dakota, down to Sioux Falls and Sioux City in South Dakota, then back to Mason City, scrupulously avoiding major metropolitan areas and their police departments. They'd stop for only a few days in each city, crank up a lab in the back of their fully-loaded RV, cook a few pounds of meth, sell limited quantities to a select circle of low-profile dealers, then hit the road again. Since they were on wheels, they'd be in and out of a police jurisdiction before the local heat even knew they were there. Sweet. Except this time the boys were careless storing their chemicals in the back of the Winnebago. While cutting through Polk County on their way to Grand Forks, they encountered a pothole and the meth lab exploded.

We found them a few clicks east of Highway 32 on CR 12, what remained of their RV was lying on its side across the blacktop. The two deputies I had met earlier—Hermundson and Moore—were already on the scene by the time we arrived. So were the Fertile volunteer fire brigade and Polk County EMS.

The Dakota was toast; the EMTs had already draped a blanket over his body. The Hispanic was badly burned on his arms, torso and face. He was crying as they loaded him into the blue and white van, but not for mercy, medical attention, or even his lawyer. He wanted to see Deputy Bakken.

"'E's my friend."

"Your friend?" said the sergeant.

Maybe the Hispanic was delirious with pain and that is why he was making what the courts call "spontaneous declarations." Most likely he saw the police uniforms and figured they were all his friends.

"'E show me good place ta camp," the Hispanic said. "Good place ta cook my goods. Dep'ty Bakken my friend."

From the expression on his face, I had the distinct impression the sergeant no longer felt that way about Bakken, if he ever had.

"I want him here, now," he snapped at the female deputy.

They paged him, radioed, and called on a land line. Only Deputy Bakken wasn't answering.

I looked upward. The clouds had parted and the sky had become a pale blue. It was turning into a beautiful day.

Three Polk County Sheriff department cruisers rushed into the clearing surrounding Bakken's trailer only to find a fourth cruiser in the driveway. Unfortunately, Bakken was long gone, and so was the Buick Regal that had been parked in the garage. The sergeant ordered an alert for the Regal. Afterward, he told Moore to search the cruiser while he and Hermundson checked out the trailer. I remained with Moore. I had managed to tag along with the deputies mostly by pretending I wasn't there and I stayed way back while she meticulously examined the contents of the cruiser. I didn't speak a word until she popped the trunk.

"What's that?" I said.

"What's what?"

"That smell."

Deputy Moore sniffed the air.

"It smells like—that's perfume." Moore leaned into the trunk. "Oh, no," she said, followed by, "Sergeant."

She explained quickly when he returned to the driveway.

"The trunk smells of a woman's fragrance—I think it's called Obsession." As if on cue, Deputy Hermundson returned to the trailer.

"Something else," Moore said. "Along the inside of the trunk lid—I think that's blood and human hair."

The sergeant reached over and slammed the trunk closed.

"Don't touch anything else," he said. "Have the car towed to our impound lot, then call the Bureau of Criminal Apprehension and ask them to send a forensics team up here."

"Yes, sir," said Moore.

"Sergeant," said Hermundson. The deputy had returned from the trailer. He was holding a small bottle of Obsession in his hand.

The sergeant looked like he was about to be sick. His expression became even worse when his radio crackled. The Buick Regal had been spotted moving at high speed on Summit Avenue toward Sand Hill River.

"Tess," I said aloud.

I had been surprised by how calmly and efficiently the deputies moved up on the scene—I had expected Barney Fife but got Steve McGarrett, instead.

It was only about 5:30, but night was already a reality. Yet in winter it's never entirely dark. The snow and ice always find one source or another of illumination to magnify and reflect and the night sky was loaded with them—stars you rarely see in the light-polluted Twin Cities. They made the area around the Edelson house seem as bright to me as Midway Stadium during a night game and I felt terribly exposed as we moved to the front.

Light also poured from the house; it fell like a blanket on the snow that laid beyond the large bay window overlooking the river. Inside, we could plainly see Tess tied to the arms of a chair. Her face was so mottled with fear and exhaustion that I scarcely recognized her. Bakken paced in front of her, talking loudly and waving his hands.

The sergeant sent Hermundson to the far side of the house and positioned Moore closer to the bay window. Both deputies were carrying .308 hunting rifles fitted with telescopes.

Moore sighted on Bakken.

"I can take him now," she said.

The sergeant rested a hand on her shoulder.

"Don't fire unless you need to," he said. The sergeant removed his gun belt and set it next to Moore's knee. "I'm going to try and negotiate with him."

Bakken turned his back to Tess and walked to the window. I thought for sure that he had seen us until he brought his hand up to shield his eyes from the light and I realized that we could easily see in, but because of the reflections, he couldn't see out.

I sighed deeply and both the sergeant and Deputy Moore looked at me like they were surprised I was there.

"Be quiet," the sergeant said. "Stay the hell out of the way."

I nodded my agreement, afraid to speak.

"Jeezus," he muttered and started making his way toward the front door. He couldn't have taken more than a half dozen steps when we all heard Bakken scream, "I want my money!" loud enough to penetrate the walls of the house and echo across the snow.

The sergeant looked up; saw Bakken take his county-issued Glock from his pocket and point it with both hands at Tess.

"I want my money now!"

"Deputy," the sergeant said.

It was early morning before they finally removed Bakken's body from the house; before the ME, the county attorney, the county sheriff, and a field agent for the Bureau of Criminal Apprehension ran out of questions to ask. One question in particular still hung in the air—What did Bakken mean when he said, "I want my money."

With a loud, sustained sob, Tess collapsed into the sergeant's arms—it was like the question had given her permission to cry. The sergeant seemed embarrassed as he gently maneuvered her to the sofa. He wrapped his arms around Tess and held her close. Tess rested her head against his shoulder and wept. After a few minutes she began talking. She said, "He told me he killed Jack. He said he found Jack and Jodi together and he killed them both. He said he did it as a favor to me, but now the police were after him. He said he heard it on his police radio. He said he needed money and he wanted me to give him some. He wanted me to pay him for killing my husband." She cried throughout most of her answer and when she finished, all restraint left her. She wept until the sergeant's shirt was wet with her tears.

I thought, Tess was more than a good actor. She was way up there with Meryl Streep and Cate Blanchett.

"You don't believe this, do you?" I asked the sergeant. "Tess and Bakken were in this together. Don't you get it? Bakken came here to get his money and Tess wouldn't give it to him."

"What money?" the sergeant asked.

"The percentage of the insurance settlement Tess promised to give him for killing her husband."

It was then that the sergeant decided he had had more than enough of me for one day and threw me out of the house.

To prove I was full of crap, Tess agreed to take a computerized polygraph exam conducted by John Hopkins University. According to the Applied Physics Laboratory Computer Scoring Algorithm—whatever the hell that was—the probability was greater than 99 percent that the subject was being truthful when she answered "No" to the questions "Did you conspire with Deputy Bakken to kill your husband?" and "Are you responsible for the death of your husband?" Despite my protests, the BCA cleared her as a suspect.

DNA testing proved that the hair found in the trunk of Deputy Bakken's cruiser belonged to Jodi Bakken and the blood belonged to Jack Edelson. Based on that and Tess' testimony, the Office of the Polk County Coroner concluded that they were both dead and classified their deaths as homicides. Despite an extensive search, their bodies were never found.

A few weeks later Tess and I met in the office of a probate attorney in Crookston, Minnesota, the seat of power in Polk County. According to the will he read, Jack left his $3,500 golf clubs to me. He left everything else to Tess—an estate valued at over $700,000 including his half of their joint property. Tess and I thanked the lawyer. As we left his office, Tess said she had Jack's clubs in the trunk of her car. I transferred them to my car.

"What are you going to do?" I asked her.

"I already put in my notice at the hospital; my house will go on the market tomorrow. The realtor thinks I'd be better off waiting until the weather gets warmer but I don't want to wait. I want to sell the house, sell the furniture and get out of here just as soon as I can."

"What about Jack's life insurance?"

"The state declared Jack dead, a victim of homicide. My lawyer doesn't think there'll be a problem with the insurance company."

"Lucky you."

"Are you driving back to the Cities tonight?"

"I think that would be best."

"You could come down to Fertile; stay in the guest room like you did during the holidays."

"If I did that, people might think we actually like each other."

"We certainly can't have that, can we?"

"Besides, you've been a widow for less than a month. What would Jack say?"

"I think Jack is past caring, don't you?"

I carried Jack's golf bag through my back door into the kitchen. Jodi met me there with a spatula in her hand and wearing a white apron.

"Hi," she said cheerfully.

Jodi looked a little like the Barbie dolls she used to collect, except for the bruises on her face, neck and arms where Deputy Bakken had beaten her. But they had already faded to a soft yellow and would soon be gone forever.

Jack appeared in the doorway behind Jodi and went to the golf bag, taking it from my hands.

"How did it go?" he asked.

"According to plan."

"Is it in here?" Jack opened zippers and flaps. Instead of balls, tees, shoes, rain gear, and other golfing paraphernalia, thousands of dollars spilled out, most of the money in packets held together by rubber bands.

"Wow," Jack said. "How much is here?"

"I didn't count it," I said. "I was in a hurry. Bakken kept the money in a lock box buried in the woods behind his trailer. The box was designed to keep the contents safe in case of fire or flood or whatever. It wasn't hard to open. I took the money from the box, ran it over to your place and stashed it in the golf bag before meeting the sergeant."

"How did you know where it was?" Jodi asked. "Even I didn't know where it was—he made sure of that."

"The first thing Bakken did when he realized that you left him was to check to see if you took his money. I knew he would. I was watching."

"Four hundred sixty-seven thousand dollars," Jack said after he finished counting. "That's more than I had hoped for."

"If the Polk County Sheriff's Department ever starts arresting some of those meth dealers instead of just chasing them down the road to another jurisdiction, they'll probably find that Bakken had been taking money from them for years."

"I want you to take some of this—you did all the work."

I shook my head. "I didn't do it for the money."

"You did it for us," said Jodi.

"What can I say? I'm a sucker for love."

"I kinda feel sorry for Tess, though," Jodi said.

"Don't be," said Jack. "She has all that insurance money to keep her warm."

"She doesn't have you."

Jack and Jodi embraced. I poured myself a cup of coffee.

"You will look in on Tess, won't you Danny?" Jack asked. "Once in a while just to make sure she's all right."

"Sure."

"You're a good friend. I think I'm going to miss you most of all."

Jack hugged me.

"Do you want to know the names we've chosen?" Jodi asked.

"No," I said. I hugged her—there was a lot of hugging going on in my kitchen. "Just have a good life, both of you."

An hour later they were gone, driving south in an aging Ford Escort I had bought at a charity auction and registered under a false name. It was the same car I had planted in the parking lot of the Fertile-Beltrami High School for Jack and Jodi to escape in. A few minutes later, I called Fertile, Minnesota.

"Hi," I said when Tess answered.

"Are they gone?" she asked.

"Just left."

"Will they be all right?"

"Bakken left them nearly a half million dollars. If they can't start over on that…"

"I kinda feel sorry for them."

"Don't. They have each other to keep themselves warm."

"That leaves just you and me."

"I'll have plenty of closet space cleared out by the time you move in."

Pat Dennis

Pat Dennis is the author of Hotdish To Die For, *a collection of culinary mystery short stories where the weapon of choice is often hotdish. Pat's fiction and humor have been published in* Minnesota Monthly, Woman's World, The Pioneer Press *and other publications. She is the editor and a contributor to the anthology of mystery short stories of crimes and bathrooms entitled* Who Died In Here? *Pat works as a stand-up comedian for special events and is married to an air traffic controller who goes to work to get away from the stress.*

Jake

Pat Dennis

The sound of the train whistle reminded Jake Johansen to kill his chain-smoking, alcoholic, meat-eating, animal-rights activist bride. He knew if he waited, his wife could easily be on the next train, holding a one-way ticket stub while mulling over the possibility of turning him in to the FBI.

"Gawd…," Kim said, drawing out her thick Chicago accent as she looked through the window at the train lights passing by in the dark winter landscape.

"Don't 'cha just wanna' go somewhere fun? Some place like Atlantic City? You got all that money hidden away, why not spend it instead of squirreling it away?"

And then, as if remembering she purported to be a lover of all things animal, "Not that I don't like squirrels, that is."

Jake stared at her in disbelief. How did this moron of a woman manage to deceive him, of all people? Yet he, Jake Johansen, who was wanted by three separate governments for computer hacking and bank fraud, had fallen for dirty emails and altered Photoshop images.

Three months earlier, and bored with his weekly two-hour drive to Duluth for ten-dollar blowjobs, Jake decided to log on to an internet-dating service for vegetarians. He envisioned finding the perfect, passive woman who would tolerate his little peccadilloes such as infrequent bathing or hacking into foreign government securities systems for fun.

He promised an "icy Minnesota paradise" and a "loving, devoted Christian-like husband" to a "full breasted female who wanted to homestead and didn't mind growing vegetables and canning preserves."

He was completely amazed when hundreds of women from around the world responded to his post. He was exceptionally delighted that many of the emails contained both obscene photographs and useful gardening tips.

"I need to ask you one more time," Jake said, staring at Kim's flat chest. "Just what did you think I meant when I used the term 'homestead'?"

"I didn't think," Kim said quite honestly. "I just kind of reacted. It sounded good, you know, like you posted on the website—"a chance to get away from it all." I just didn't know that by 'all' you meant everything, including cable TV."

Jake sighed. What a waste of time, space and money. He had spent three months of his life learning to fall in love with Kim only to find out that it took him less three weeks to learn to hate her.

And then there was the cost! It wasn't that he didn't have money—he did—3.7 million in a Swiss Bank account. But Switzerland was thousands of miles away and until he figured out a foolproof way out of the country he had to watch every penny. Besides, more then anything in the world, Jake didn't like being used.

Jake had foolishly paid for all of Kim's expenses for the three days they "got to know each other" in Chicago before they married. He even bought her a generous trousseau at Wal-Mart, consisting of a pair of boots, three sweatshirts, and a bottle of Obsession perfume.

To top it off, acting as if she knew her groom was a millionaire, Kim insisted on ordering pay-per-view movies while on their one-night honeymoon at the Best Western. The movies were a total waste. They weren't even porn and unless actors were naked, Jake had no need for them. Marrying Kim cost Jake as much as sixty visits to a parka-clad alleyway hooker.

"Once again," Jake said, leaning towards her over the green, cracked Formica tabletop, still wondering how this woman who seemed to be so funny and just right for him in emails was so, so wrong for him in person. "Explain to me why you say you're a vegetarian?"

Kim sighed, bored as usual. "Because I don't eat meat—you know, meat? Steaks?"

"And hamburgers aren't meat?" he asked, watching her shove down the last of the frozen White Castle hamburgers that she'd purchased on their last trip to town.

"No. They're hamburgers. Besides, I'm a vegetarian, not a fanatic," she answered.

Actually you're not anything, Jake wanted to say.

Everything about her was fake; her cleavage, she created by using strips of duct tape that pulled her miniscule breasts together; her purplish hair that turned out to be a wig; her tattoo reading "Vegan For Life" that washed off during their first shower together; and her personality that shifted easily from one viewpoint to another, depending on her mood.

Jake had never known any one quite like her. In a way he was fascinated by her perfect shallowness. If he wasn't afraid that she would share with the police what he had shared with her during a night of drunken ardor, he would probably just let her go back to her old life.

On their first night as man and wife, Kim explained that living in the Windy City had become too difficult. It was a daily struggle just to buy food, booze and two packs of cigarettes on a cashier's salary. By the end of every month she could only made ends meet by turning tricks or asking Old Man Severson if he'd like to buy her dinner.

Old Man Severson understood dinner meant a fancy meal where Kim would ask for a doggie bag and he would ask if he could come up for a chat. By the end of the evening Old Man Severson would mumble something about how sorry he was that he missed her birthday, Valentine's Day or Fourth of July. He would place a few bills on the nightstand and tell her to buy herself something nice. And she would—usually another month's rent.

If Old Man Severson hadn't died on her, literally, she would never have left Chicago.

"His dying changed everything," she told Jake.

Of course when most brides admit such abhorrent past behaviors, most normal husbands are somewhat disturbed. But Jake Johansen wasn't normal, far from it.

Kim turning a few tricks didn't bother him. Jake assumed most women did. In fact, he was glad she shared her past with him. After another pint of Jack, he eagerly, and mistakenly, shared his own.

Ten years earlier Jake was just your everyday 28-year-old perverted IT specialist, living in his mother's basement and addicted to reruns of *Baywatch*. One day, trying mainly to impress a chat room of hackers, Jake created a computer worm, nicknamed "Pamela Lee" that infected around half-a-million computers. The next morning he managed to infiltrate the personal accounts of the Osmond Family and transferred millions to a bank account in Zurich. Instantly, Jake Johansen became an international hero to both hackers and lovers of rock and roll music everywhere.

Jake had been on the run ever since, working day labor across the country, then finally hiding out in a three-room cabin in northern Minnesota. Although he had been able, through the Internet, to connect with a teenage kid who produced dead-on driver's licenses for thirty bucks, Jake had yet to find a foolproof passport. Once he did he would be out of the U.S. of A. for good.

But the years of enforced isolation had gotten to him. He yearned for both a woman and a partner in life. And nothing would be better to Jake then one of those tattooed, nipple-pierced, purple-haired, twenty-some-year-old vegetarians that worked at co-ops or collected money for PETA.

Jake hadn't always been a vegetarian himself but found that he eventually realized he liked animals better then people. When he discovered that the two people he did admire—Bob Barker and Adolph Hitler—were vegetarians, he felt he had but little choice to join the movement.

"Can I get on the computer?" Kim said, interrupting his thoughts. "I wanna send some emails."

That was another thing. Kim spent half her day on his computer. Whenever he would enter the room she'd hit the screensaver button so he couldn't see what she was doing over her shoulder.

"Emails are private," she'd bark. "I don't look at your stuff on the computer so don't look at mine."

He had had it. Twenty-four days of nasal whining, bad sex, and the smell of hamburgers had brought Jake to his boiling point. There was no way he would take this loser to Europe. Even her nipple rings had turned out to be clip-ons.

Jake poured her a glass of red wine. "Good for your heart," he mumbled, trying to hide his disgust. It would be easier to kill her if she still thought he loved her.

"I don't know if wine goes with White Castles. You got any beer?" she asked.

"No," he answered. "I didn't plan for defrosted fast food."

What he did plan for was a sweet, simple murder. In the tool shed was an axe, recently sharpened for the occasion. Later that evening, Kim would retire to their bed and fall asleep while reading old copies of *People* magazine. Once she dozed off, one quick hack to the neck would end all of his problems. Then he figured he'd cut her up and toss her parts into the lake. Fish bait is how he would remember her.

"I'm going to the tool shed," he announced, opening the front door and staring outside, surprised to see that another two inches of snow had fallen and more surprised to see footprints in the snow, a man's footprints, where there shouldn't have been any at all. Jake hadn't left the cabin all day and the nearest neighbor was a mile away. He and Kim didn't have visitors. Jake felt his guts start to swirl.

Ever since he met Kim he had been off his game, losing his edge. He was more concerned with getting rid of her then his own protection. The footprints could belong to the authorities, probably did belong to some nosy cop. Jake was assessing his desperate situation when Kim took him totally off-guard by her announcement.

"Did I tell you Sarah's coming to visit?" she said as she grabbed a toothpick and struggled with a piece of gristle that had stuck between her front teeth.

"Sarah?" he said whirling around. "Who the hell is Sarah?"

Everything was going wrong. There were footprints where there shouldn't be any and now a potential visitor.

"Sarah, my friend from Chicago? Duh!"

"Sarah's coming all the way here?"

"Yep."

"Why?"

"Why not? Geeze. What's up your butt?"

He turned around. He was halfway out of the front door, heading into 25-degree temperatures, yet small rivers of sweat rolled off his face. He whispered, "Kim, there are a man's footprints in the snow."

"Don't worry. They're mine," she said. "I used your boots to go to the mailbox this morning. Didn't you see me?"

"No," he answered. "Why didn't you wear your own boots?"

"Yours were closer. I didn't want to get mine wet, in case I want to return them."

"You're in friggin' Minnesota. Nobody returns boots in Minnesota. Besides, you bought them in Chicago, remember? You gonna' drive to Chicago to return a pair of boots?"

Idiot, Jake thought to himself. He had to get this over with quickly. He needed to kill her before Sarah arrived and then, if necessary, do Sarah as well.

Sarah! She had never even mentioned Sarah before. Some close friend she had to be!

Jake slammed the door and walked out into dark, towards the tool shed. He started thinking about Sarah and what she might look like. He wondered if she was a redhead. He'd always liked redheads. Her breasts had to be bigger then Kim's. Even the postman had tits bigger then Kim's.

He pulled his jacket tight around him. The tool shed was twenty feet away. He could tell Sarah that Kim drowned while walking on the thin ice. He might even be able to manage a few tears if it would guarantee him bagging Sarah. What woman couldn't resist a grieving widower?

He produced one final smirk on his face at the stupidity of women everywhere when the tool shed door swung open and Sarah stepped out, holding a .25 Beretta in his hand.

"Who in the hell are..."

" Sarah V," the man answered as he pulled the trigger.

"V?" Jake said stumbling as he jammed his hand over the hole in his chest, trying to plug up the hole with his fingers. "Sarah V, the hacker?" he said between his gasps for air, remembering the name of the legendary hacker whose nickname reflected a love of jazz.

"One and the same," Sarah said as he grabbed Jake's collar and started dragging him toward the lake.

"Was—was this a set-up?" Jake asked as he felt his legs give out and his body become extremely tired. He suddenly wanted to sleep forever.

"Why do you think Kim was so perfect for you? She planned it that way. She's been trying to find you ever since you stole the money," Sarah said as he pulled Jake onto the pier. "She recognized your writing when you posted for a bride on the net. She said the posts had the same grammatical errors and bad syntax as the ones that bragged about doing the Osmond heist."

Jake was surprised when he found he could push his fingertips deeper into his chest. Blood made them slippery. "It was just about the money?" he mumbled, choking on his own blood.

"What isn't?" Sarah answered reaching the end of the pier.

"But," Jake said pausing, pathetically aware of his bad luck with the other sex, "she's my wife."

"Mine too," Sarah answered as he kicked Jake onto the ice-covered lake. He fired three quick shots into the thin ice surrounding Jake and smiled when he heard the cracking sound. The weight of Jake's body did the rest. Sarah headed back to the cabin.

"Too bad we had to kill him," Kim said, as she packed her bags and worried that murder could easily become a habit. This was the second murder she had been involved in that year alone. She'd abruptly killed Old Man Severson when he refused not only to pay her but had the nerve to blame it on her expanding cellulite. Kim knew she didn't handle insults or people very well. Maybe that was why she chose early on in life to be a computer nerd rather then a cheerleader.

"Johansen never connected the dots? Never figured out that you were here for the bank numbers?" Sarah asked, lighting a cigarette as he watched his wife finish packing.

"Nope. He thought I was just another stupid broad. Did I tell you the numbers weren't on his computer after all? They were hidden in the 'secret compartment' of his wallet. What a moron!" But then Kim found herself softening a bit. After all, Jake was dead and she knew you weren't suppose to talk bad about the dead, even if you had made them dead.

"There was something kind of nice about him," Kim said as she folded sweatshirts in half and placed them in her luggage. "He never once mentioned that my breasts were small, my purple hair a wig or my tattoos phony. I guess tattoos were a turn-on for him."

"But, for a while there you were his ideal woman."

"At least on the web," she answered, zipping up her jacket and putting on leather gloves. "There's a McDonald's in town. If we hurry, we can make it before it closes."

"I thought you gave up meat," Sarah said, picking up Kim's bag. He knew Kim expected him to act like her servant and he didn't mind. He, like most men, would do anything for love.

"Meat, silly!" Kim laughed as she opened the cabin door. "Meat, not hamburgers."

The Clues

A headless Barbie doll
A page torn from a dictionary
Footprints in the snow
The sound of a train whistle
A temporary tattoo
The scent of Obsession
A wig
A soiled ballet slipper

Made in the USA
Middletown, DE
04 April 2023